CASH FOR LIFE

a novel

by

Janice Barrett

Library and Archives Canada Cataloguing in Publication

Title: Cash for life : a novel / by Janice Barrett.
Names: Barrett, Janice (Dramatist), author.
Description: First edition.
Identifiers: Canadiana (print) 20240415892 | Canadiana (ebook) 20240415906 | ISBN 9781927882993
  (softcover) | ISBN 9781998494002 (Kindle) | ISBN 9781998494019 (EPUB) | ISBN 9781998494026
  (IngramSpark EPUB)
Subjects: LCGFT: Thrillers (Fiction) | LCGFT: Novels.
Classification: LCC PS8603.A7689 C37 2024 | DDC C813/.6—dc23

Dedication

There would be no book. There would be no me, if not for my sister Jackie Kevill. She kept me alive physically and emotionally for the last twelve years. Jackie has given up hundreds of thousands of hours to look after me. We have sat in too many ER hospital waiting rooms in different cities for hours. She's taken me to continuous doctor appointments with the Family Doctor, Respirologist, Cardiologist, Neurosurgeon, Endocrinologist, Optometrist, Ophthalmologist, ENT specialist, Diabetes Clinics, Sleep Apnea Clinic, CPAC machine Specialists, Rehab Clinic, X Rays, many MRIs, too many Cat Scans, Lab visits, Lawyers, Real Estate properties to find me a home, and countless other appointments. She took me to my book launches, to listen to live bands and many outings to keep me sane and distracted from my illness. To dedicate this book to her is minuscule compared to all she has given me. I know ultimate love because of her. Thank you, sis for the sacrifices you made for me. I am forever grateful to you for keeping me alive and happy. I can't begin to express what your friendship has meant to me. I love you forever.

Other Works by Janice Barrett

Authorized Cruelty

Chapter 1
1963

Jackie sobbed. She sat on a swing in a park, feet dug into the ground, while a steak knife rested on her tiny wrist. Unsure of how to do it, she scratched the serrated edge over the wrist. Then, she wailed, forcing herself to push. She felt the stinging wetness of tiny drops. She needed to do it. Tears and snot streamed. A noise frightened her. A head floated in the air rushing toward her. Startled, she froze. Grief silenced her. The head hovered. His black hooded sweatshirt and pants blended into the night.

He sat on a swing beside her—still. "That's the wrong knife."

Jackie looked at the blade held in the carving position against her skin.

He laid the knife on its side and glided a thumb over the sawtooth. "With them teeth, you gotta saw into flesh. Can you do that? Back and forth pushin' hard four or five times." He waited for an answer. "Gonna shred skin, ripping out bloody insides, and stringy shit. If you don't got the stomach and can't finish, you bleed out. Painful way to go. Box cutter blades—much better, quicker. Got one in my showroom. Give me the shank and I'll get it for you."

Jackie handed him the steak knife. He tugged the black hood off his head. From the glow of the nearby streetlight, Jackie recognized Gino.

"Heard you cryin'." He took a small flashlight out from a pocket, picked up her wrist, and examined it. "Why?"

Jackie wiped snot on her sleeve whimpering, "I want to be with Mommy and Daddy."

"Where are they?"

"Heaven."

"What happened?"

"Car accident. The police said if I got no relatives, I'm an orphan. They were going to take me, but Henrietta wouldn't let them. She told them not to wake me 'cause it was too late and to come back in the morning."

Gino took a cloth out of another pocket wrapping it around her wrist. "It's a scratch. Nothin' to worry about."

Jackie looked at the awkwardly tied knot, without knowing if she should believe him. "Mom said you're a drug dealer and a hoodlum."

Gino lit a cigarette. "I'm a businessman. There's my showroom." He pointed to the vehicle parked under the streetlight half hidden between trees.

"You call that a showroom? It's a truck."

"Hell yeah, it's a truck. For a speedy getaway if I need it. Won't lose the inventory that way. Smart, eh?"

Jackie picked at the frayed edge of the cloth. "Mom said you can't be trusted."

She hung onto the swing's chains, turning around in circles, and twisted them.

"Ask anybody, I never screwed nobody. If people buy something that's broke, I make good on it with my trade-in policy. My truck's been parked in the same spot for years—shows I'm dependable."

Letting the chains unwind, she spiraled around in the other direction. "Mom wouldn't buy anything from you."

He took hold of both chains above her hands, stopped the momentum, and gained her attention. "Knew you was a tough cookie first time I saw you."

"How?"

"You don't give up."

"Give up what?" She leaned back looking up at the stars.

He sat back on the swing beside her. "Means you're not a quitter. I was about twenty-two and you was maybe four. Playin' in front of yer house. You was tryin' to scrape a wad of gum off the sidewalk."

"I don't remember." Jackie sat up, curious. She loved hearing stories about when she was little.

"You was hunkered down, arse swayin' between yer knees, pushin' on a yellow plastic shovel to get the gum up. The shovel kept bucklin' so you got pissed off and threw it on the road." He laughed. "But you was stubborn and wouldn't give up. Found a popsicle stick and used it to pry up the gum." He laughed again.

"What's so funny?"

"It was the fuckin bow on top yer head. You was gruntin', exertin' so much pressure on the popsicle stick when the gum come up you landed arse over tea kettle, with the bow teeter totterin' on yer nose making you go cross-eyed lookin' at it."

They both laughed.

"Shoulda seen yer face light up when I gave you a stick of Juicy Fruit gum."

"I remember. You were always giving me gum."

"Stuff from the sidewalks got grit in it. Don't need to be chippin' no tooth." He smiled showing off his chipped tooth.

"I remember when I was six and Emanuel Miceli tried to run me down with his two-wheeler. I always heard him coming, but that time, he didn't have a card clothes-pegged to the spoke of his bike."

"Yeah, he used the king of spades, the man with the axe. Thought he was king shit, makin' that sound like a Tommy-gun comin' after you kids."

Jackie spun around, plowed her feet in the sand, and faced him. "He was bigger than us too. He knocked me down, then took off back-peddling. I saw his feet flip the pedals forward so he could take another run at me."

"Yeah, he's still a shithead."

"I didn't even see you until you pulled him off the bike and punched him."

"You was too busy pickin' gravel outa yer knees."

"But he never picked on me again."

"I always got yer back. Just like now. Have to sleep in the showroom on account of the old lady kickin' me outa the house."

"Yeah, everybody knows about it. Mom was glad, thought she'd seen the last of you on our streets. Aren't you too old anyway to live with your parents?"

"In Italy, sons live with their folks till they're thirty."

"That's weird."

"The old lady don't understand. This is my territory, I got to make sure no one takes it over. I got to live here to do that. Protect what's mine."

"Mom said we'd never get rid of you."

"She's right. Twenty-nine's too old to move and stake out new territory. Up and leavin' would cost me half my sales. How long you seen me work our street?"

Jackie remembered the last time she skipped rope. The verses to double-Dutch singsongs drowned out the normal street deals. When the rope tangled around her legs, she looked up and saw their neighbour, Marg, mini-skirt hiked up while she showed off fish-net stockings and rhymed off prices for services to a customer. As always, Gino lurked in the background. Jackie didn't think anything of it that day. But she realized now that people on their street didn't do nothing for nothing.

"I don't know. You've always been around."

"That's right." Gino stood up, rubbed his ass, and stretched. "Hang on."

He clutched both chains which she held, rocking back and forth. Jackie pumped her legs. She was high enough now, so Gino grabbed the edge of the wooden seat and thrust her upward.

"I laid claim to our block when I was just a kid in high school. Even flunked a couple of grades to stay in school longer 'cause sales is about connections and location to keep the gravy train movin'."

She looked at the metal bar overhead afraid she'd fly over the top. A grunt interrupted the words when he pushed again.

"I give people what they want. They want a TV, radio, watches, jewelry, I got it. It's called economics. You'll learn shit like this in

school. People demand and I supply. It's the way the world works."
He stopped pushing and walked around to face her. "Some world,"
he grumbled. "When we're both homeless."

"I got a home."

"They won't let you stay in it. Not without someone to look after
you. Like the cop said, you're goin' to an orphanage."

"But I don't want to."

"Makes no difference."

By three a.m. their street was in heat with shrieking sirens,
whistles, and seductions that caterwauled like cats. Gino flipped
the hood up—masking his thoughts until words mumbled past the
what-ifs. "You do got a home."

"So, you said I can't stay in it."

"Not by yourself. Maybe…"

"Yeah."

"Nah, it won't look right. People will talk. What'll they think?
I'm not gonna look like one of them."

"Who?"

"You don't want to know."

"Yeah, I do." Jackie skidded her feet to a stop.

"We could help each other. You got a home and I need one."

"You're not getting my house!"

"We got to make this a win-win. Means we both get what we
want. So, what do you want?"

"I want to stay here."

"Okay, to stay here, you need someone to look after you."

Jackie looked him up and down. *Mom said Gino was trouble.
She'd be mad at me for bringing him home. But maybe Mom
couldn't see him from heaven.*

"If they take you to the orphanage, I can break you outa there.
Get forged papers to convince them, nuns, to release you into my
custody. The deal is good for both of us. Nobody wins if you're stuck
in an orphanage and I'm on the street with no home base. What do
you say?"

"It's my house."

"I know already. But I don't see nobody else offerin' to cook yer meals, clean yer clothes, and do a whole lot of other shit. We can be partners. We don't got a lot of time if the cops are coming back soon. Do we got a deal or not? I ain't gettin' any younger." Gino stuck out his nicotine fingers. "Deal?"

"Deal." Jackie shook his hand.

Chapter 2

Lying under a cot, so the other kids wouldn't see her cry, Jackie pretended she was in a coffin, crossing her hands over her chest the way her parents were laid out. As if by mimicking their state and thinking about them, she would be with them. They looked strange, like store window dummies, resting on those satin pillows. She wanted to poke their faces and make sure they were real.

Blue threads dangled from the mattress tickling her cheek with each snorted breath. She turned and saw large sensible black shoes plodding closer, as a black habit skirt swished toward the cot.

"Get out from under there now, or you'll get the strap."

How did she know?

Jackie hated it here. She hated the kids, hated the nuns, and hated being lined up like dolls on a shelf for people to pick from. Even the beds in the orphanage weren't like the box spring mattresses at home. Layers of pee-stained circles reminded her of those big, all-day suckers with rings in them. The faded blue ticking in the mattress changed to the colour of nicotine by the stench of nightmares from kids too scared to walk the halls at night to go to the bathroom. She never peed on the bed at home.

"Dust yourself off and fix your hair. You have a visitor."

Jackie followed Sister Mary Agnus down the stairs to the receiving room. It was the first time she'd seen Gino in a suit and not in his regular biker clothes.

The sister addressed Jackie, "I'll let you get reacquainted with your cousin."

"Thanks, sister." Gino bowed his head reverently to her.

Jackie couldn't stop a smile from spreading. She couldn't believe Gino got away with the forged papers and conning Sister Mary Agnus with the too-tight suit. Acting like he was respectable.

Gino didn't speak until the nun left the room. "So, how'd you like it here?"

Jackie turned around to see if anyone could overhear their conversation. She'd gotten the strap once and didn't want it again.

"I don't."

"They say the older you are the harder it is to get adopted. Everyone wants a baby or a little kid."

"Do we still have a deal?" she asked.

"Yeah. I'm tired of pissing and shitting in the bushes and not having water for showers."

Jackie's squinted eyes and pursed lips made freckles ride along her pudgy cheeks. "What took you so long?"

"Things done right, take time. I signed all them papers what gave me custody of you. The nuns are happy. All you got to do is pack up and we'll get outa here."

***

It was a quiet uncomfortable drive from the orphanage to Jackie's house. Gino broke the silence when he pulled into her driveway and asked, "Still got the key?"

Jackie didn't answer. She rummaged through a book bag and produced a key on a chain. Gino didn't take the key from her, but let her be the one who opened the front door into the kitchen.

It was strange not to be greeted by her mom. The cookie jar on the counter was empty. They pulled out chairs sitting across from each other. He read the Hamilton Spectator while she ate Alpha-Bit cereal. The rustle of newspaper exaggerated the quiet between them. Jackie noticed the dirt in the creases of his palms.

"Aren't you going to wash your hands?"

"What's it to you?"

Jackie didn't like him using Mom's China sugar bowl. It was for good company.

"This is my house."

"Didn't say it wasn't. Wanna go back to the orphanage? 'Cause I'll take you back."

Gino picked up the newspaper, snapped it, and straightened it up. He looked over the top of the paper at Jackie and the cereal box.

"Who knew Alpha-Bet cereal was Alpha-Bits? Ate it when I was a kid. Thought it was Alpha-Bet. Should be Bet. What do you think? Think it should be bet?"

Jackie stopped gazing at the picture of Davy Jones from the Monkees on the back of the cereal box and turned it around. The front said Alpha-Bits. She thought it was Alpha-Bets too. "What's the difference?"

"Big difference. Nobody wants a bit. But a bet, everyone wants. You wanna bit of the paper?" Gino asked.

"No."

"Want a bet?"

"Sure."

"See, I told you. Bet is better than bit." The paper was open to the court section. "Bet you can't tell me how much time you'd do for a B and E."

"Five years."

Jackie was eleven, but she knew what the letters stood for.

"Nah. You got to figure everythin' into the mix. Is this a first-time, second, or repeat offender?"

Jackie turned the cereal box around to ogle Davy Jones. She couldn't wait until the box was empty so she could cut out the forty-five, cardboard-record to play it.

Gino smiled at the dribble of milk running down her chin. "First-timers get a slap on the wrist. Repeat offenders, now they're different. Depends on who they got defendin' them, who the judge is, and if they ratted out their friends for lesser charges."

With the same hand, the spoon was in, Jackie wiped a sleeve across her chin mopping up a trail of milk. "It's not fair. You didn't tell me that before."

"You didn't ask."

"You're cheating."

"That's bullshit. Just 'cause I know how the system works don't mean I'm cheatin'."

"You got the upper hand."

Gino put down the newspaper, took off the jacket, tie, and shirt, and exposed a black T-shirt underneath. Leaning over, he fished a lighter and a pack of Players Plain cigarettes out of the jacket pocket.

"So, I'll teach you. Then no complainin'. Right?"

"Okay."

"A young judge, like this here Mountney, believes in rehabilitation, older ones know better." He tapped a cigarette out of the pack, lit it, and inhaled deeply. "A teetotaller will always convict a drunk driver, never just a fine, and a woman judge will slap the max on any of them child-abusin' scumbags." With a tilted head, he puffed smoke rings above Jackie's head.

Relieved to hear he was unsympathetic toward child abusers, she felt more comfortable. Pushing the chair closer to the table while leaning an elbow on it, she cupped her chin in hand.

"See, it was no fair because I didn't know."

"Okay, try this one. Assault with a deadly weapon. Man clobbers a best friend with a baseball bat."

"First-timer?" Jackie asked.

Gino turned his head spitting a piece of tobacco off his tongue. "No, repeat offender."

Gross. Mom wouldn't like him spitting in the house. She'd make him wash the floor. "Is the judge old or young?"

"Old. But I know this case. The dude says he was drunk when he did it. Claims the best friend was havin' an affair with his wife. And had it comin'."

Jackie looked at the last page of the newspaper and scanned columns of numbers indicating baseball team standings, before asking, "Is the judge a teetoddler?"

Closing the paper, Gino laughed, "Totaler, teetotaler. Nah. He's a booze hound."

Thinks he's so smart. Living in everyone else's home? Too dumb to get one of his own. "Okay, I say the mark gets four years."

"I figure two." Gino laid the paper flat on the table pointing to the verdict. "The judge ruled two, but he'll be out on probation in six months to a year. Good thing you didn't bet against me, 'cause I'm good at this shit. Career criminals are the easiest. Followin' their rap sheet is like readin' their resume. Listen, I don't want to take advantage of you."

"Because I ain't no mark."

"Didn't anybody tell you ain't's not a word? 'Cause I'm not no mark."

There's the smug look again. He's not the boss of me. Right, we're partners! "You're not my father."

Gino leaned across the table, scowling at her, and rolled the cigarette pack into the black sleeve.

"I'm not scared of you." Jackie crossed her fingers behind her back.

She looked past him to a pink skipping rope looped around the hall closet doorknob; orange handles dangled.

"Don't wanna be no father to a scraggly, mouthy brat like you. It's yer house. I ain't tryin' to take it away from you. But I got to pay for it."

Jackie went back to dreaming about Davey Jones and his band.

"Pay attention. I got to do things different here. I'm not lettin' them junkies batter down my door at all hours of the night lookin' for a fix this time. The street life stays on the street."

Jackie's fingers tapped along the grooves in the chrome banding that edged the red, Formica kitchen tabletop.

"I'm gonna hire me a kid to work the streets at night. If anyone comes to my door..."

"It's my door." Jackie slammed the spoon on the table.

"Yeah right, our door, I'm not gonna sell 'em shit. It's what pissed off the old lady. Got me kicked out."

"It's not my fault your parents kicked you out."

Gino flicked the lighter extending the flame. He puffed on a cigarette, blowing smoke in Jackie's face, and made her eyes water. She ducked behind the cereal box.

"I'm not blamin' you." He laid the lighter on the table. "Don't blame my folks either." Gino moved the cereal box. "I'm not askin' you to be a runner for me. As long as you don't give me no shit, you get to be just a kid."

Jackie raised the bowl, tilted it to her mouth, and drank the last of the milk, licking the bowl clean. Tobacco smoke lingered in the air making her cough. She looked past Gino to the oven and thought of how the kitchen always smelled of freshly baked bread or cookies and she wondered what Mom would think.

Chapter 3

Jackie felt comfortable and safe being home, in her own house, surrounded by neighbours and friends. Playing street games, she used to play with friends, meant she hadn't lost everything and everyone.

Gino came and went whenever his business allowed. He arranged for Henrietta, their neighbour, to keep an eye on Jackie, feeding her if he didn't get home in time for dinner. But when he was home, they played cards or board games. He made sure she got dinner, did homework, brushed her teeth, and always kept her mesmerized with stories or advice.

"So, how's school?" Gino asked, plopping down a plate of bacon and eggs.

"Billy Thompson was pulling my hair again and bugging me. I told him what you said but it didn't matter." Jackie licked ketchup off her fingers.

"Don't worry about it. I'll look after it." Gino busied himself making a peanut butter sandwich, wrapped it in Saran, and stuffed it into a paper bag. "Apple or orange?" he asked.

"Apple." Jackie used her finger to scoop the last of the egg onto her fork.

"Get a move on or you'll miss the bus," Gino said.

Jackie gathered up homework, crammed it into a book bag, grabbed the lunch, and headed out the door. When the bus pulled into the schoolyard, she was shocked to see Gino standing off to the side of the playground. She watched him glaring at the boys as they piled out of the bus. He waited for her to reach him.

"Which one is Billy?" Gino followed the pointing finger.

"The kid with the red shirt and blue cap?"

Jackie nodded.

"Wait here."

Jackie glanced over at the yard monitor when Gino yanked Billy by the arm, moving him to a secluded side of the building. Only a few words were exchanged before Gino picked Billy up by the ankles, and swung him around, threatening a beating if he puked on his boots. He dangled him upside down pretending to lose his grip with a downward jerk of his arm that made Billy screech. Afraid someone heard, Jackie peeked around the corner at the playground thankful the yard monitor was busy. He was breaking up a fight between two boys which held everyone's attention. She turned back as Gino lowered Billy to the ground. He jumped and ran past her.

Gino ruffled Jackie's smoothed-brown locks. "He won't be botherin' you no more. Any more problems, you tell me about them."

Annoyed, he messed up the hair she'd tamed before breakfast, she brushed away his hand.

"Have a good day."

Jackie followed as he walked away. He turned around, smiled, and waved before walking out of sight.

Looking at the potted plant life on the windowsill, as it basked in the sun, in Mrs. Milne's grade three class, she wished all problems could be handled as easily. Jackie liked the way Gino settled a score. She smiled at the thought of Mrs. Milne being swung around by her ankles, dangling upside down. Every time she saw Mrs. Milne, she relived that day. Even though it happened when she was in grade three, the memory was still vivid. The terror stayed with her...

Mrs. Milne stood rigid, pointer in hand, eyebrows were the only part of her body that moved. Stern, thin lips were pursed for ridicule. The pointer slammed against the blackboard—the sound echoed a reminder that the strap was within easy reach.

She sat in the seat as the normal mantra flitted through her head. *Please don't ask me, please don't ask me,* when Mrs. Milne called her name. So afraid, she didn't hear the question, as she stood paralyzed by the desk. If she was asked to repeat it, Mrs. Milne would know Jackie hadn't been paying attention. The teacher glowered at her.

"Well, what's the answer?"

Her voice was terrifying. Jackie looked down at her scuffed shoes touching the cardboard that covered the hole in the bottom with curled toes.

"Look at me when I'm talking to you. I'm waiting." The pointer sliced silence, skimmed Billy Thompson's head, and made him flinch. "No need to be sitting in a seat if you won't pay attention. Go under my desk, now."

Jackie followed the direction of the pointer afraid she'd be smacked alongside the head with it. Pushing the teacher's chair aside, she ducked under the large wooden desk. Enclosed on three sides, fluorescent light peaked between wooden chair rungs, creating shadowy bars on the dark oak.

"Who else wasn't paying attention?" Mrs. Milne asked, calling Michael Forte's name.

The shrill sound bounced off the imaginary wooden prison flicking goosebumps on Jackie's arms. She heard the question this time and knew the answer even before Michael mumbled it. Sitting on the cold linoleum, her arms hugged her knees. The teacher's voice got closer. A black, box-pleated skirt plopped into the chair. Fingers gripped the edge of the desk as she pulled herself closer. Jackie tucked in her feet when casters skittered toward her. Mrs. Milne slid down in the seat, feet stretching, kicking stinky white soles toward her. Wedged into the corner, Jackie's back jabbed into a screw. Pebbles stuck in the shoe's treads scraped her arms and legs from repeated kicks to her body. Crouched in the darkened corner—afraid—Jackie waited for the bell that would end the torture.

When she told her mom, she clutched her hand marching her back to school. Jackie was left in the hall while her mother spoke with Mrs. Milne. She threatened if she ever raised a hand to her daughter or did it again, she would be sorry. "I could have your job," Mom screamed.

Gino was like Mom. He righted wrongs. Except Mom was a talker; Gino was a doer who never yelled. But they both got the job done. I wish Mrs. Milne was around today so I could tell Gino.

Chapter 4
1976

Jackie stood patiently in front of Queen's University's main entrance while Gino held up a parade of people until he was satisfied the angle was perfect before he snapped a picture. Even though there were only eighteen years between them, Gino was the proud father who took more headshots of her tousled hair poking out from a stiff cap at the university convocation than any other mother who preened over a daughter's coiffed locks.

After the ceremony, Gino took Jackie to an expensive steakhouse restaurant.

He looked down at the place setting. "Never been to a place as fancy as this. Look at all them forks and spoons. What person needs all them to eat?"

Jackie was aware of the waiter who stood stiffly at Gino's elbow with a white linen napkin draped over his arm. Annoyed, Gino tapped a Player's Plain out of the pack. The waiter at the ready lit the cigarette. Gino gave Jackie one of his many hand gestures, part of their secret sign language, to indicate what he thought of the waiter. He crossed two fingers into an X. A warning.

Gino turned. "Am I paying you to eavesdrop? Back off."

Then he turned to Jackie. "You was the prettiest girl up there. I'm proud a you. Don't know anybody who went to university. When I was a kid, I always wanted to be a big brother. Then you came along, and I got to be one."

"You were more like a dad."

"I'm too young to be your dad."

"When I was little, you looked old to me."

"I hated being by myself. Always wanted a little brother to boss around."

"So, you got me instead."

"Did you hate being a only child?"

"No. I hated being around the other kids in the orphanage. With just you and me, I got all the attention. Just like with my parents."

Gino wiped the tear from an eyelash.

"You're such a suck." Jackie smiled at him. "How about a toast?" Jackie raised her glass of wine tapping it against Gino's bottle of beer. "To the best dad ever."

Gino played with his silverware. "You are the only good thing in my life."

The waiter picked up Jackie's napkin hat, snapped the folds out of it, and laid it across her lap. Jackie stopped Gino's hand when he reached toward the waiter.

"Keep your hands where I can see them." Gino addressed the waiter.

The waiter backed away visibly shaken. Jackie smiled.

"So, what now?" Gino asked.

"Find a job, I guess."

"You got a bright future. I've been thinkin' a that. Do you know why I made you go to this here university out of town?"

"You thought it offered a better program."

"What would I know about university? It was because of my business. When you was little nobody bothered you. Cause how would it look, a tough guy pickin' on a little kid? But now yer grown, anybody who wants to get back at me, knows you're my soft spot. They'll come after you. I can't protect you. I got to struggle just to hold my territory. Somebody's always tryin' to push me out. I don't want them threatenin' you to get to me. It's not safe for you in Hamilton. You got a chance for a better life. A respectable one. With decent people who ain't never been to jail."

Jackie laid her fork on her plate picking up her glass. "You've got more morals than most of those church-going do-gooder hypocrites who keep you in business. The Merchant of Misery, that's what the holy rollers on the block call you behind your back.

But they don't mind rummaging through your truck to get a stolen TV or radio, do they?"

"This ain't about me. We got to think about yer future. Our streets ain't no place for a university graduate who wants to get a career and be successful. You don't need no junkies goin' after you to find me. You got to go out on your own now. Cut the ties to our street."

The waiter returned and with a flourish presented their food, refilling their water glasses. Gino tapped his beer bottle pointing at Jackie's wine glass. "How about a refill?" His eyes never left Jackie. "You been away for years already. It should be easier to move on. It's up to you where you want to live, but you need a fresh start in a city where nobody knows about me or what I do."

"I don't want to leave Hamilton."

"There's lots of cities close by you can move to and I'll visit you."

"Why should I move? I want to live in my house."

"I've been thinkin' it's time to sell your place now. You can pay back the student loan then have lots left for a down payment on your own home."

"I don't need you to plan my life."

Gino stuffed a wad of steak, dripping *au jus* into his mouth. "I'm scared for you. Do you know why my parents kicked me out?"

"Because of junkies knocking at their door at all hours of the night."

"It was the simple answer for a kid. You're grown now and old enough to know the truth."

Jackie put down her fork, swirling her glass of merlot. Her eyes never left his, not even when she set the empty glass down.

"An asshole tried to move into my territory to take over."

Gino stopped talking when the waiter came over and set their drinks down. Gino waved him away. The waiter stepped back, but only two paces behind him. Gino turned around. "Hey, you doin' surveillance I should know about? You're fuckin annoyin'."

The waiter withdrew. Jackie hid her smile behind her napkin while Gino continued.

"'Cause I'm not connected to the mob, I got no protection. The asshole beat up my dad real bad. The fucker wouldn't come after me, 'cause he was too chicken shit. So, the old lady kicked me out and wouldn't have nothin' to do with me."

"It doesn't mean it will happen again."

"Right, 'cause I'm not gonna let it. Same shit different day. With all these hippies and free love, demand's up. Dealers are greedy."

"You got through it before."

"It cost me my family. It's why my folks moved away. Saw the old lady on the street one day. She walked by me and wouldn't talk. Turned her head, like she couldn't stand to look at me."

"She must have forgiven you by now."

"You don't know the old lady. When we moved here after the war, being Italian, we was treated like the enemy. At the time, the war was an open wound and we was the puss running out of it. Neighbours treated us like we was friends of Mussolini. Like we started the war. They called the old lady *IL douche*."

"Mussolini was a long time ago."

"Not to the old lady. Some things stick in your craw. She said I was actin' like Mussolini taking over the block. Like I was provin' the neighbours right and it looked bad on her. Like it was my fault they called her *IL douche*, when they'd called her that since I was ten."

Jackie sipped her wine engrossed. Gino seldom talked about his parents.

"The old lady was always lecturin' me sayin' I was goin' to hell. Makin' out like her family was angels and their shit don't stink. But Dad told me her brother owned a restaurant in Florence. He kept two cash registers. One for cash and one for credit. Only reported the credit sales to the government. Once a month, he'd drive a thousand kilometres to Monaco stashing the money in a bank account there. Monaco got no tax laws. But to the old lady, he was an angel. And me, I was the devil. But we're doin' the same illegal shit."

Gino mopped up the *au jus* with a chunk of French bread. "The old lady screamed at me, 'It's what happens when you act like Mussolini. Good people like your dad get beat up.' She blamed me. But Dad said it wasn't my fault. They beat the shit out of him."

"I can look after myself."

"That's what Dad thought. I'm not gonna let it happen again."

Gino got up from the table, and dragged the chair beside Jackie, wrapping an arm around her. Tucked into the warmth, frizzy hair wilted with his horseradish breath. "I love you more than I dreamt was possible. You're my life. The only person I ever cared about."

Jackie felt the wetness on her cheek and knew the tears weren't hers.

"I don't want you to move away," Gino said. "But we got to think about what's best for you. It won't do you no good in life to be the daughter of a drug dealer."

Jackie squeezed his hand. Her long slender fingers cupped around his stubby stout ones for a perfect fit. *When did this happen?*

Gino blew into his napkin, placed it in the empty breadbasket, and motioned for the waiter.

"We're done with this." Gino pointed to the breadbasket.

The waiter frowned at the snot-filled napkin in the basket. Gino smiled at him.

Jackie handed the basket to the waiter. "Thank you," she said.

Gino's grin widened at the waiter's disgusted look and slid his chair, scraping the wooden legs on the tile floor, moving it back to where it belonged.

"Don't let your food get cold." Gino nodded at Jackie's plate. "Now's the time to put the deed to the house in your name and sell your parent's house."

"What about you? I'm not kicking you out of our house."

"It's not our house, it's yers. You never let me forget it. Remember when you was a teenager? You threatened to kick me out." They both laughed. "It's what I liked best about you. You stood your ground. You got spunk. Always liked that about you even when I was on the receivin' end. No one's gonna take advantage of you. That's the way it should be. But you got lots of heart too."

Jackie reached across the table squeezing his hand. "I love you too."

***

By the time they arrived back in Hamilton, Jackie convinced Gino it was better if he continued living in her house and paying toward it until she was ready to buy a place of her own. Within a brief time, she secured a job with the Unemployment Insurance Commission in St. Catharines. Jackie picked out an affordable two-bedroom apartment for when Gino stayed over on the weekend. They both packed up her life.

Chapter 5

Paula met Gino through her girlfriend Cathy Ermeta, a hooker who flaunted herself on Barton Street. Cathy provided free babysitting and a place where Paula could dump off Theresa. It was difficult to find a babysitter when one laboured split shifts in a restaurant. Cathy was the perfect friend. She worked nights.

Paula loved the bar scene but the girls at the bar were youthful, and thinner and made it impossible for her to compete for any male leftovers when the lights came on at the end of the night. Fed up with having no prospects after last call, Paula usually left, broke and single.

According to Cathy, it wasn't a bad thing Gino never went to the meat-market bars Paula frequented, because then he wouldn't know how many times she'd been around the block. *Wasn't that the pot calling the kettle black?*

Paula learned Gino went to a local pub where the only thing that got picked up was a pitcher of beer. With no music, dancing, or flirting, the only boobs watched in the place were the boob tubes in each corner of the room. Not the bump-and-grind Saturday night she preferred.

Cathy set up a blind date for them and chose this location, so they could get to know each other without screaming over the music. The bar patrons were like an extended family to Gino; so it was comfortable for him, like sitting in his living room with the television on visiting with friends.

Cathy warned Paula to tone down the makeup and wear something conservative. "Gino doesn't want to be in a relationship with a hooker. Not saying you are one. Just saying you don't want to look like one. Go figure, a drug dealer with scruples."

Gino picked up Paula at her apartment. He didn't drive in front of her building honking the horn like most guys. He even opened the car door for her. It made her feel important. It was a good start to the evening. There was no instant attraction for either of them. Stout overweight guys like Gino were a dime a dozen. But he at least was the big Kahuna on the block with a steady supply of cocaine, her drug of choice. She needed to get back to a double-income lifestyle.

Paula knew she'd hate the bar the minute Gino opened the door, and she heard Tanya Tucker's song, Delta Dawn, playing. She wouldn't be another cast-off like her, whining about her misfortune. Paula hated country music twang and down-on-your-luck songs. It was her life they were singing about, and she didn't want to be reminded. She liked rock and roll. The louder the better.

Customers all turned when they entered the place. "What? Are we the entertainment?" Paula asked.

"The guys like to check out who comes in. Everybody knows each other." Gino escorted her to a quiet table in the corner.

She wasn't going to settle for a beer when he could pay for high test. Clancy, the owner, came and took their order. Gino introduced him. Paula liked this VIP treatment. They ordered drinks and food. It was delivered by Clancy himself.

"Food's on me," he said, giving the table one last swipe before he set the dishes down, and winked at Gino.

"Thanks. I'll remember it."

Could get used to this. Why remember it? Like he owed Clancy. What a schmuck. You don't thank the guy. You take it for granted. You'd think for a drug dealer he'd know how things work. "Do you bring dates here often?"

"Not really."

Paula sipped her Rye and Coke. *Gino needs a swagger in his step. You don't get ahead by being humble and thoughtful. Another old dog to teach new tricks.* She smiled. Gino smiled back.

Paula was surprised Gino never married. She'd been married twice and was looking for number three. After dinner, people stopped by their table to have a few words. Gino introduced her each time.

"You must be pretty important to get this kind of attention," Paula said.

"I'm just one of the regulars."

Throughout the night, Paula made mental notes: *low self-esteem, easy to manipulate, probably browbeaten most of his life. Needs his ego stroked more than his cock. My type. Just like numbers one and two. Except Gino likes being needed, looking after people. A perfect match. I like being looked after.*

"You're more than just one of the guys. These people look up to you. Respect is hard to get. Folks are drawn to you. Maybe it's because you're a business owner."

"You're right. I am a businessman. Ain't nobody seems to get it, except you," he grinned. "Most people figure a dealer's got shit for brains. I'm not like the rest of them dealers snortin' away their profits."

"I like a man with smarts who can make things happen. You've got great business sense. I hear people say you're fair. You know how to treat them."

It was a perfect first date. How could it not be, when Paula drooled compliments and acted like he was every woman's wet dream? And she was the one who lucked out.

Over the months of dating, she saw how people admired Gino. She felt being his wife would garner the same respect. It was easy for Paula to fake the lovey-dovey crap with Gino because he was desperate for love with all the trimmings. Paula sensed he liked the idea of having an instant family because he always wanted to do family shit: bowling, the zoo, dinner, and a movie.

He couldn't get enough of Paula's praise—sucked it up like a junkie with a straw and was attracted to her because of the accolades. Her hard features softened with each compliment and her brazen attitude mellowed as she agreed with him on every point. In Paula, Gino liked having someone who believed in his abilities and who looked at him like Jackie did, as invincible. Physical attraction was an immature thing of the past. It didn't matter.

They saw each other almost every day. Addicted—he used her for a confidence fix. Paula knew he was hers. She'd done this twice before. Men were gullible when it came to their egos. Paula knew how to massage them.

Their sex was great; at least she didn't have to fake it. Gino was a pleaser in every way, and she liked revving him up. Paula convinced him this was what life would be like with her. She set the mood for their future taunting him with false expectations. She wasn't sure how much longer she could keep up the charade. Cutting off snide remarks drained her. The sooner they were married, the better.

Chapter 6

For two years, Gino visited Jackie twice a month on the weekends playing their newspaper game, "Time for the Crime" spawned from their first day together. Life began to change when Gino met Paula and her daughter Theresa. Instead of visiting twice a month, he was coming on the third Friday of each month. He left earlier than normal on Saturdays which allowed for more time with them. Jackie was painfully aware it ate into their time together.

Paula had muscled her way into Gino's life, squeezing Jackie out.

Gino took Paula to the places they used to go. Niagara Falls, their special place, was now Paula and Theresa's. Nothing was special anymore. Nothing was theirs, Jackie and Gino's. Paula had taken over the traditions they started. She was a constant intruder who wouldn't leave and who took Gino away from her. Theresa was the same age as Jackie when she and Gino began living in her parents' house. Conversations were all about them now. His world revolved around Theresa.

Over the last year, however, it seemed like he was doing more things with Theresa than with Paula. The relationship dynamic seemed off. Jackie heard the sadness in his tone when he talked about Paula.

"I love Paula, but I'm not stupid enough to think it was my good looks what got her." He winked rippling acne scars that pockmarked much of his face.

Jackie knew Gino was lonely ever since she went away to university. He missed family life.

"She's lucky to have you."

"Life's better now with them."

"Don't let Paula take advantage of you. Making you a free babysitter so she can go out drinking."

"I like spendin' time with Theresa. She's a great kid."

"But she's not your responsibility." *I'm his daughter. He can't replace me with her.*

"Paula's got no money for a babysitter."

Jackie hunched over The Hamilton Spectator checking the court section for any new rendered verdicts. A lined sheet of paper sectioned off with headers read: PERP, CRIME, G's verdict, MINE. Jackie read off the charges of the alleged perpetrator. The bet was always two bucks but occasionally went up to five on the more high-profile cases.

"She's taking advantage of you." Jackie filled in the name of the perp reading off the crime.

"A body can only struggle for so long. So, she takes advantage. It's her survival instincts 'cause she got Theresa to look after."

"Verdict?"

"Guilty," Gino answered.

Jackie went to the fridge and got him another beer. "You never believe anyone is innocent."

"Don't matter guilty or innocent somebody's gotta pay. And everybody's guilty a something."

"That's why I'm winning more cases than you."

Gino kept his head down like he was reading the page. "We're talkin' bout marriage."

"What?" The glass bottle hit the table in front of him harder than she intended. "It's too soon."

"We're not kids."

With fingers still gripped around the beer, she took a long swig. "Why haven't you told Paula about me?"

"I will when the time's right. When I know for sure."

"Know what? If you can trust her? Why would you get married if you can't trust her?"

His silence aggravated her more. "So, when will you get married?"

"Soon."

She took the bottle with her when she sat down. "But I haven't even met her yet."

"And you're not gonna."

"But the wedding..."

Gino stood and walked to the fridge, getting himself a beer, since his seemed to be attached to her hand. "Not gonna be no wedding. Just, I do's, at city hall to make it official. No party. We're not kids anymore. Just another day. It's the way we want it."

"What about me?"

"Nothin' will change. I'll still come every third Friday and we'll still have holidays at a cottage. I'll tell Paula, I'm fishing with the guys, so we'll spend our two-week holiday together."

***

Three court cases concluded since the previous month when Gino last visited. He owed her four dollars. After picking out their movie, Jackie went to the fridge plucking a Coke from behind the Molson Golden, Gino's favourite brand. There was so much to tell him. She'd met someone, unlike anyone before. Refined, intelligent, from an upper-class family. He'd traveled all over. He was the kind of man Gino would want for her. A month was too long. She was rankled thinking about how Gino would settle for someone like Paula. Why he couldn't see what a user she was, was beyond her. But maybe he did and wouldn't admit it. Paula didn't deserve him.

She finished the last of her Coke when Gino swaggered in wearing a permanent-press smile.

"What's up?" Jackie asked.

"We did it. Got married last weekend."

***

Gino was right. Nothing much changed in the year since he got married. He continued to visit Jackie every third Friday and they went on their holiday at a cottage. Jackie's life was busier now with her boyfriend David. Their relationship became serious.

Jackie left the kitchen and stretched out onto her expensive sleek, leather couch with chrome legs, admiring the TV before she turned it on. The quality of the furniture and Tom Thomson prints contrasted with the chipped plaster walls, cheap linoleum floors, and metal Venetian blinds. Who knew how many decades ago the place was last painted? Instead of squandering money on a high-end apartment that would yield nothing when she left, Jackie chose to invest in furnishings.

When she started on her own it was easy to settle for this place since she decorated the apartment with old second-hand furniture and some stolen property from Gino's truck warehouse. A faded floral couch with worn arms, a stained coffee table, and dented lampshades suited the apartment. Gino should be more selective. After all, jail time was still jail time whether the loot was top-notch or cheap second-hand stuff.

Chapter 7

"You're supposed to be the man, Gino. The breadwinner." Paula slammed her fist onto the kitchen table. "I'm only asking for crumbs."

Gino moved his 38-caliber gun aside, spreading out the newspaper. Paula sat across from him. "Maybe if you made more money, we wouldn't have to worry about you being," she leaned in closer over the table "short."

They both knew the inference of her jab. She used it often enough. "It won't cost you anything to expand your territory. Stop thinking small-time."

Gino held up the newspaper in front of his chest to block her out.

"I'm talking to you." Paula stood, hands on hips.

She flicked his lighter, igniting a flame at the bottom of the fold in the middle of the pages. Black smoke with a mixture of blue and orange flames shot up the back of the newspaper. Luckily, Gino was close to the sink and dropped the flaming pages into it, smothering it underwater. Charred black bits floated in the smoke-filled sink.

Paula walked over to the sink and stood behind him. Not wanting to get bushwhacked again, Gino turned around and scowled at her before yanking a tea towel hanging from the bar of the oven door.

"Bad enough, I gotta watch my back on the street, now I got to at home."

She moved closer to him tilted her head and flaunted her three-inch taller frame. She loved reminding him, that five feet four was insignificant for a man. His height bugged her more than him.

"You think kids are cheap?" Her breath was sour.

Gino waved the tea towel, dispersing the smoke, ignoring her.

She yanked the towel from him. "Theresa always needs something. You wouldn't know about it because she never comes to you wanting things. I'm the one who's got to keep shelling out money for her."

Gino didn't look up at her when he walked back to the table. He lit a cigarette and put the lighter into his pocket.

An empty coffee cup clattered on the saucer when she picked it up for a refill. "You can make big bucks by taking over just a few more blocks. You got enough of them street kids to do it. Just kick them in the ass to get them moving."

Gino put his cigarette into the ashtray. "I'm not getting into a war over territory. They turn out bad. Where's your pay cheque?"

"In your goddamn fucking stomach. It's been four days since I got paid."

"Yeah, it's why I'm askin'. For most people, a pay cheque lasts a week. What are you spendin' your money on? 'Cause it sure ain't groceries. There's nothin' to eat in this place."

Gino noticed her mood swings were worsening. The impulsive behaviour of setting the paper on fire was a sure sign.

"You swore you weren't using again."

"Make them bastards earn their money instead of letting them pick your pocket, nickel and diming you to death with excuses and lies," she said.

"There ain't no talkin' to you when yer like this. I don't need you tellin' me how to run my business."

"You don't want to look after your own family, but you'll act like a big shot bailing out those street kids who run for you. But when it comes to me, you pinch the nickel so hard it makes the beaver piss."

Gino sighed. He'd spent years wiping off the street life at his front door, only to let Paula trek it through his house. He turned around when he heard a floorboard creak. Theresa ducked down on the stairs.

"Come here." Gino handed her twenty bucks. "For whatever you need."

"But I don't need anything." Theresa tried to hand it back.

"See, she doesn't need anything because I give her everything." Paula's voice became louder—shriller. "It's me who's tapped out because of her. She's fine because I've been making sure of it. You think because she's not yours you don't have to look after her?"

Gino ruffled Theresa's hair. "I want to look after you. Get a treat for yourself at the corner store. Take your time. Whenever you need money come to me, not your mom." He winked.

Home was Gino's escape from the chaos of the streets and business. Like being in a boat on the water, feeling the calm ebb and flow of the lake. With Paula there was no ebb and flow, no give and take to family life, only turbulence.

Theresa didn't move. The fear in her eyes made Gino give her a nudge toward the door. "Run along and take your time comin' back."

"What the fuck are you doing giving her money?"

"You just told me, to start lookin' after her. So, from now on, she can get any money she needs from me."

"Twenty bucks! What kid needs twenty bucks? I'm the one who needs it. I'm the one who's tapped out. You dole out money to me like I was a kid on an allowance, then give the kid whatever she wants. If you got money to throw away on a kid, you got money for me."

Gino put his money back into his pocket.

"What's the matter, you're not short, are you?"

He made no move to reach into his pocket.

"I work hard around here for shit." Her cheeks were turning bright pink. "The one chance I get to go out and enjoy myself, I can't because you come up short. Should have known you'd always be short."

The snarl in her tone was a dead giveaway. Paula looked around the kitchen. She was a thrower, Gino knew. Spider veins in her cheeks and nose grew creating a pink mask over her face. Prime conditions.

"Who are you to dictate to me?" Paula lunged over the table.

Gino turned, reaching for the marble ashtray, and didn't notice Paula snatch the 38-calibre until it was too late. She pistol-whipped the side of his face loosening a couple of teeth. The hard metal crashed into Gino's cheek, teeth cutting jagged slices into the soft inner tissue splattering fatty pockets of bubbly flesh. Blood filled his mouth. He ran to the sink spitting blood into the tarnished metal basin while blood gushed from his nose and split lip. Piercing pain shot up his nose and across his brow. Gino worked his tongue around the swelling gums as he took hold of a clean tea towel and sopped up the blood. Although the words were muffled by the cloth, there was no mistaking his anger.

"This fuckin' shit ain't gonna happen in my house."

When he grabbed her, Paula froze letting him seize the gun from her hand. He put his bear paw hands on her arms shaking her. His thumbs gouged into her soft meat while his body tensed with restraint. He wanted to hit her, but she was a street fighter. He'd sworn not to bring street life into his home. Besides, no kid should come home to violence. His hands stayed where they were, with fingertips dug in. He couldn't stop clenching his teeth even though the pressure sent waves of throbbing pain through his face. He glowered at Paula.

She was frightened, but something was unnerving about her grin. "Can't hit a girl. It's your rule. I heard you telling Theresa. Don't stay with nobody who hits you. You're a loser, Gino, and always will be. Can't even win a fight against a woman."

He reminded himself to calm down. It was a while before he could take his hands off her. When he did, Gino saw a small round bruise from where his thumb was.

"Now, tell me what you've been doing with my money?" he said.

Chapter 8

Jackie picked up the TV guide and flipped through the listings. Normally the TV was a distraction, its grey noise filled the space in her small apartment. To quiet her fears, she looked from one yellowed photograph to another trying to conjure up faded memories of her parents now bleached clean through the years.

In the photo, her mom looked uncomfortable and stiff without an apron hung around her neck and Kleenex poking out from a pocket or sleeve. The dress her mom wore was the same one she had been buried in. Except for her mom's frizzy hair, Jackie was more like her father, big-boned, tall, and athletic-looking with breasts that wouldn't fill a C-cup.

When she was little, Jackie would perch on a stool at the end of the counter and help make cookies. Her mom claimed a cook's best tool was her tongue. Jackie snuck chocolate chips into her mouth before they went into the batter, but she was never scolded for it.

She hugged the picture to her chest at 7:20 p.m. Maybe Gino was lying in a ditch somewhere, dying. She held her breath. Jinxed. Afraid the thought would make it happen.

"Please," Jackie said. "Please protect Gino and keep him safe for me." Hoping by saying the words out loud her parents would hear them. If anything happened to Gino, it would be her fault because he was coming to see her.

More guilt, like when she was a kid and thought her parents' automobile accident was her fault. She wasn't even in the car. She was at home tucked in bed under the covers, but still, it was somehow her fault. Because someone was late it didn't mean they were dead, she told herself. She put the photo back on top of the TV. They should be eating by now.

Gino lived in a routine. Habits were the ways people knew where and when to find him. He drank in the same bar. Ate dinner at the same time. Ruts and routines created expectations. Gino should have been here by 5:30 p.m. at the latest! Panic flicked Jackie's skin taunting goosebump memories of waiting for her parents to arrive and then finding out they never would.

Life was better haphazard. Nothing planned. No waiting for the axe to fall. No on-edge nervous energy gnawing at the inside of a cheek. She wished for a picture of Gino to snuggle up with. But he made sure no connection could be made between the two of them. Since she graduated from university, he has been obsessed with keeping their relationship secret. He wouldn't let her introduce him to any of her friends.

When Paula came along, he put their photographs in a safety deposit box at the Bank of Nova Scotia and gave Jackie the only key. She felt like he was deleting her from his life. He never said the words "in case he died," but now she was sorry she wished for his pictures. Jinxed.

Jackie shut the TV off and went into the kitchen, checking the wall clock, 7:50 p.m. She folded up The Hamilton Spectator and opened The St. Catharines Standard newspaper to the movie section. They both loved action and adventure detective stories. Her chin dimpled, puckered by quivering lips. Gino called it her pout-a-puss face. But they both knew it happened just before she cried.

A slow thud hammered the steps, struck the concrete, and echoed up the stairwell. The sound of Gino's steel-toed biker boots drifted through the ajar front door. Jackie rushed out and met him. "Holy shit! What the hell happened to your face?"

"You know mine's a rough business."

"No one ever beat you like this before. Who did it? What was it about? What did you do?"

"It's nothin'." Gino was winded when he arrived at the apartment.

"Who did it?"

"I'm not talkin' about it, so don't ask me no more. And get that pout-a-puss look off your face."

"I can't imagine what the other guy looked like. Sit down. You're out of breath."

Gino put on a lot of weight since she went away to university because no one kept him in shape.

"Maybe instead of dinner and a movie, we should go for a walk or play catch, the way we used to. Do you remember how to ride a bike?" Jackie asked.

Once his breathing slowed to a regular rhythm, Gino said, "I could ride circles around you."

Jackie smiled. "Remember when the kids wouldn't let me play baseball until you came out with me?"

"Even in my best henchman stance, you was still the last kid picked. Never seen anyone with two worse left feet than yours."

"Nothing's changed. They call me Miss Klutz of the UIC. I was going on break the other day and tripped on the metal foot stand holding the baffle board upright. It went over and almost took out a claimant. But he didn't look as bad as you."

Gino held the side of his face. "Don't make me laugh. If I remember right, I was the one had to be the ump what kept you in the game. If I never taught you how to kick up dust slidin' into home plate you woulda been tagged out a bunch a-times. But I learned you to do what it takes to win. Never mind them good sportsmanship rules."

"Maybe it's why I liked playing catch in the backyard or riding our bikes. Non-competitive sports." Jackie pointed to his face. "Is that why you were late?"

"Shit happens." Gino turned the newspaper around so he could read the movie listings.

"So, why were you late?"

"Paula always starts somethin' just when I'm trying to get out the door."

"What's her problem?"

"Same as always. I don't want to talk about it. Where we goin' for dinner?"

"Vito's. It's a new place on Victoria Street. They have great French onion soup and lasagna."

"You know what I like," Gino said, as Jackie opened a Molson Golden and put it in front of him.

She threw the beer cap in the garbage. *If he doesn't want to talk about the fight, it must have been a whopper.*

Jackie sipped her beer. "To be over two hours late, it must have been some fight."

"Now don't you start? I've got my fill for one day."

"You think the problem will disappear if you just stop talking about it?"

"Oh, I know it won't go away."

"Then tell me what's wrong."

"It don't concern you."

"You've looked like shit in the last few visits. Have you seen a doctor lately?"

"Enough." Gino guzzled the rest of his beer.

"I'm not stopping until you tell me what's wrong. I worried about you this whole month. And it's not just today. It's been ongoing for the last three months. For you to be two hours late, it has to be really bad. Do you want me to get ulcers over this? I can't take not knowing anymore. I can't sleep at night. Look at me, I've lost weight. How long are you going to keep doing this to me? How much more do you think I can take?"

She was good. Knew how to break him down. He couldn't stand the thought of hurting her. She sucked in her cheeks making herself look emaciated. Meanwhile, she gained five pounds since last month.

"Alright. I'll tell you. But it's my problem and I can handle it. I don't want you interferin'. Paula rang up twenty-thousand dollars on my credit card."

Jackie took another swallow of beer. "I imagined you dying of cancer or some inoperable disease. At least, this isn't life-threatening. No wonder you looked so depressed." *Always thought Paula was a gold digger.*

"How did she get your credit card?"

"She don't got no credit ratin' so couldn't get a card of her own so, I added her to my card."

"Didn't you notice all the things she was buying?"

"It was all cash withdrawals. And she pays the bills."

"So, what was she spending the money on?"

"Drinkin', drugs."

Jackie leaned over the table. "What will you do?"

"Pay off the credit card."

"What about Paula?"

Gino lit a cigarette inhaling deeply. "She's my wife. I just got to make sure she don't get her hands on any more money. I look after payin' the bills now."

"It will take you forever to pay back twenty-thousand dollars."

Gino shrugged. "It won't take long. Sales have been good."

"We could sell my house. I could give you the money."

"I told you it was yer house. I ain't takin' yer house or yer money."

"But you paid the bills, taxes, and upkeep over the years."

"The price of doing business."

"You've been paying all these years on the house without being compensated."

"That's what a dad is 'posed to do." He'd thrown his trump card, smiling, even though she knew it must have hurt.

He cornered her. If she insisted on paying him back, it would be like saying he wasn't her dad. She wouldn't do that to him. It was what he counted on.

All through the movie, Jackie thought about how she could help him. Gino always said, talk is cheap, show me. She needed to show him she loved him and would do anything to help him when he was in trouble.

After the movie, Jackie lay in bed and pondered a solution. Somehow stealing from the government wasn't like stealing at all. Members of Parliament exhibited no qualms about taking her money every pay cheque and squandering it on lavish dinners, booze, high-priced hookers, and vacations. She wasn't stealing money, only the paperwork to make it. It wasn't like she was stealing for herself. She wouldn't do that. It wasn't Gino's fault his wife was a conniving bitch who would steal him blind. So why should he have to pay?

A man was responsible for his wife's debt. It's the way the law worked. This was the one time in life she was given an opportunity to do something for Gino. She wasn't about to let him down. She tried not to think about the risks and punishment, not wanting to see her name in the newspaper and a part of their game.

The next morning, Jackie waited until Gino was sitting at the kitchen table with a coffee before she told him about her plan.

"I can get blank Record of Employment (ROE) forms from the stock cupboard at work."

"So?"

"People who aren't entitled to unemployment insurance (UI) can get it with this form."

Gino's puzzled look made her explain further.

"Okay, if someone gets laid off, they apply for pogey, right?"

"Yeah."

"They get a record of employment from their employer."

"Yeah."

"Then they apply for UI, fill out the cards, and get paid up to fifty weeks of benefits."

"So, you tellin' me I can get pogey if you give me the form?"

"Yes. But we're not doing a one-time thing. You have to think bigger. Your customers can collect. I want you to sell these forms. I'll complete them to show your customers worked and are entitled to maximum benefits."

"So, I'm selling these forms so my customers can get pogey?"

"Yes."

"No. I'm not doing it."

"Why not? It's perfect."

"This is my problem to solve. It has nothin' to do with you."

Jackie worked on Gino for another hour trying to convince him she would be protected since he was the only person who could turn her in. Nothing worked. She knew she would be late for her date with David, but she needed to convince Gino to go along with her plan before he left.

"Even if someone catches me taking the ROEs, I can explain, I'm mailing them to an employer. No one will suspect I'm stealing them. They're just another form in a stockroom piled high with forms. No one considers their real value. It's why they aren't locked up the way they should be."

Gino picked up his overnight bag. "I got to go."

Jackie tugged on his arm holding the bag.

With his free hand, he hugged her. "We're not endin' up pen pals in prison. I didn't send you to university so you could end up a thief. Enough! I don't want to hear another word about it."

He hugged her goodbye.

Chapter 9

Hair still wet from the shower; Jackie got dressed. With pantyhose stuck to damp legs, it slowed the progress as she tugged them. She threw clothes on, then raced back to the bathroom and dried her wet hair. After wiping steam from the mirror, Jackie looked into the misty crystal ball image left by her palm rolling curlers around her hair.

When she heard the knock at the door, Jackie yelled from the bathroom for David to come in. He was punctual as always. The noise of the hair dryer couldn't muffle him.

"You had all day to get ready. We're going to be late."

She turned the hair dryer on max, damn the frizzy split ends. "Turn the TV on, I'll be out in a minute. Get yourself a beer."

"There's no time for beer." He continued pacing. "Is this going to take long?"

Hot air burned her ears, while she made a mental checklist of the make-up and jewelry she would snatch on the way out the door.

"I'm going to the garage. I'll pull up to the front door. Meet me there."

"Are you sure you don't want a beer?" Her last-ditch effort to stall.

Jackie hopped into the car with rollers in her hair, clutching her make-up bag. "These things always get started late."

"I guess it will be now since I'm the Master of Ceremonies. They can't start without me."

Jackie applied her eye shadow. "Bowling banquets are notorious for starting late."

"Not when I host them."

Traffic was brutal. Cars deliberately got in their way slowing them down. David honked his horn repeatedly. Jackie took the rollers out of her hair. Waiting for a red light, David looked over at Jackie's finger-combing results. "Your hair looks good," he said.

"Thanks."

Stuck in traffic and late and still he made her feel good about herself. He knew how self-conscious she was of her frizzy poufy hair.

"You know, you're a nice guy. I'm sorry I made us late. I really do feel bad about it."

"Well don't. It won't change anything, and I don't want it to spoil the night."

Jackie put the rollers and make-up into a grocery bag. *Great. More guilt.* "Are you nervous about the speeches?"

"No. I've done this for years. It doesn't bother me. I don't write speeches. I like to wing it."

"I don't know how you can do it. No one could pay me enough to stand up there."

"What's the big deal? They're all people you know."

"Yeah, but I just couldn't do it."

"Well, luckily you don't have to."

They pulled into a packed parking lot. Jackie bolted out of the car, then slowed down when she saw David's relaxed stride and kept pace with him. So much for her prediction.

"We're only ten minutes late. Who knew everyone else would be on time?"

David opened the foyer door for her. She heard voices drone and dishes rattling making her anxious. David planned on giving the speeches before dinner. He would be upset if dinner was already being served. Rushing down the steep narrow stairs, Jackie's heel caught on the lip of the metal edge. She groped for the rail but felt nothing as her body pitched forward tumbling down the steps. She landed at the bottom of the staircase, which opened into the main room, with her legs spread and her head flung forward, smothering her face with long softly curled hair that spilled into her lap. She looked up into the shocked faces of the two people who took tickets at the door. Not the grand entrance she hoped for. Nothing said classy like being spread-eagled in front of an audience.

David rushed to her side. "Are you alright?"

"Yeah. I'm fine. Just help me up."

David slipped his hands under her armpits hoisting her up onto her feet. "Are you okay? Can you walk?"

"Damn."

"I'll help you to the table," David said.

"No. I'm fine. I got a run in my pantyhose. Go to the podium. Break a leg, just not mine." Jackie was relieved dinner was not being served.

When she settled in at a table, David smiled back at her. Jackie forgot about a drink but wouldn't attract more unwanted attention, so she stayed put. The speeches were brief. David was good at that. He announced the awards. Nicknamed the "Gutter Ball Queen" for the last two years, what other award could she expect except "Best Sport." Jackie stood but couldn't get her balance. From the corner of her eye, she saw the person beside her shift in his seat and drag her chair out of the way.

"And you're my best sport too," David said.

Jackie felt her heel wobble making her unstable. She must have done something to the shoe in the fall. Feeling the foot slide on the smooth linoleum floor, she grabbed the edge of the table with both hands, white-knuckling it to hold her weight, with her head down.

David's voice boomed over the microphone, "I love you. Will you marry me?"

She looked up, brushed hair from her face, and leaned to one side putting too much pressure on the stiletto. When the heel snapped, Jackie slid with the grace of swing dance precision underneath the table, clearing her head by a fraction of an inch. Hearing the collective gasp from the audience and not wanting David to be standing at the podium worried his proposal might be turned down, Jackie yelled, "Yes," her voice muffled by the draped white linen. The straight-edged white tablecloth now resembled scalloped edges from where it was lifted by the now laughing on-lookers.

"I'll help you up." It was Peter who sat beside her.

She looked at his black dress shoes smiling at the cartoon character socks beneath the navy pants. Jackie picked up the broken heel lying beside her. Why she tried to pull off "classy" in these too-high heels was beyond comprehension. Her body wouldn't let her do classy.

"No, I'm alright." She couldn't face people yet, but it wasn't like she could sneak out unnoticed now. In between bouts of laughter, David announced, "It's usually at last call when people end up under the table."

***

The next morning, cuddled into the heat of each other's bodies, Jackie's left hand reached out of the covers with the diamond ring poised to catch the splintered light. Wiggling the ring finger, she saw a glint of colours change as they bounced off the diamond cuts before the ring slid to the backside of her finger.

David pulled Jackie closer. "I'll get it sized. Do you like it?"

"I love it. I just love it. It's beautiful. I'm sorry I screwed up your proposal. I feel like such a klutz."

David entwined their fingers. "It's part of why I love you. I never know what to expect. At least there are no permanent scars. Someday you'll look back on it and laugh."

"Don't remind me. You know you wheeze when you laugh that hard and right into the microphone. No wonder I needed to be coaxed out from under the table."

His laugh turned into a wheeze again. He released his fingers, wiped both eyes, and then cupped her breast.

"So, when should we do it?" David said.

"I'm ready now." Jackie rolled over to face him.

David's good looks made most women take more than a second glance. Jackie noticed some women out right stared at him. She was lucky to be the one he chose.

"Oh, you mean the wedding," she teased.

"A year seems reasonable. We need lots of lead time for all the preparations."

"But just a small wedding. Your family and our friends, right? Something simple, not too fussy."

Jackie hated the pomp and ceremony that forced friends to choose sides at the church when the ushers asked, friend of the bride or groom. It reminded her of dividing up teams for baseball. Would their friends pick David over her? With no relatives to claim as her own, Jackie didn't want the pressure of wondering if she would have enough people on her side of the church to fill two pews, while his side clogged up thirty.

"I'd like a small church, quaint and cozy. With only a best man and maid of honour, no big wedding party or ushers to escort people into the church. The reception should be all about great food and dancing. I don't want long, formal speeches."

Being walked down the aisle with Gino by her side, his arm tucked around hers was Jackie's only wish. But how could she tell David about Gino now? In their two years of dating, she never once mentioned his name or his visits every third Friday of each month. She told David she belonged to a book club who met then. When they started dating, Jackie told him her parents died when she was eleven and she was put into foster care, bumped from one home to another. She claimed, for the most part, she was treated well, and it seemed to be all the information David needed. The lies started innocent enough. After all, she had no idea that David would be the person she loved today.

Throughout their relationship, Jackie was glad he never questioned her past again because it made for fewer lies and less guilt. But how could she start a new life with him blanketed in those lies? But she wouldn't compromise Gino, not even for David. He wouldn't understand. Through her own doing, Gino couldn't exist in her life, except for a few stolen Fridays.

David got out of bed.

Jackie propped her head on an elbow. "Where're you going?"

"To get a pen and paper so we can make a list of the guests."

Jackie watched him go into the small bedroom across the hall that was set up as an office. Trying to make partners at Halloran, Holbrook, and Barns accounting firm, David would bring files home with him, so he could work into the night. David claimed the only way to get ahead in life was to work harder and longer than anyone else, which didn't leave a lot of social time for them, especially during income-tax season. The small bedroom office was a reminder David would want to work, and she would have to leave soon. They only spent Sunday morning together, then after breakfast, Jackie was expected to leave so David could finish his work. But his work was never-ending. Maybe he would make an exception today, and she could stay for the rest of the day. After all, he had just proposed to spend the rest of his life with her.

While Jackie stretched out in bed, David pulled the nightstand over to write on it and sat on the bed. On a piece of paper, David drew a line down the middle of the page, labeling one side as mother and the other side as father. Below each parent, he listed his aunts, uncles, and cousins on each side, so as not to miss anyone. Then below he added his list of friends and associates.

"So, who do you want to invite?" David said.

She didn't want to do this now. The thought of a wedding without Gino made her sad. But when David started something, he followed through with it. He was driven. A long-term planner. It was one of the things she liked about him. He was dependable and predictable. He offered a stability she could never get with Gino.

"Ryan and Lillian, Mike and Krista, Katie and Andy, Megan and Peter, Caroline and Tommy, Candice and Jason, Emily and Daniel and Christopher and Letia."

"That's it?"

"Yeah. They're all my friends. And most of them you haven't met because they're from my university days."

Maybe, when the time was right, she could tell him Gino was the only foster father she'd been close to. He had been in Italy for years and just returned. Then Gino could walk her down the aisle.

Jackie looked over his list. "Do we really need all these people? I was hoping to keep the list small. I want an intimate wedding with close friends and the immediate family. I thought seventy-five people would be nice and manageable. Your list looks more like a hundred and seventy-five."

"This is the rest of our life. We have to invite the right people."

"But I haven't even met most of these people from your work."

"You never know which one could influence my future, so it's best not to leave out anyone from the hierarchy."

"I think if we don't hang around them regularly, then we shouldn't invite them."

"You do want me to make Partner, right?"

"Yeah, because you're smart and a hard worker, not because you kissed the right person's ass."

"In my business, sometimes it's what it comes to."

"Well, I don't like your business."

"It's what will put the champagne and caviar on our table."

"I like beer and pizza."

"But why settle for less when we don't have to?"

She looked at him as he lay down on the bed. *Pizza and beer are settling? Not when it's what I want.*

Pulling her beside him, he kissed her neck. "I want to give you everything you want in life because I think you're worth it."

Jackie arched her spine offering him more. How could she argue with that logic when he was just thinking of her?

Before heading to the kitchen for breakfast, the couple got dressed. David put bagels into the toaster and got cream cheese from the fridge. He handed Jackie a knife to cut up fresh fruit.

"No big breakfast to celebrate?" Jackie said.

"I got to hit the books. You know the routine. It's Sunday."

"Bacon and eggs take too long?" Jackie stopped coring the apple. "It's a three-minute egg."

"I have a lot of work to do."

Jackie put the fruit on the table. David finished his bagel. She sat down in front of the plate and watched the fruit disappear.

"Done like dinner." David brushed crumbs off his hands like symbols that skimmed each other making a big show of being finished. His finale.

Jackie took the first bite while he loaded the dishwasher. The song lyrics, "Isn't it romantic," to some old song, she couldn't remember the name of, flitted through her head. In the windowless kitchen, the diamond engagement ring didn't sparkle as brightly as it did before. The luster off the promise.

She loaded the dishes in the dishwasher and closed the door harder than she intended. *Wham bam thank you ma'am and don't let the door hit you on your way out.*

Chapter 10

Heavy black smudges of ink were ground into the table, next to her teacup, from countless editions of the morning newspaper, marking Jackie's spot at the kitchen table. She laid her hand flat on the tabletop admiring the ring. She didn't want to part with it for the time it would take for sizing. She looked between her spread fingers at the ink stains that started when she was an obnoxious, know-it-all 11-year-old orphan.

Jackie took her ring off, lying it on a shelf next to the books. She thought of the standing lie with David about book club every third Friday of each month. Funny how he never asked who was in the club or what book she was reading. Jackie looked over at the three paperback novels sitting on the open kitchen shelf. David deserved to know who he was marrying. They were the same three books she brought when she moved in. After two years of being in a book club, she should have been able to fill four shelves. Why didn't he notice? Maybe she should buy more books. Or maybe just tell him the truth.

Jackie looked over at the stack of stolen records of employment forms with unemployment insurance applications piled beside them on the table. She had never stolen anything before. Not even a penny candy from the corner store. Never even got a parking ticket. She obeyed the law, yet here beside her was her graft.

It was a good thing, Paula hated cottage life with bugs and fishing. It made Jackie's time at a cottage with Gino special. Something Paula couldn't take away from them. Jackie was glad to be getting away from the scene of the crime with the loot. Gino would be picking her up soon. They were heading to a rental cottage on Baptiste Lake for a week's holiday. Hopefully, she would be able to convince Gino to take the stolen forms off her hands. But for right now, she couldn't get herself and the stolen goods packed and out of the city fast enough.

Lost in worry, she didn't hear the knock at the door and jumped when Gino appeared in her living room. "Are you ready?"

Gino gripped her suitcase, headed down the stairs, and loaded it into the trunk as Jackie trailed behind. She clutched the plastic bag filled with papers. While Gino drove down the highway, Jackie checked the side-view mirror. She envisioned blaring sirens and being pulled over by police cars forcing them over to the side of the road. It wasn't until they were on the back roads surrounded by thick forest and huge rock cuts that she'd made her escape. Watching for deer offered a distraction from the plastic bag at her feet.

After arriving and unpacking, Jackie presented Gino with her plunder.

"There's fifty of them. No one will miss them, and I can't take them back, so you might as well use them."

"My problem ain't yers to solve." Gino took the bag and tossed it on the coffee table.

Jackie clenched her jaw. *I risked everything for it.*

"It can wait. We're here to relax and forget about our troubles. I'm puttin' burgers on the barbecue. You can get out the fixins."

The next morning, they drove into Bancroft, to get groceries and beer. Later in the afternoon, they went fishing, hoping to catch dinner. They ate burgers again. Determined to catch a fish, Gino convinced Jackie to head out with him again.

In the boat, Jackie reached for a worm in a tub at the bow, baiting her hook when she seized the side of the boat and steadied herself. Gino gave the speed boat, that churned up the water, the middle finger.

Waiting for the waves to calm, Jackie said, "I've been thinking a lot about this con. It can work. It's simple and clean with little risk and a big pay-off."

"You don't think I can look after my own shit?" Gino tugged on his line jerking it out of the water. "Don't need your help."

"But this will solve your problem."

"Kids don't tell parents what to do."

"I'm not a kid anymore, so stop treating me like one. I did everything you wanted. Moved away and stayed out of your life. You don't want me around, I get it. I don't fit in with your new life."

She couldn't look at him and turned to cast her line, brushing away a tear.

Gino looked out over the water, watching his bobbing lure. "Where'd you get this idea? I ain't said nothin' like that. Would I be sittin' here beside you if I didn't want to spend time with you?"

Jackie tugged on the pole. "Do you think I'm too stupid to help?"

Gino reeled in his line. "You're not gonna stop, are you?"

"No. And you're trapped here with me. No walking away unless you're Jesus," she laughed.

Gino laid his pole across his lap. "Okay, you win. Tell me about your plan."

"I filled out all the record of employment forms along with the unemployment insurance applications. The only things I can't complete are the name, address, phone number, and social insurance number of the buyers and the first and last day worked. Those things have to be filled in when the customer buys them. I put in the pen I used, so there's no difference in ink when you add those things. I think I did a good job of forging your writing. I got enough practice from all the times I did it for school with notes to the teachers."

Gino raised his eyebrows smiling.

"You'll have to make sure the dates on the application coordinate with the record of employment. Everyone gets laid off with a recall date. This way the office won't be hassling them with a job search. The less contact with the office the better. I figure you should sell the set for five hundred dollars."

He sat forward on the seat. "Little high, ain't it, for a couple pieces of paper?"

"Not when you consider the buyer will get paid fifty weeks, at the maximum UI benefit rate. This means he'll get one hundred and forty-seven dollars a week for fifty weeks for a total of seven thousand three hundred and fifty for the year. So yeah, five hundred is dirt cheap. It's not like a standard con. There's no mark getting hosed out of five hundred dollars. He'll recoup his money back in four weeks of payment. Then he has forty-six weeks of pure gravy. It's not like a stolen TV or stereo. No one's coming back pissed off because the picture isn't clear enough or there's too much static. It's nice and clean, no refunds necessary."

"At five hundred a pop, it won't take me long to pay off the credit card. But I'm not sayin' I'll go along with it; I'm just tryin' to get the details."

Jackie bobbed her pole in the water, not interested in catching a fish.

"This is the beauty of it. I got you fifty records and applications to sell. So, with fifty at five hundred dollars each, your take will be twenty-five thousand dollars. It's even more than what you need. It shouldn't take too long to sell fifty. You can be in and out of business fast. Less chance of getting caught. There's less risk and more profit in this than in your stolen property."

"Won't the office know these record forms are missin'?"

"They aren't missing. They're accounted for."

"What do you mean?"

"We have a logbook. I put in an entry showing fifty were requested by one of our largest companies in St. Catharines. They are always ordering them. I supposedly sent them out to their payroll clerk, the same one who normally orders them, to the regular address so it won't be suspect."

Gino beamed. "Except them forms never get there."

It was a proud kind of beam. The one she recognized every time she hit the baseball and made it to first base. The same one plastered on his face on graduation day.

"But nobody knows except you and me. And fifty is the customary amount the payroll clerk would order. I forged the signature of another UI clerk. I don't like her anyway." She looked over at her bobber, the rhythm mimicked her thoughts. *Even though I don't like her, she doesn't deserve to be a scapegoat. What if we get caught? Am I doing the right thing? Of course, not. It's fraud. If he says yes, I'll be squirming like bait, or he could say no, and I'd be off the hook. Government assholes, can't plug the holes, making it too easy. I owe Gino.*

"Even if someone thought this looked strange, and by the way it doesn't, they would go after the payroll clerk or an employee at the St Catharines company or the person's name I forged on the requisition form. I'd be in the clear. But they'd never think to link the St. Catharines UIC office to a fraud that happened in Hamilton.

"Because your buyers will be from Hamilton, I used a Hamilton employer on the ROE. Arpico Steel is perfect because it's so large it makes for too many suspects to weed out. But the beauty of it is, the only trail the police can follow is to Arpico which has nothing to do with this, so they'll never find anything."

Jackie watched a family of ducks slice through a sunset-cast ribbon of orange that coated the lake and showed off their silhouette against a grey sky as their boat floated and bobbed like their lure.

"It's getting late. Time to head in," Gino said.

Once docked, Jackie hefted the cooler out from between the boat's wooden seats, setting it next to a fire pit near the water's edge. Fastidious about the fishing poles and gear, Gino wouldn't let Jackie carry them in case she got them tangled or snagged. Gino built a fire while Jackie broke off a couple of twigs from a nearby tree and grabbed a bag of marshmallows she stashed in the cooler with their beer.

Surrounded by darkness, heat from the campfire kept them warm. Jackie blew on the charred marshmallow at the end of the stick putting out the flame. Gino pulled his evenly roasted golden brown marshmallow out of the fire presenting it to her. "Try mine."

"I have my own."

"You want to hope whatever man you marry likes burnt offerins'."

Jackie considered telling Gino about her engagement. But she wanted the ring on her finger when she told him. Besides it might give Gino another reason not to go along with the scheme.

"Mine's got more flavour, like barbecue."

"I ain't never served you barbecue like that. Charcoal flavour don't mean it's got to look like charcoal."

"You keep it up and I won't be having you over for dinner."

"With them cookin' skills, you ain't hurtin' my feelings."

Their laughter carried off into the night, rode the wings of bats, and taunted the wailing loons. Stars were bright and many. Water lapped rhythmically, gurgling out of breath onto the shore.

Gino threw another log on the fire. "What if the cops pick me up with the goods? What do I tell them about how I got these record things?"

The wind shifted setting up a smoke screen between them. Jackie waited until it cleared so she could see his face.

"You say you got them through a guy who works at Arpico Steel. You've never seen him. You do an exchange: drop off his cut and pick up more forms in Building Three at locker thirty-six. That's all you know."

"Is there even a locker thirty-six there?"

"Of course, there is. You don't think I'd leave you hanging, do you? I've been there a couple of times and checked out the place and Building Three would be a good spot for an exchange, and locker thirty-six was open. I bought a combination lock for it and put it on. The combination is 20 right, 43 left, and 16 right. I wrote it down for you, so you can keep it in your wallet and pull it out if you get caught. Which isn't going to happen, by the way. I just knew if I added that part you might be more willing to go for it. I've covered all the bases. It's foolproof."

Jackie knew by the long silence he was second-guessing himself.

"How did you get so damn smart?"

The pride in his voice made Jackie smile. "I picked up a few things from listening to you over the years."

"Thought I'd protected you from my life. Didn't want my shit rubbin' off on you."

"You taught me how to look out for myself and it's a good thing."

Gino shook his head raising his eyebrows. "You're my girl. If you're sure this can't backfire on you in any way, then I guess I'm in. I only need the twenty Gs, so I'll give you the last five."

"No. I'm doing fine. I don't need it."

"You got to take a cut. I'm not gonna let you risk jail time with no reward. Your cut is five G's. I won't do it otherwise. Ready to go in?"

Gino disappeared into a cloud of smoke when he doused the fire with sand from a large coffee can kept nearby. They hiked up the hill. Gino led the way with a flashlight and leaned on a walking stick he fashioned from a tree branch. The beam of light swayed with his lopsided gait each time he put pressure on the makeshift cane.

"When did you start needing that," Jackie asked.

"It's just this goddamn hill. After a while, it gives me a charley horse."

The porch light shone down the path, allowing Gino to shut off the flashlight before they reached the front stoop. Jackie set the chess board between them at the kitchen table and opened a beer for each of them.

"You know, you could let your dear old dad win every once in a while."

"You mean like you did with me? Show no mercy. Wasn't it your rule? Do you know it was years before I learned the right way to play this game?"

Gino laughed. "But I never lost in those days."

"I thought there was something wrong with me because I couldn't remember the different moves each piece made. I never figured you kept changing the moves to win."

He laughed. "You were a sucker then. Couldn't have no little kid beat me. How'd it look? You outsmartin' me. You was easy to string along then. Your head was filled with all that pretend shit playin' with em Barbie dolls a yers."

He moved his Bishop and she scooped it with her Knight.

"Check. I remember what you used to say when I'd dress Barbie in a gown. *Pretty ain't always good and too pretty hides something bad.*"

"Sounds like somethin' Confucius would say. Maybe I read it in a fortune cookie. Can't remember now. But it's good advice."

"Checkmate." Jackie gathered the chess pieces and put them away before they headed off to bed.

***

It was hard to believe it was the last night of their holiday. They were so busy with swimming, fishing, campfires, and fireworks during the week, that they'd forgotten to play their customary game of "Time for the Crime."

"Did you bring the newspaper?" Jackie asked. "We can't leave without settling the score."

"Shit, I almost forgot about it. I'll get it. It's in my bedroom."

The cabin was small enough that they could easily speak with each other from different rooms. Jackie moved to the living room and looked out at the lake.

"I missed this at university. I couldn't get anyone interested in playing. They didn't like the commitment of following the verdict and lost interest."

"Kids nowadays don't want to wait for nothin'." Gino came out with the Hamilton Spectator and laid it on the kitchen table. "But them's the ones that'll be the next mark. They don't stop to figure things out."

The first time she heard the slang word "mark" was the first time they played this game. *Am I setting him up as a mark?*

"'Cause they don't see nothin' coming. I learned you, to watch your back, position yourself so's you see what's comin'. Preparin' you. So, you know the risks and punishment."

Do I have his back?

Gino scraped a chair on the floorboards moving it beside his own. "Stop daydreamin' and get over here. The verdict's in on Harold. Get out yer money. I picked out another good one. Big case. Gonna be a long trial. Think we should up the ante on this one? Maybe make it five bucks."

Chapter 11

Jackie hadn't heard anything since Gino took the plastic bag with the ROEs and UI applications home four weeks ago and set up his new business venture. They agreed to have no contact except for their regular third Friday.

When Gino arrived, Jackie couldn't wait to hear about sales.

He settled in at the kitchen table. "Nice chairs."

With feet set apart and arms crossed, she stood over him waiting. *A frigging month worrying, and all he has to say is nice frigging chairs!*

She smiled at him. "I just got them. They're the latest. Real modern."

"Gonna get a matchin' table?" He lifted the newspaper. "This one's seen better days."

"You're right. We saw the best days at this table."

"I couldn't believe you wanted it."

"I wasn't going to let Paula throw it out. I don't think I'll ever get rid of it. Too many great memories."

"Yeah. We've seen more'n our share, for sure." Gino pulled a pack of Players Plain out of his pocket.

Jackie sighed, hands on her hips.

Gino opened the newspaper to the movie section ignoring her.

"Soooo." The syllable stretched out as far as her open arm's length.

"*The Enforcer* looks good. It's billed as the 'dirtiest' Harry of them all. Can't beat Clint Eastwood."

Jackie picked up the ashtray from the kitchen table frowning at the pack of cigarettes. He wasn't getting what he wanted until he started talking. He folded the St. Catharines Standard and reached for The Hamilton Spectator. Jackie shifted her weight and huffed.

He raised his head, stared into her eyes, and challenged her. He believed a glower worked with people the same way it did animals—got them riled up.

"The ashtray stuck to your hand?"

"You'll get it when you start talking."

"Been talking to you since I got here."

Gino ignored her, flipping the pages to the court section to see if there were any more rulings on the latest perpetrators in their game.

She caught the smile tweaking the corners of his mouth.

"I feel lucky this month." He compared their tallies on the newspaper bets, figuring out who owed whom.

"You need luck. Why you figured the judge would let Watkins off with a light sentence is beyond me," Jackie said.

"Watkins was only rightin' a wrong."

"I told you, judges today are cracking down on this kind of stuff. It's not like the old vigilante days. Even if you right a wrong, the fact you use force to do it makes you as wrong as the first guy. That's the way it should be."

"This new generation of do-gooders is screwin' around with the natural way of things. If some scum bag attacks you, I'm gonna beat the shit out of him."

"It makes you as guilty as him. Both of you get charged with assault."

"That's where this whole system is screwed up. Somewhere along the line, these judges are blamin' both people equally, when they should be lookin' at who threw the first punch or who started things first. Nail the first guy's ass to the wall, but leave the other guy alone, 'cause he's just tryin' to set things straight."

"That's why you owe me another four dollars. You better get with the times because you're losing more bets than you're winning."

"All these wet behind-the-ear judges don't know what justice is."

Guzzling his beer with a deep sigh afterward, Gino went back to the paper and wrote the name of the perpetrator and the crime committed. Leaning back in the chair, stretching his legs, Gino took another gulp of beer and considered his prediction on the judge's rulings for the next month's bet.

Jackie never knew him to take so long.

She ground her teeth as she waited for the list of perpetrators to grow. Gino turned the pages to the comic section. He never read the comics. When he put the beer bottle to his mouth for another swig, Jackie said, "Stop jackassing around and tell me, how's business?"

Gino put the beer down before a big grin threatened to swallow the bottle whole and lit up a cigarette. "Easiest sell I ever made."

Jackie put the ashtray on the table and sat.

"Soon as people find out about it, they want in. Everyone wants to screw over the pogey office. Never made so much money so fast like this before. Sold thirty-nine already. The credit card is almost all paid back. Put the money down on it right away so I don't have no big interest payments."

"Where are you selling them?"

"Docks off Burlington Street. I'm gettin' a lot of them, seasonal workers. They don't got enough weeks in to get pogey. Some union guys too. Word's gettin' around fast. I should be sold out in a week."

"What will you do then, when people come asking for them?"

"Sorry, outa business. When they're gone, it's over. I got to hand it to you, been on the back side of business all my life and never seen a slicker run operation. Anythin' out of the ordinary at work?"

"You worry too much."

"I always have when it comes to you. I'll be glad when the last of them forms is gone. Then I'll stop worryin'."

Gino got out of the chair giving Jackie a big bear hug. "You got me outa a big mess. Thank you."

"It wasn't your mess. Paula created it. You haven't told her anything about this, have you?"

"Do you think I'd risk you gettin' caught? I told you, she couldn't know about you. It's why I kept you away from city hall when we got married. And made sure you never came home. I loved Paula when we got married, but I knew enough not to trust her. Leastways, not with yer life. She got no breaks in life, so she weren't above screwin' people over to get what she wanted. Shit, what could a guy like me expect? It weren't like some good woman was gonna take up with me. It's slim pickins. Most don't want the trouble my business brings."

Jackie hugged him. "Any good woman would be lucky to get you."

"Paula can't know nothin' about you. If she ever finds out, I'll say I don't know nothin' about you or where you is. Tell her we fought and you don't want nothin' to do with me."

Jackie hugged him again. She figured it wrong. He wasn't pushing her away to make room for his new family.

"She don't know who you are and it's the way I'm keepin' it. It's why all our pictures are in a safety deposit box."

"It would have been nice to have a couple."

"Why, so you could put them next to your folks? People would ask questions. David would want to know who I am. I told you before, you get them after I die. It's the only way you can be safe. Remember, I do all the worryin' for both of us, so you don't have to. It's all under control."

"If you haven't told her about me, what does she think you do every third Friday?"

"Make my buys."

"You've been telling her that for two years?"

"She don't bother about what I do. She likes it when I'm gone. Then she don't gotta make dinner. She can go to the bar and I'm outta her way."

Jackie felt her heart sink. Gino deserved so much more than this. He just wanted someone to love who would love him back. She couldn't understand how he, who made his living off people, could have been so taken in by Paula.

It could be why he lectured her on dating only guys from the right side of the tracks and hid from her life, so no one knew they were from the wrong side of town.

Then Jackie remembered the news and flashed her ring under his nose.

"When did this happen?"

"Last month, but I waited until I got the ring back from the jewelers."

"Have you set the date?"

"Not yet. David says we'll need about a year of lead time. I think a late summer wedding would be nice. But I want you to walk me down the aisle. You have to be there to give me away."

"I'll walk you down the aisle but never give you away. You're stuck with me for life, kiddo."

"Good, that's the way I want it. David's taking me golfing again next weekend. I love it. He's patient and the perfect teacher. And he loves dancing and concerts. We have so much in common. And he's fun."

"Imagine me around all those muckity muck people. He's not like most accountants, is he? All dollars and no cents?" He spelled the last word out. SENSE.

"You don't have to spell it. I get it." Jackie smiled. "Relax. You'll like him," although she doubted it.

David wasn't a guy's guy. He didn't watch sports on TV or play poker and drink beer. He liked to boat but not fish and would never get into a fistfight.

"Come on," Gino said, wrapping his arm around her back. "We better get goin' if we don't want to miss the movie."

Chapter 12

Gino took Paula and Theresa to all the attractions in Niagara Falls. Paula had never seen Theresa so excited before. It was great how they got along so well. She didn't have to worry about Theresa anymore. Gino would always look after her. It was a relief.

When Gino parked the Pontiac at the bottom of Clifton Hill, Paula looked at the gaudy bright storefronts, museums, and tourist traps that flanked both sides of the street.

"Look, it's Frankenstein," Theresa pointed. "He's beside the haunted house. I want to go there."

"Been there, done it." Paula shook her head. She decided she'd wait in a bar until they finished traipsing around.

Gino looked at Paula. "It's your last chance. Sure you don't want to come with us?"

She lit up a cigarette. "I'll wait in here," she motioned to the dark, dingy-looking bar.

"Ripley's Believe It or Not is another good one," Gino said when Paula opened the door.

Paula sat in front of the window, ready to do her part, waving goodbye to the two as she ordered a Rye and Coke.

She knew Theresa was the buffer who kept their relationship stable. Gino wanted to raise a kid and he was a perfect dad. If she were single, the two of them would never have made it through the first month of dating. She knew his soft spot. Too busy being a father he didn't notice her disinterest in him. He was getting what he wanted; she was the one who made sacrifices. After all, Gino wasn't the man of her dreams. She'd mistakenly thought she'd hit the jackpot and married him for his endless drug supply. But he padlocked the back door.

Married life with Gino was not all smooth. *Thought he was king shit controlling my supply. He's a meal ticket—nothing more. Not even a good one at that.*

Paula thought, they could've made a lot more money, but Gino lacked ambition. She tried to persuade him to branch out, take over a few more blocks, and expand his territory, but for Gino, the good life wasn't about bigger and better. He was content to rule the block and look after the street kids who ran for him. Gino would always be small-time, but she concocted big-time ideas. Gino tried to tell her the logical reasons why those ideas wouldn't work but she wouldn't listen. At least he was a built-in babysitter, and she could come and go as she pleased, so the times when she was too high to come home, she stayed overnight at Cathy's apartment.

Staring at people walking by, Paula took particular interest in a street kid who hung around. Too disinterested in attractions to be a tourist and besides, he didn't have the look. She recognized his look. The same way Gino realized she was a user, so he hid his stash. The kid watched people, waiting for someone. She knew the setup, watched until the buy was made, and then Paula hit the street and made her purchase.

A trip to the washroom and the fix was in. Life was more relaxed now back on her bar stool in front of the window, as she drank another Rye and Coke. Watching the dealer, she was reminded of a conversation she had with Cathy. They were stoned but she recalled details. Paula complained that she couldn't get high with Gino.

They had laughed when she'd said, "Whoever heard of a dealer who wasn't a user." She was spaced-out enough to confess, "He caught me stealing from his stash."

Cathy didn't say anything. Her eyebrows crawled like centipedes up her forehead.

Paula explained, "If he wasn't tight as a whore's pants, counting his pennies, he wouldn't have noticed me skimming off his bottom line. Then poof. The supply gone in a flash. Quicker than any line snorted."

The centipedes crawled again.

Paula got in her face and broke the silence. "You set us up and got me in this mess. With no drugs or money, what good was he? Dead weight. It'd be better if he was dead. Get something for his carcass then. The house, life insurance."

I always got my best ideas when stoned. But Gino shut them down telling me they were crazy. I was crazy. Thought he was so smart cutting me off. I showed him, wracking up the credit card. Bastard thinks he's got me, cutting up the credit card and having the mail delivered to a post office box. I'll get the fucking key off his neck and get back the credit card.

Distracted, Paula didn't notice them walk into the bar until Theresa rushed up to her.

"You wouldn't believe what we saw. I loved the wax museum, Houdini's Hall of Fame, and I want to break a Guinness World Record."

"I'm glad it was fun, sweetie."

Paula looked over at the grin on Gino's face.

"Ready?" Gino said.

Paula swilled the last of the drink and headed home to their battlefield of wills and one-upmanship. She was used to a regular fix and when Gino tightened the purse strings life got harder. She needed more to take the edge off living with him. Snarled words, criticisms, and belittled sarcastic remarks were the only forms of conversation. Fights were constant because Paula wouldn't go back to begging for her own money and having to explain what she spent her money on. Those days were over.

She wanted a way to divorce him but still get a big payday. Unfortunately, with the twenty thousand debt, she was out of luck. She needed to relax and think. She needed her fix. She'd spent most of yesterday ransacking the house looking for his stash but couldn't find it. *Smug bastard. Hiding it. Thinks I can't be trusted. Calling me a loser. Like he's better than me because he doesn't use. Calling his customers losers too. Like his shit don't stink.*

The next morning, Paula waited until Gino and Theresa left, and then she called in sick at work. She searched for the life insurance policy and the deed to the house. Her insides were a pressure cooker as she rifled through drawers while her hands shook, as jitters reacted to gut-twisting pain.

Fucking Gino thinks he can control me. Dry up my source. Dry me up. I'll get his money, then get whatever shit I want. Won't have to settle for what he peddles.

When she found a large manilla envelope in the nightstand drawer, her hands trembled scattering papers to the floor along with keys. She knelt picking up insurance policies for the car, and house. Miss-matched odd keys laid on top of everything from their marriage certificate to appliance warranties. But still no deed to the house or life insurance policy. It would be difficult to ask Gino about it without making him suspicious.

Why wouldn't it be here with the rest of the stuff? It doesn't make sense.

***

The credit card company was very obliging when she told them she accidentally washed her pants with the card in her pocket. They would send out another one today and it should only take a couple of days to get it.

Two days went by and Paula needed to get the key to the mailbox so she could get the credit card before Gino saw it. As always, Paula had a plan. After dinner and clean-up, Gino and Theresa played their board games while she watched TV. Paula waited until Theresa went to bed and Gino joined her to watch TV before going into the kitchen.

The Canadian Tire would be closed in a couple of hours. She read the instructions on the bottle of sleeping pills. To speed up the process, she ground up three additional pills over the recommended dosage into a bottle of beer.

"I'm having a beer," Paula said from the kitchen. "Want one?"

"Sure."

He was out in no time. She took the keychain from around his neck and closed the door so as not to wake Theresa. Paula drove to the Canadian Tire store a few blocks away and got a duplicate key made. Standing under the buzzing fluorescent lights, she planted her feet trying to counteract the feeling of Mexican Jumping Beans that took over her insides. While the key machine etched out her future, she looked at the Dutch Boy paint chips and perused colour choices imagining life in one of those brightly painted rooms in the advertisement. When the clerk handed her the key, she thanked him, rushed home, and replaced the original. Gino didn't stir when she pushed his head on his chest, flopped the cheap metal key and chain around his neck, and fastened the clasp.

The next morning, Gino woke up stiff and groggy. "Why did you let me sleep all night in the chair?" he said.

"I'm not your fucking nursemaid."

He looked at the clock. "No time for a shit, shower and shave."

Gino dressed and headed out the door. Paula called in sick at work to go to the post office with the key. It was simple enough to get the mailbox number, people were so gullible. Paula sized up the postal clerk behind the counter as she approached: early fifties, mousey looking with those pinched features, married maybe 20-25 years, enough time to be resentful and pissed at her husband.

"Oh, I can't believe it." Paula walked up to the clerk, shaking her head.

"What's wrong?"

"My husband gave me the key to pick up the mail, but I forgot the mailbox number." Paula smiled and dangled the cheese to get the mouse. "Guess I'm so used to tuning him out, I let it go in one ear and out the other."

The clerk laughed.

If you can get people to laugh, they trust you. She'd played enough people to know. It always worked. The clerk gave her the number. Among the expected bills was a notice for renewal on a safety deposit box at the bank, but no credit card yet. She took the renewal notice to get the number for the safety deposit box.

Maybe his stash was there. Another fucking key! Then she remembered all the single keys Gino kept in the nightstand drawer. *Maybe it was one of them.*

She didn't know how safety deposit boxes worked and whether she would be able to access Gino's without his permission, so she went to the bank to find out. Under the pretense of getting a safety deposit box, the bank clerk gave her all the paperwork, including the paper to add a co-applicant to an already existing account. She filled out the co-applicant form, which would allow her access to Gino's safety deposit box, forged his signature, and dropped it back off at the bank.

The next day Paula gathered the five loose keys in the envelope and went to the bank. None of them fit the safety deposit box and it was getting late. Theresa would be off the bus soon, so she needed to get back home.

Theresa walked through the doorway, all excited—talking too fast and waving a paper in her face. The endless babble drove Paula crazy. Mexican Jumping Beans were back in her stomach. Theresa agitated them. All she heard was blah, blah, blah, when Theresa shoved the paper in her face again. Paula was aware her body shook, aware her hand aided it, accelerating it, when she plucked Theresa by the arm, dragged her into the living room, plunked her into a chair, and turned on the TV.

Paula returned to the kitchen. She tried to think. Figure out a way. Theresa stomped back into the kitchen, arms flapping, the white page at the end of her fingertips fluttered and reminded her of a flag. But instead of surrendering, Theresa demanded to be heard.

"Sign it. Just sign it so I can go on the trip. It's a permission slip. I can't go until you sign it."

Fucking kid wasn't going to stop.

Paula opened the junk drawer looking for a pen. Rummaging through discarded crap: lighters, paper clips, hairbands, and elastics, she spotted a single key.

"There's a pen," Theresa reached into the drawer and put it in Paula's shaking hand. Theresa went back to the living room with the signed page as Paula took the key out of the drawer examining it.

Why wasn't this key with the others?

Paula looked at the clock. "I'm going out. Be back soon."

The bank clerk warned her they'd be closing soon so she wouldn't have long to be in the vault. Paula was shocked when she opened the box and saw a bank book for a separate checking account set up by Gino.

She'd been fired from enough jobs to know what record of employment forms and UI applications were. But the paperwork was already completed waiting for a name and some personal information to be filled in. She couldn't put it together until she checked out the bank book deposits followed by debits to the credit card company in neat columns. Gino was making a bundle off this latest con and she was getting nothing. She didn't get a chance to go through the rest of the stuff underneath the UI applications and ROEs when a bank employee barged in telling her they were closing so she must leave. She'd have to come back again to see what else was in there. Maybe she'd find the life insurance and deed there too.

When Paula got home, she was surprised their neighbour Henrietta was in the kitchen. Theresa explained Gino came home and got Henrietta to look after her because he wanted to leave. Then Paula remembered today was the third Friday of the month. She'd have to wait until he got home to find out about this scam.

Chapter 13

Gino was barely through the front door when Paula said, "It's about time."

"Did you miss me?" Gino hung his coat on a peg and then walked toward her.

"Don't I always?"

The sweet tone of her voice stopped him as he braced himself, ready for impact. Paula knew the night before when he left, it was to make his buys, so he should have more forms.

"How many more record forms and applications did you get?"

Gino looked over at Theresa sitting on the couch watching TV. "Hey, Kiddo."

Without taking her eyes off the TV, Theresa's hand waved in the air. Gino raised his eyebrows, nodding his head toward the kitchen. "What are you talking about?"

"You don't think people talk to me? I have friends; I hear things. This one is a real money maker. So how many more did you get?"

"Yer not makin' no sense."

"I know you're getting five hundred a pop for them. So, where's the money?"

Gino shoved Paula against the kitchen countertop and whispered, "Who the fuck are you to question me?"

His scare tactics couldn't dampen Paula's enthusiasm. "This one's a real money maker."

"Told you, I don't know what yer yabberin about."

"You want me to dog your trail? I'll find out who's supplying you and get some for myself."

His shoulders slouched.

"Too short..." Paula bit back the rest of another joke. "So, how many more did you get?"

"None."

"Why not?"

"I don't got to answer to you." Gino stood with his knuckles pressed into his sides. They disappeared into his fleshy stomach. "When I sell the last of what I got, I'm closin' up shop."

"Are you crazy? They're making you a shitload of money. Why would you do that?"

"This has nothin' to do with you. It's my business only."

"This is the jackpot of all jackpots. It's cash for life, Gino. Think about it—cash for life. The pogey office will always be there. You'd be a fool to give this up."

"I don't want to hear no more about this. When the forms are gone, I'm done."

"If you don't want to do it, tell me where to get those forms. I'll do it and give you a cut. Hell, I'll give you all the money. Just tell me where to get the forms."

"When I went to get the forms from the supplier, his buddy told me the cops picked him up. If I'd got there sooner, they'd of nabbed me too."

"Isn't there someone else you can get them from?"

"It's too risky. The cops are all over this one. So, when I sell the last of 'em, I'm out of business. What's for dinner?" Gino said.

"Get it yourself. I'm not a damn restaurant. Theresa and I ate an hour ago. If you wanted dinner, you should have been home on time."

Paula envisioned money rolling in from this cash for life con. She'd already picked out the new car she'd buy and the house they'd move into. For the first time in her life, she thought she'd be set, thumbing her nose at everyone else. But everything Gino touched soured. As long as she lived with him, she'd have nothing. Gino was making life too difficult.

***

The first thing Monday morning, Gino went to the bank and checked out his safety deposit box. An ROE was on top and the bank book was underneath. It was not the way he left it. He rifled through the applications, to the stack of ROEs. Digging further, he found the life insurance policy, deed to the house, and pictures of him and Jackie all seemed undisturbed. Taking out the UI applications and ROEs, he stuffed them into a briefcase. He got another safety deposit box put the life insurance, deed, and pictures in it, and then mailed the only key to Jackie with instructions.

Gino came home to the smell of his favourite dinner, garlic bread, and lasagna. Theresa sat at the kitchen table doing homework when Gino entered the room. She looked up at him grinning. He smiled back, did two eyebrow raises and she gave him the thumbs up. They mimed signals and secret gestures Paula gave up trying to figure out.

"What you doin'?" Gino leaned over her shoulder.

Theresa pointed a ruler at her math textbook. "Fractions."

"The only fractions I know are the ones you put a cast on," Gino said.

Theresa laughed. "That's fractures," she said.

"Clear the table and set it," Paula instructed Theresa.

Gino winked at Theresa.

After dinner, Gino sat with his feet on the recliner, which took the pressure off his full belly.

"When you finish your homework, I'll have a game of Rummy with you," he said.

Theresa and Gino played cards in the kitchen while Paula watched TV in the living room. The evening passed pleasantly except for the few times when Paula hollered at them to keep the noise down when their laughter got too loud. After Theresa went to bed, Gino went into the living room.

"Cathy's got a new boyfriend," Paula said.

"You mean a new pimp?"

"No. A boyfriend. He's an insurance salesman."

"Oh, so he's a John."

"Cathy says he's great. I was thinking about having them over next Saturday for cards. What do you think?"

"Insurance salesman, it's all I need. Those guys are all the same. Always tryin' to sell a policy. Ain't met one yet that didn't try to sell me somethin'."

"He can't sell you what you already have. You have life insurance, right?"

"A course."

"Then what's the problem? If it's upsetting you, I won't bother." Which was just as well, seeing as how Cathy didn't have a boyfriend.

"Good."

The next morning, Theresa sat at the kitchen table eating Rice Krispies when Gino came downstairs, dressed for the docks.

"Morning," Gino said. Paula didn't look at him as she made a peanut butter sandwich for Theresa's lunch.

Gino took the kettle from the cupboard and plugged it in. From years of being in the same position, the kettle permanently steamed a patch of filmy white on the dark wood cabinet above the counter.

"Pull the kettle forward so the steam isn't hitting the cupboard door."

Paula nagged the same line every morning. There was never any reaction. If she didn't do something now to change her life, everything would go on the same way and fifteen years from now she'd be staring at the dishes through the hole he would eventually make in the cupboard door.

"Apple or orange?" Paula said.

"Orange. Can I have a cookie too?"

Paula gathered everything and put it into a brown paper bag. "Get your book bag, the bus will be here soon." She balled a tea towel in her hand mopping sweat, then squeezed the towel to hide the shakes. "Have a good day."

Gino curled two fingers wiggling them. Theresa responded with the same gesture. It translated to, don't take no shit. Paula knew the signal. She overheard Gino and Theresa laughing about this kid, Billy Thompson, a bully Gino picked up by the ankles and swung around. He said the two wiggling fingers reminded him of Billy's legs squirming trying to get away. Gino grinned every time his fingers wiggled to make the gesture.

Paula cleaned up the kitchen, wiping the table around him. She squeezed the tea towel, nails biting into her palms, that mimicked the ache chewing at her insides. Gino scooped out another spoonful of sugar from the bowl and spilled some on the table.

The shakes were her dipstick, a marker indicating she was down a few grams and needed to be topped up with cocaine—to even her out. As far as Gino knew, she'd cleaned up her act. And since the shakes were her reaction to withdrawal, he wouldn't be suspicious. He was used to seeing her body tremble sporadically. If Gino saw the shakes, he'd tell her to tough it out. But he didn't use, didn't understand. He'd cut off more of her money, forcing her to go cold turkey—threatening Cathy again. But cold turkey never lasted long. Paula was always able to figure out a way to get a fix. Like when she convinced Cathy to give her money for the drugs she bought from the dealer in Niagara Falls. Cathy left today to visit her mom out of town for a week. Choked off from her supply, Paula shot daggers at him.

Gino laid his dripping spoon on the spot she just cleaned. He read the newspaper not aware of what she was doing and was unprepared for the dishcloth she flung at him.

"I'm sick of cleaning up after you."

"I ain't never asked you to. I can look after myself."

"Oh, I'd like to take care of you." Paula gritted her teeth.

She knew most of the guys who would pull the trigger for a price, but so did Gino. Those guys liked him, so the odds of finding someone to do him in were slim. Even just asking around, would get back to Gino. If she wanted it done, she would have to do it herself.

"Are you just gonna stand there starin' at me with that stupid grin on your face?"

She didn't move just continued staring. The grin got bigger.

Gino wiped off the table and threw the dishcloth into the sink before he headed out the door.

Butting out her cigarette in the ashtray, hands shaking, Paula turned the TV on. She couldn't concentrate on solving the Password clues hunched over as she clutched her stomach—the pain too real. Anxiety was building faster than nausea. A voice was back in her head insisting she needed a fix. It wouldn't stop. It was right. She needed to get topped up and knew what she'd have to do. With Cathy gone for the week, she must go back to old habits from her early teenage years and earn the money she needed for drugs. She drove out of town to turn tricks, so Gino wouldn't find out about it.

Hours later, back on the living room couch, with the shakes gone, she tried to forget about the old sweaty bodies that had laid on top of her as she played out Gino's murder, editing and refining as she went. Before Theresa came home from school, Paula created a plausible scene for her chalk outline. The only problem was it must be done while Gino still had the record of employment forms and applications. She needed to turn him in for this because it was the only job he worked alone. She didn't want to make more enemies by implicating others in his drug dealings.

Gino startled her when he walked in. "How was your day?"

"Best day in a long time, things are looking up."

"Glad to hear it."

"I was talking to Cathy today. She's disappointed we can't get together Saturday, but she said her boyfriend was wondering who we were insured with?"

"See. Didn't I tell you? He wants to sell us a policy. Did you tell her?"

"No. She said something about him doing a comparable for us."

"Not interested."

"She said we could save a lot, especially on life insurance. Is the life insurance with the same insurance company as our auto?"

"Yeah, but I'm still not interested."

"Okay." *Problem solved. Might not have the policy, but I know it's at the insurance company that has our auto coverage.* "So how were sales today?"

"Great, sold another five. I guess word's gettin' around."

Paula took the casserole dish out of the oven. It translated to $2,500. It was a shame to give up the rest of the money, but she must if she wanted to turn Gino in. For an arrest, he was required to have the stolen properties on him.

"So how many forms do you have left?"

"Six."

***

Each time she reviewed the details of the plan, there were more complications, which required her to come up with yet another new and improved scenario. If he sold the same amount tomorrow, he would only have one record form left. If she didn't act now, she might not get another chance.

Chapter 14

After Gino left the house for the docks the next morning, Paula rushed upstairs to shower and dress. There was so much to do. She walked from their wartime house down the block to a busy gas station on Barton Street. She waved and called "Hi," to Ronnie who pumped gas, before opening the old, battered phone booth door. If Ronnie thought it was strange for her to use the phone booth when she was so close to home, he didn't say anything. The guys here all knew her. For years this was the only place Gino would bring the old Pontiac in for servicing. It was an easy walk down the street to pick up when it was ready, and the guys here knew not to mess with Gino.

"Police Department." Paula wasn't prepared for the cheerful sound.

"I'd like to report a crime," she said.

"Hold the line please while I transfer the call."

"Detective Murphy. How can I help you?" a gruff voice asked.

"I'd like to report a crime." Paula heard the shuffle of paperwork.

"What's your name?" Murphy said.

"I have to be anonymous."

"So, what's the crime?"

"I guess it would be defrauding the government."

"In what way?"

"Record of employment forms have been stolen from the Unemployment Insurance Office. They're filled out so a person can get pogey for a year, without ever working." Paula smirked. "The buyer pays five hundred for the completed forms."

"How many are we talking about?"

"He's gone through close to fifty, but he only has a few left. He should be out of them by today if it gets busy."

"Who's selling them?"

Paula hesitated a moment and prepared for the investigation with a deep sigh.

"What's his name?"

Another deep sigh preceded the sound made by the dime she tapped against the chrome ledge. More tapping, like it was a hard decision. Make him sweat.

"You need to promise me you won't pick him up at home. He has a daughter. She doesn't need to see her step-father handcuffed by police." Paula made her voice sound shaky.

"Okay, we won't pick him up at home. We'll play by any rules you want. His name?"

"You need to promise." Worry and nervousness in Paula's voice were evident.

"Okay already, I promise. Good enough?"

Her silence made him prompt again. "I have to know his name."

"Gino Amodeo," Paula almost whispered.

"Where can we find him?"

"The docks, off Burlington Street."

She was heady with excitement at the thought of the cops picking him up. She wished she could be there to see the look on his face. He thought he was too smart to get caught.

"Is he connected?"

"Do you mean with the mob?" Paula let the shock register in her voice.

"Yeah." The officer sounded exasperated.

"No. I mean, I don't know. No, he couldn't be,"

She looked at her watch. "Will you be picking him up soon?"

"Can't say for sure. Is there anything else you can tell us?"

"Don't hurt him."

"Does he work with anyone else?"

"He works alone."

"Is he armed?"

"I don't know."

"Do you know how he gets these records of employment things?"

"No."

"Is he there every day or does he change his location?"

"No, he's always at the docks. He knows a lot of the guys from the union down there."

"Do you know who his customers are?"

"Seasonal workers, union guys, sailors who decide to stay for a while, and anyone else who needs easy money. Word gets out on the street. People don't think much about hosing the government."

Paula checked her watch again. Time enough for a trace.

"You won't hurt him? He's a good man and a good father; he's just treading down the wrong path and I'm afraid he'll get himself killed. I couldn't stop him, but you can. I have to save him from himself."

She could almost hear the halleluiah bible-thumping chorus and wanted to add, that the devil made him do it.

"Don't worry. If you need to get a hold of me for any reason, my name is Detective Anthony Murphy."

Paula hung up the phone and dialed the number for Budget Rent-a-Truck. She spoke to a clerk who informed her of their reasonable rates and assured her that small trucks or moving vans could be rented anytime. It was happening. She was setting everything in motion. Was she crazy? Could she pull it off? She wanted to tell Cathy about her plan. She needed someone to confide in. But Cathy would want some of the money. Might even threaten to rat her out to the cops if she didn't get half. The daydream was getting real. Paula didn't know if she could go through with it. She hated Gino, but she didn't know if she could pull the trigger and watch him die. But she wanted the money. And she wouldn't share it. After two years with Gino's hoarding ways, she was owed that money.

Chapter 15

Gino drove down the pot-holed road to the docks on Burlington Street and parked in front of the building housing Union Local 786. Over the years, the windowpanes were layered in thick grey soot which made it impossible to see inside the building. The workers checked in daily with their Union Local to see if there was any work for them. It was a large local, with many members who created a steady flow of traffic making it easy for him to blend into the crowd. He heard snickers and overheard one man say to another, "Looks like a kid with a lemonade stand," when he passed by them.

Once outside, Gino walked by a row of large shipping crates and watched while one was hoisted by a crane and deposited onto an old, rusted barge. A lot of men were milling about with little work getting done. Walking along the shore, his heavy work boots sank into the sand. Rotting fish decorated with seaweed floated in coloured rings of pollutants edging the bay to wash up on shore. Gino was reminded of gasoline rainbows on the pavement when he side-stepped the colourful scum of roiling water that licked up sludge from the shore to backwash it into the undulating ebbs. The smell was putrid.

At dock 17, Gino set up a folding lawn chair and put a briefcase on a TV tray. Hopefully, he'd finish his business today. His business was slow but steady. He watched a man coming toward him. He exhibited the right look: scuffed worn work boots, coveralls, sleeves rolled up. But he could tell the closer he got by his nails. Dirt always gets under the fingernails here. At least he was alone. Gino wouldn't do business if two guys came. He'd act like he didn't know what they were talking about when they asked for the pogey forms. Cops travel in twos for backup.

The man stood beside the TV tray. "Heard you're the guy to see." He took his hand out of his pocket wiping his palm across his chin leaving a dark smudge. "Got laid off and don't got enough weeks for pogey."

Gino noticed the dirt around his cuticles and under his nails. "It's five hundred dollars upfront."

The man took a wad of twenty-dollar bills out of his pocket and counted them into piles of hundreds on the TV tray. After Gino examined the money and re-counted it; he put it in his pocket, opened the case, got out a completed ROE, and filled in a few details in the blank spaces.

"Give me your social insurance card." Gino printed the number clearly on the ROE and the application.

"What's your address and phone number?" He worked between both forms. "I'm makin' today your last day worked." He dated the application form turning it around to face the man before handing him back his ID. "Sign here," he said as he watched the man write Anthony Murphy. With his hands so close to Gino's nose, he caught a whiff of a familiar smell. He was reminded of his father and Sunday mornings when he polished his shoes before church. Another man approached as he gave Murphy the employee's copy of the ROE while keeping the employer's copy.

"Done deal," Gino said. "Take this to the UI office on Rebecca Street. It will take four to..." The smell was shoe polish. He looked at the man's cuticles. The second man was closing in.

"Nice doing business with you Giovanni," Murphy said, as he showed him his badge. Before Gino could bolt, the other man flung him onto the ground, buckling the TV tray legs around his body. He cuffed Gino's hands behind his back, read him his rights, and pulled him off the ground.

When Gino was taken to the police station for interrogation, he told them the story Jackie concocted about an exchange of money for ROEs at Arpico Steel. When they questioned him further about the exchange they asked for the locker number. After giving it to them, he pulled the paper with the combination to the lock out of his wallet and handed it to the officer. Gretzinger made Gino write up a sworn statement corroborating the information he supplied. The cops were planning on staking out the locker to nab the suspect. In his statement, Gino claimed he didn't know who supplied him with the ROEs. He'd only spoken to the man over the phone.

When he was granted his one phone call, he was tempted to call Jackie and warn her but decided against it. He didn't want her phone number to show on police phone records. She couldn't be connected to him in any way. He called Paula instead so she could make bail. He gave her the name of a lawyer and said they were holding him overnight.

***

The lawyer couldn't give Paula a time when Gino would be released tomorrow but said he would call her when he found out. Not knowing when to expect Gino made Paula anxious. Her plan hinged on a sequence of events happening. But there was so much she had no control over.

Paula went upstairs to their bedroom, knelt on the floor, and hauled folded moving boxes out from underneath the bed. She put the boxes together, loaded them up with clothes and toiletries, and dragged each one downstairs to the front door. Paula packed Theresa's clothes in the same haphazard way. Although she was exhausted, knowing she was almost free of Gino was exhilarating. Paula looked at the time. Theresa would be off the school bus soon. She couldn't have her come home to a houseful of boxes, so she met her at the corner with an overnight bag.

They ate an early supper at a diner around the corner from Cathy's place.

"Why do I have to stay at Cathy's?" Theresa used her sleeve and mopped ketchup oozing from the corner of her mouth.

"Use the napkin. I told you already. I'm meeting with the girls and Gino is out of town."

"I'm old enough to look after myself. I don't need a babysitter."

"Cathy will make sure you get to school in the morning, so you don't have to take the bus."

"Whoopee do."

"I don't need your attitude right now, so knock it off. After school, you can come home on the bus like always."

Theresa finished the rest of her burger and fries in silence. When the bill was paid, Paula marched her daughter to Cathy's place and left, with little said except, "Thanks, Cathy. We'll catch up later about your time away." Paula handed Theresa the overnight bag. "See you tomorrow after school."

Once home, Paula packed the kitchen. She decided to take all the good stuff and leave a few of the mismatched dishes and glasses for him. It wasn't like he was getting them anyway. After all, he wouldn't need any of it not when he was six feet under. She kept the pretense as if she was dividing things, so the scene she was setting looked right. She wrapped her favourite casserole dishes in bathroom towels. Frying pans and pots along with the rest of the kitchen paraphernalia were categorized into good or bad condition, special, and not so. The good and preferred things were thrown into moving boxes. She would leave the appliances for Gino. Paula didn't have enough strength to scour away pit marks and permanent stains on the rusted white enamel stove from years of use and neglect. There would be no need to empty the fridge. After she got the insurance money and house, she'd have money enough for nice new avocado-green appliances. She wanted a fresh start. Maybe she could buy a new townhouse. She didn't want his old kettle. It would remind her too much of him. Paula looked at the clock, 11:10 p.m. She was tired. The food in the cupboards could wait for tomorrow. Exhausted, she headed upstairs to bed.

Chapter 16

Paula got up early, raring to go. Slicked with pink nail polish and lipstick, effervescent in pink pants and matching poncho, some women would be described as a tall drink of water, but Paula was more like a stout gulp of Pepto-Bismol.

She called a taxi and was on her way to pick up a small moving van rented over the phone yesterday. It was going to be a busy day. The taxi pulled up to the door at 7:55 a.m. Paula counted out the fare. When the rental agent unlocked the front door at 8:00 a.m., Paula was the first in line. With the paperwork concluded and a key in her hand, she headed out to the lot and gave the form to the car jockey. Paula jumped into the van. Experienced with bigger trucks before, she wasn't intimidated by its size. Checking her watch, she drove the six blocks to her house, and then backed into her driveway, avoiding the low-hanging branches of their silver maple tree.

The lawyer hadn't called yet to say when Gino was going to be released. She was going to have to wing it. Paula called the Unemployment Insurance office.

"Casual labour office," she said.

Waiting to be transferred, she thought, yeah right, an office. One guy behind a desk in a cubicle. Some office! She knew these labourers would never work long enough to get pogey. Most were homeless addicts who could only work a few hours, nothing steady. She wasn't looking for dependable, just bodies to hear and be disinterested enough not to react to her scream.

"I need to hire two men to help me move boxes and furniture into a van."

For the next hour, she packed canned goods and food items from the cupboards into the sturdiest boxes. *The movers should have been here by now.*

She hoped all the days spent planning and organizing this scheme would work otherwise she'd be the one on the floor dead. And Gino would be counting his blessings. She finished putting together the last of the flattened moving boxes before the doorbell rang.

Paula didn't react to the men who stood on her front porch. She wasn't shocked by the look or smell of them. She could tell they slept on cardboard in alleyways. She knew their type from sleeping on the streets as a teenager, knew that exposed skin iced to a winter sidewalk could thaw when curled up in a laundromat dryer for a quarter. And she knew by the look of them, they'd do anything for their next bottle—anything that got rid of the shakes.

"Pogey office sent us for a moving job." The sallow-skinned man belched acrid gases of digested alcohol from a split lip.

"You can wash up at the kitchen sink." Paula led the way. "Load the boxes at the front door into the moving van first, and then start upstairs in the bedrooms."

While the movers were busy, Paula went to the bedrooms. Using adhesive-backed red dots which she purchased days earlier in an office supply store, Paula placed a red dot on each piece of furniture to be carried out and into the moving van. The movers finished loading the boxes at the front door and met her upstairs.

"Take only the furniture and lamps with a red dot on them."

The unhealthy-looking man nodded his head.

"Good. Now get your asses moving," she said.

Paula went back downstairs to finish off the kitchen. Occasionally, when she heard the men shuffle and grunt under the weight, she checked on their progress.

"Is this going to take long?" She crossed her arms and tapped her foot.

The men walked with their heads down.

By the time the upstairs furniture was arranged in the moving van, Paula had finished packing the kitchen and progressed to the living room. Red tagging the furniture was easy. Only the newer, better pieces of furniture were tagged. She kept a room ahead of them. Paula noted the time before taking the battery-operated kitchen clock from the wall.

"Can't you move a little faster?"

Neither of the movers looked at her. Paula nagged between the six trips each of the movers made from the kitchen to the van. She packed the upstairs and kitchen first and saved the living room, which was at the front of the house, for last. She was in the living room with a clear view of the street and their driveway. Paula felt relieved knowing Gino couldn't sneak in without her seeing him. Gino would have to park in the driveway below their living room window since she had parked the van on the far side of the two-car driveway.

The last red-tagged piece of living room furniture was loaded into the vehicle. She wasn't sure if the men sweated from exertion or forced detox. Either way, they looked exhausted and thirsty, but she wasn't about to offer them a break or even a glass of water. It was 1:05 p.m. She looked down the street. Not knowing when Gino would show up kept her on edge. She didn't know what she would do if Theresa came home before Gino. If he wasn't here by 2:30 p.m., she would ask Cathy to pick Theresa up after school.

"The only thing left is the shed out back. Do it first, and then dismantle the swing set."

Since her witnesses were out back and away from the impending crime scene, she had one less thing to worry about.

Paula pushed back the curtains over the kitchen window. She watched the movers walk by Theresa's swing set. Those concrete foundation blocks leaning against the rusted swing set poles infuriated her. The poles should have been cemented into the ground. Gino always did things half-assed. When Theresa swung, the poles lifted out of the ground, then back in again with the motion. How many times did she bug Gino to cement those damn things? Now she was glad he hadn't. At least dismantling the swing set would keep the movers busy in the backyard away from the house.

The old poorly-constructed shed was off to the right corner of the property, surrounded by tall weeds. Paula opened the window. *What the hell were those two idiots doing, saluting each other?*

Then she realized, they shielded their eyes from the sun. There was no padlock on the door, and rusted hinges made it droop lopsided in its frame. The bearded man heaved upward on the door and opened it. Like yellow highlighter, the ray of sunlight stroked the rusted garden tools, wheelbarrow, lawn mower, and flower pots. The movers disappeared from view into the shed. She chuckled, imagining what they would do upon sight of the two full twenty-sixers of Canadian Club planted there earlier.

Paula paced the living room, her fingernail picked at a hangnail on her thumb. Her eyes flitted from ripped skin around the thumbnail to the Timex Watch around her wrist. Ten minutes since the movers went out back. When Paula lifted the living room window, she saw her neighbour's curtain move and knew Henrietta lurked behind it. Paula was surprised Henrietta didn't come over when she'd pulled up with the moving van. Henrietta lived for gossip. But most people in this neighbourhood were smart enough to see when trouble brewed and wise enough to stay clear of it.

Paula watched for Gino's car. A drop of blood slid along her jagged raw cuticle. She backed away from the window out of Henrietta's sight. Like a well-choreographed dance, she practiced her movements to ensure she would end up on the floor underneath him.

How long?

How long did she have before Gino would be home? Every time a car came down the street, Paula felt like a rubber band had been stretched tight around the top of her head and made it pulse, while a pressure throbbed. When it wasn't Gino's car, the band slackened in relief and left only a tingly pins and needles numbness.

Again, from the top.

Her index finger, pointed with thumb up, mimicked the gun: bang, back in the pocket, fingers tugging the poncho from front to back as she turned her back to him. He'd slump over her, and they'd fall to the floor. Him on top of her.

When the next car came, the band twisted tight, gouging into anxiety, and pinched nerves. Running to the kitchen window, she swallowed hard, trying to clear the thrumming static clogging her ears. The movers were nowhere in sight. Back in the living room, she checked her watch, fingers yanked the poncho. When she heard another car coming, her body shook with aspirated breath rattling inside her chest until the street was silent again. *Was Gino even being released today? Could all of this have been for nothing? What if the cops kept him another day and not the customary 24 hours?*

Paula felt the threads of truth tugging on her reality, threatening to unravel her plans. She rolled the neck of the poncho and saw the tag confirming she had it on backward.

Sprinting to the kitchen, she looked out the window and saw the sallow-faced mover. He walked toward the house. She felt dizzy. Static in her ears returned.

What the fuck! He couldn't come in. Gino would be home any minute.

She dashed out the backdoor and jogged toward the mover. Barely contained hysterical jitters vibrated her head and hands.

Fucking mover. Didn't they find the booze?

"What are you doing?" she hissed as he advanced.

The mover stopped. "Got to take a piss."

Thankful for the smell of alcohol, Paula said, "You can't come in. You can piss or shit in the backyard for all I care because you're not getting in."

Paula noticed his eyes staring down at her and she remembered the gun in her pants pocket and looked down to make sure the poncho covered it up. She tugged a bit on the garment to readjust it.

Could he see the gun's outline? "Get back to what you're doing."

He looked at her again with an unsettled sense, then turned and walked away. Paula ran back into the kitchen, pulled the curtain away from the window, and watched him take a leak against the shed. She picked up a tea towel from the counter and dried her sweaty palms. Bolting to the living room, with the towel in hand, her heart raced when she heard Gino's car and saw it come into view. No time left. Paula grabbed the windowsill for support and felt the vibration from the Pontiac's dual exhaust, as Gino parked the car.

Damn Lawyer! She watched Gino get out of the car and look into the moving van before he came up onto the front porch. Across the road, in her house, Paula saw Henrietta pleated into her living room curtain looking out—spying.

Paula got a stabbing pain and twitch in her right eye. The door opened and closed. She raced to the foyer, fell against Gino's chest, and sobbed.

"I don't know what the lawyer told you, but we don't got to skip town. Don't overreact. It'll be just a little jail time. Calm down," Gino said.

Paula felt his hand rubbing her back. She typically wore tops stretched tightly across her thick torso and wasn't used to the yard of material hanging down from around her neck.

Paula screamed, "No, No," as she pulled the gun out of her pants pocket. Cautious to aim the gun on a slant, her hand shook when she slammed the muzzle against his barrel chest and fired. Following her choreographed dance, she automatically put the gun back into her pocket. The impact from the bullet sent Gino sprawling backward onto the floor. His eyes mirrored her stunned look.

"Fuck!" She mopped up the blood on her face and neck with the tea towel and left it on the floor beside him. Adjusting the poncho, so the blood splatter was on her back, she hissed at him. "You couldn't even get this fucking right."

He should have slumped over top of her, taking her down to the floor. She needed to get underneath him. It was the only way it would look like self-defence. Laying next to him, Paula turned on her side tight against Gino's body, pulled his arm, and rolled him over on his side. Listening for a creak in the back door, she tugged repeatedly on his arm until his body toppled over her back, flattening her to the floor.

The movers must have heard the scream. It was loud enough. But as predicted, they didn't come to investigate. Gunshots and street violence were part of their life, nothing new or out of the ordinary. They knew not to get involved.

Henrietta would have heard Paula scream. The old lady had radar hearing and picked up on all the whispered gossip. She'd probably be reluctant to do anything until she heard the gunshot. Only then would she call the police.

Gino's laboured breath wheezed against Paula's ear. The warmth of his blood spread across her back and she was grateful the initial blood splatter would be absorbed into the gush of blood smeared between their bodies.

Paula felt Gino struggle for deep gulps of air as he tried to clear his throat but only managed a croaking choking sound. She heard a gurgle before blood bubbled, and sputtered out of his mouth, puddling in her hair.

"It's self-defence, Gino. So, who's the stupid one now?" Paula asked. "I'm getting the house and your life insurance. I'm getting it all."

Paula looked over her shoulder into Gino's shattered face and was surprised to see him cry. She had expected anger, even rage, but never the softness of sorrow.

She heard a faint crack and felt a warm flow of urine trickle between their bodies when Gino expelled his last breath crushing her against the dirty linoleum floor. Paula shifted and tried offsetting his weight when she felt something jab into her stomach. She had forgotten about the gun. It had to be between their bodies. She worked the gun out of her pocket and pulled up her knees so she could use her back as leverage. Over and over again, her knees slid back, rubbed raw by the gritty dirt on the linoleum while Gino's

Harley Davidson belt buckle scoured her back like steel wool. When she inched under Gino's body, she slumped her back and created a hollow where she could put the gun.

With the weapon finally in place, exhausted, Paula collapsed underneath his weight, her cheek pressed into the dirt on the floor. When she turned her head, grit stuck to her cheek and made a scraping sound against the floor. She was surprised to see the build-up of yellow wax on the linoleum. She never noticed how bumpy the floor was. Like blackheads nestled into facial pores, dirt was pitted into the wax. No wonder the floor never looked clean. So much for linoleum, her next floor would have a smooth flat surface. Hardwood maybe. She could afford it now.

When she heard police sirens, she knew people scattered to their homes and cars, squashing any potential street deals to be done.

Two police cars pulled up to the house and blocked the path of the moving van and Gino's car, to ensure no one from inside the house could use those vehicles to escape. Four police officers rushed onto the front porch.

"Police. Open up," one of the officers shouted.

"Help." Paula's hysterical, mournful cries bleated out the words, "He's dead."

"Is there anyone else inside the house?" the officer asked.

Paula's sobs had become gut-wrenching spasms of grief.

"Ma'am, calm down. We can't do anything until you answer the question. Is there anyone else with you?"

"No." Paula puffed the word out. "Help me."

Her soulful plea got a reaction. Between the strands of hair camouflaging her face, Paula saw the looks the cops exchanged before one pointed to Paula's shoes peeking out from under Gino's bell-bottom pants. Two officers cleared the house and made sure there was no one else inside, while the other two knelt over the bodies. One officer felt for a pulse in Gino's neck, then shook his head.

"He's dead."

"Get him off." Paula's broken sobs turned to loud hysterical screams. An officer knelt beside her and looked into her ghoulish mascara-smeared face and garish, bright blue eye shadow that accentuated the blue veins around her eyes.

"Are you hurt?" the officer asked.

"Get him…" Paula's words faded with a grunt.

One officer straddled Gino's stout body while the other one clutched Paula's left wrist.

"Just a minute. I need to get her other arm."

She felt the officer tighten his grip on her slippery skin.

"He's got her pinned. Lift him a bit." The officer braced his feet, ready to pull.

"When I say go, you drag her out," the officer straddling Gino said.

The gun was digging into her back, but when the officer lifted the corpse, it rolled onto the floor with a thud.

"Go."

He hauled her along the floor until she was freed of Gino's weight.

Chapter 17

The officer helped Paula stand and sat her in a brown leather recliner. Round holes left by cigarette burns ran along the arm of the chair. Kneeling beside it, hand on the arm of the chair, the officer's fingertip slid into a hole. "Are you alright?"

She looked down at herself. "I think I'm okay." Her hand went around to her back. "Something hurts there. And my knees are sore."

The officer lifted the poncho revealing raw scratches and he noted her scraped knees after raising her pant legs.

"What happened?" the officer asked.

Paula took a couple of ragged breaths and calmed herself.

"Take deeper breaths," the officer said.

"When Gino came home, he was furious." Paula took another deep gulp. "He knew I turned him in. He was committing fraud. I had to." She panted out the words. "Why would someone at the police station tell him it was me? I was supposed to be anonymous."

Flipping open his pocket notebook, the officer took down her statement.

"Called me a fucking bitch. Said he was going to kill me. When he reached into his pocket, I could tell he had a gun."

Paula paused and waited for the officer's pen to catch up with her words. When the pen stopped, Paula waited until the officer looked at her. She wanted him to see the anguish in her face when she said, "He was furious. Going to kill me." She spoke in such disbelief of what had happened it sounded real, even to herself. "Just as he brought the gun out, I knocked it from his hand. It fell to the floor. We both dove to get it. I reached it first and I don't know what happened. Gino twisted my hand behind my back. He was on top of me so fast. One minute we were standing, and then we were on the floor fighting. The gun ...” She cried and couldn't continue.

“I'll get you some water.” The officer returned and handed her a glass of water. He waited patiently until she was finished and then he set the glass down on the floor. “Better?”

Paula nodded. “Yes.”

“Okay, what about the gun?”

“The gun was in my hand when it went off, but my hand was behind my back, and I couldn't get turned around because he was on top of me. I don't even remember pulling the trigger, but I must have.”

When two detectives who gave their names as Anthony Murphy and Daniel Gretzinger, arrived on the scene, the officer who had been questioning Paula stood and walked over to them.

The officer gave his opinion from what he could tell, it looked like self-defence. The officer explained how she was pinned under Gino, stomach to the floor when they arrived, with the gun sandwiched between them. He described how the gun rolled off her back when they lifted Gino's body, the blood stain on the back of her top, the lack of blood on her front, the scratches on her back, and the scrapes on her knees. “Oh, I almost forgot,” he said. “He accused her of turning him in. Something about fraud. She said he was pretty worked up about it. He just got released.”

“Thanks,” Murphy said.

The two detectives checked out the body on the floor before they turned their attention to Paula. While they were interrogating her, another officer brought in the two movers from the shed.

“Look what I found.” The officer escorted the movers in while carrying the two empty bottles of Canadian Club Whisky.

“They're the movers,” Paula said. “Where were you?” she hissed at the two men. “This happened because you were too slow. I should have been out of here before Gino got home! It's your fault. If it weren't for you two, Gino would still be alive!” She burst into tears.

“Where did you find them?” Murphy said.

"Backyard. I looked out the kitchen window and noticed the shed door was open. They were sitting in a corner, so you wouldn't see them from the house. They each had a bottle. Claim they found them in a flower pot."

"You know anything about the booze?" Murphy said, turning to Paula.

"If I thought Gino had booze out there, I would have taken it too."

"You know anything about the gun? Where he keeps it."

"I have a kid. I told him not to bring it in the house." *Gino's dresser drawer in the bedroom, detective.*

Detective Gretzinger took the movers one at a time into the kitchen to interrogate them separately while Detective Murphy got out his notepad to question Paula.

"It was you who called in the anonymous tip, wasn't it?"

"Yeah."

"I want you to tell me everything you did from the time you called the station until now," Murphy said.

After the facts had been gathered, Detective Murphy told Paula to change her shirt because they would need it as evidence.

"I need pants too. He pissed all over me. Can I have a shower?"

"No shower, but we'll get your clothes," Murphy called to one of the uniformed police officers.

"All my clothes are in the moving van. They'll be at the front of the truck because the movers loaded them first," Paula said.

Detective Murphy turned around as Detective Gretzinger followed the movers through the living room.

"Hold on," Murphy said to the movers. "I want you to find a box of her clothes. She says the box should be at the front of the moving van."

Murphy waved off the uniformed officer. "I don't need you anymore."

The movers came back with a box Paula confirmed was her clothes.

"You two can go now," Murphy said to the movers.

Paula went to the bathroom, changed her clothes, and kept the door open a crack to hear their conversation.

"What'd the movers say?"

"They complained about her being a bitch. Apparently, she was on their case, wanting them to speed things up."

"What's your take on this?" Gretzinger said.

"Looks like self-defence. Do you think Gino heard us?"

"The interrogation door was closed."

"I don't remember if we closed it. I don't think I did. Did you?"

"He could have opened it."

"He could've heard what I said about a marriage certificate."

Gretzinger had laughed when Murphy said it should come with a warning, everything you say or do can be used against you. But with Gino lying dead the joke wasn't funny.

"We'll never know now."

"All this shit happens an hour later. Why else would he accuse her of ratting him out? He must have heard me."

"Maybe he was pissed she was leaving him." Gretzinger looked over his shoulder down the hall for Paula. "No point worrying about it now. Forget about it."

Murphy raised his voice. "You almost done in there?"

When Paula walked out of the bathroom, Murphy said, "We have to bring you in for questioning."

"My daughter'll be coming home from school soon. She can't see him like this."

"Is there someone she can stay with? Someone who can pick her up?"

"Yeah. What about the moving van? I'm paying for it by the day."

Lines above Murphy's nose turned to deep ruts when he looked over at Gino's lifeless body.

Paula followed his gaze. "I didn't mean to." The puffy saggy skin above both eyelids was smeared black from mascara. "Gino looked after finances. I never had to worry. Now I got no one. I ...I can't afford a moving van for more than a day. We were supposed to be gone. It's not my fault the fucking movers were slow." Her ugly cry was working. Murphy's face was softening.

"It has to be cleared by forensics. When does your daughter get home?"

"Soon."

"Wait on the front porch."

An officer was positioned outside. Paula sat on the porch steps, but moved out of the way, when a man wearing a coat labeled, Coroner, arrived. She checked her watch. The school bus would arrive in ten minutes.

The front door opened again. "We need to see you in here for a minute," the coroner said. He had his camera ready. "I need to get a picture of the scratches on your back and knees."

Paula lifted her top while he took three pictures from different angles. He knelt to get pictures of each knee.

"Thanks," he said. "You can wait outside for your daughter."

After some mumbled conversation inside, she was called back. "Mrs. Amodeo, can you come in here for a minute?" Murphy said. "We just have a few more questions for you. Why did you send the movers into the shed?"

"To get the lawnmower and other shit. They're expensive. Gino never used it anyway. And why should I have to buy another swing set? I was leaving him the appliances, so it was only fair I get the rest."

"The movers were in the shed for a long time. Why didn't you check on them?"

"Did you see them? Not the brightest bulbs. And fucking slow. I figured they were dismantling the swing set and knew it would take them a while so didn't bother checking on them."

"You were planning on taking the swing set?" Gretzinger opened his notepad.

"It wasn't cemented in. Gino was too lazy to do it. Theresa would have a fit if I left it behind. And have you seen the prices of them? Not going to buy a new one when she's outgrown this one in a couple of years. I'm not made of money. I figured those good-for-nothings were having problems taking it apart. Do you think I had time to follow their ass around? I had all my own shit to do. I wasn't babysitting them."

Gretzinger closed his notepad without writing anything down.

"Thanks," Murphy said. "You can go back outside."

Before Paula made it out the front door, Murphy said, "Oh, I almost forgot. Did you scream anything before Gino was shot?"

"Scream anything? If I did, I don't remember." Paula's brows furrowed in deep concentration. After a few minutes, she let a choked sob escape. "I remember thinking, oh no, when I saw the gun, but I don't know if I said it out loud." *Muddy the waters just enough to make it seem real. Too squeaky clean smelled of a setup. Any good con could tell you that.*

Theresa got off the school bus and walked down the block to their house. Police cars and an ambulance were parked outside, and bright yellow tape was wrapped around the silver maple tree, strung to the end of the front porch. Paula knew she had seen enough in their streets to figure out something bad had happened. Theresa ran the rest of the way home and stood beside the tree.

"Where's Gino?" Theresa cried.

"Come here, sweetie." Paula patted the porch step beside her. Theresa ran into her mother's arms, crying.

"I know, baby, I know." Paula rocked her little girl in her arms, swayed back and forth, and kissed her head. "Sh, sh, sh, quiet now."

Chapter 18

Jackie's spoon clicked against the porcelain teacup as she opened the latest edition of the Hamilton Spectator. She turned to the court section to see if she had won any money.

Turning back to the front page she said, "Made another six bucks," to the headshot of a C.E.O. from a Comtex Plant. Skimming down the page, a bold headline, FATAL SHOOTING, caught her attention. These were the interesting ones, following the cases, learning about how the crimes were perpetrated, and the lives of the victims. Gino always came up with his version of how things went down. He was good at figuring out motives. These cases were the long-drawn-out ones. And her favourite. Jackie trailed her finger under the words in the article, a habit from her primary school days.

An anonymous caller contacted the Hamilton-Wentworth Police Department to report hearing a single gunshot. Upon arriving at 876 Barton Street East, Hamilton...

Jackie's finger stopped under the address. It was Gino's address. Her finger continued... police found a man and a woman. A physical altercation that ended with the man being shot to death. At this time, the police have not released the victim's name. The woman has been taken in for questioning.

It couldn't be Gino. He was coming this weekend. Probably some strung-out junkie. But Gino had a rule. No business in the house. Why hadn't Gino called her?

The newspaper had been lying on her coffee table since yesterday. Already old news. The Hamilton Spectator was the source for their games, so there was no urgency to read it. Still, in her pajamas, Jackie threw on a coat, laced up her running shoes, ran to the corner store, bought the latest edition of The Hamilton Spectator, and then ran back home again.

Hunched over, she searched for the follow-up article. It was no longer front-page news but relegated to the second page.

Police are investigating the shooting death of 43-year-old Giovanni …

Jackie gasped. *Gino.* Looking down at her finger, frozen under his name, she continued reading.

Giovanni Amodeo of 876 Barton Street East, Hamilton, passed away on June 9 at 2:25 p.m. in his home.

She cried long and hard as if there would be no end. The newsprint letters blurred into a grey nothing like her life. An emptiness. Her family was taken from her again. Time was lost in sorrow until there were no more tears left. Her body was a dry, hollow shell, the pearl cut away. She tugged a paper towel from the roll on the table, wiped her eyes, and blew her nose so she could continue reading:

The woman at the scene was identified as the wife of the deceased, Paula Amodeo. She was brought in again today for questioning and was released. She declined to give any details, except to say she is not charged with any crime. She asked that her and their daughter's privacy be respected at this time.

Their daughter! I'm his daughter, not Theresa. The words screamed at the page. Spittle misted the article. Jackie rocked in the chair hoping for comfort, but felt alone. Tears started again. *A break-in. It had to be some junkie looking for a fix. Gino protected Paula. Why wasn't the headline, Man Shot to Death Protecting Wife?*

She had to know what happened. Who killed Gino? Henrietta would know. The page slid from her grasp as she jumped and got the address book. Scanning the pages for Henrietta's phone number, she was uncertain if the old woman would remember her. Old people forget or get Alzheimer's. It was seven years since Jackie last spoke with her. She felt guilty about not staying in contact, but Gino had insisted. He was afraid Henrietta would absentmindedly mention her to Paula. Henrietta knew everything that happened in their block. When she was little, Jackie loved it when Gino arranged to have Henrietta babysit her.

The phone rang seven times before it was picked up. "Hello."

Henrietta sounded impatient and annoyed as if to say, this better be good and worth her while. Like she was so busy at her age. Henrietta was the only person left who shared Jackie's childhood. She started to cry with words choked off by emotion she hadn't expected.

"Who is this?"

Henrietta used the same scolding tone from those childhood days. Jackie couldn't say Gino's name. It hurt too much. She would never stop crying if she said his name. And she had to know.

"If sniffling's all you're going to do, I'll hang up."

Jackie's words bleated like a goat. "No, no." She held Henrietta's attention.

"Jackie, is it you?"

"Yeahhhh," the syllables stretched through the sobs.

Jackie heard the catch in Henrietta's voice. She waited out the silence and knew Henrietta covered up the speaker, not wanting Jackie to hear her cry.

In the past, when they'd sat on the couch watching TV, Henrietta would wrap arms around her. Jackie wished she had those arms around her now. Henrietta always gave a squeeze with her hugs. They both needed hugs. Jackie needed it now.

Jackie heard Henrietta's ragged deep breath. "I didn't know how to reach you. Gino wouldn't give me your number. He should have adopted you legally so there was a record. So, the police would have contacted you."

"You know he couldn't. He gave those nuns those forged documents. He couldn't risk being found out."

"He should have given me your number."

"I was afraid you'd be mad at me for not calling or wouldn't remember me."

"Not remember you! I fed you enough times to remember you. I'm not senile yet. Just because I'm old doesn't mean I'm feeble-minded."

"Sorry, I should have known better."

"Gino said, he told you not to call me. He was afraid I couldn't keep you a secret. I know he was trying to protect you from Paula. But I wouldn't have told her about you."

"I just read in the paper about... about... Is he really dead?"

"I can't believe it either. It doesn't seem possible. I keep looking out my window watching for him, waiting to hear the confounded roar from his car. Then I remember. He's never coming home."

"Why? Who did it?"

"It wasn't just anybody. It was her, Paula."

"But the paper said Paula's been released."

"The cops should have kept her in the hoosegow. It's a good place for her if you ask me. I never did like that one. Try as I may, I can't understand why he ever took up with her. If you ask me, she was behind their financial problems."

"How did you know about his financial problems?"

"I heard them arguing in the backyard when I was walking by. He was doing just fine until he met her. In two years, she managed to turn Gino's life upside down. Always poking her nose in where it didn't belong. Stirring up trouble in the block."

"Who called the cops?"

There was an understanding, of what happened in the neighbourhood, stayed in the hood. The only person from the block who got turned into the cops was the guy at 859; the house with the fake red brick exterior the kids used to peel like cardboard when it rained. He molested the Boudreau kid. No one complained about the do-gooder who snitched on him then.

"It was me. I knew something was up when I saw the moving van."

"Moving van!"

"I was listening for his old Pontiac. Him and his dual exhaust. The noise is so loud it rattles my windows. I told him he needs a stronger muffler."

"Paula wasn't charged, so who did it?"

"It was her, Paula."

"It doesn't make sense. Why would Paula kill him?" *Gino was finally getting them out of debt. She had nothing to fear from him.*

"I only know what I saw. Paula was the only person I saw go in your house, except for the two grubbies she hired to help her move."

"Gino never said anything to me about moving."

"Why would the movers do it? Besides, I didn't see them for at least an hour before he... he got shot. And poor Gino would've only had enough time to walk through the front door before Paula shot him dead. Not even enough time to start a fight or get a word out before he's lying in a pool of his blood. They need to lock her up and throw away the key. Mark my words, that one's just plain evil."

"Why was she moving? I saw Gino last month and he didn't say anything was wrong. If she was planning on moving out, he would have told me. You know Gino would never move out of the block. He'd die first." Jackie clasped her hand over her mouth, pinching her cheeks to hold back the tears. "It's all my fault." *If only I hadn't given Gino those ROEs.*

"Don't be silly. Get that idea right out of your head. If Gino heard you talking like this, he'd come right down from the heavens and slap you on your head."

Jackie's chin dimpled into her pout-a-puss face. Gino would never have done it. But she remembered getting her fair share of those smarten-up taps from Henrietta.

"What's with you, girl? Don't be talking such nonsense. It's got nothing to do with you. It's Paula's greed at the bottom of this."

Henrietta reinforced Jackie's guilt. The con and the money were the cause of Gino's death.

"Do you know when the funeral is?"

"There's no funeral as far as I know. When the coroner released his body, I heard Paula was hell-bent on having him cremated."

"No service?"

"You know Gino better than anybody. Do you think he would have wanted a service?"

"No. He used to say when it was his time, he wasn't falling for the last big con. He wasn't sticking someone he loved with a huge bill so he could lay on satin sheets he'd never feel. He always said, no oak coffin with chrome hardware for him, just the fires of brimstone and a toast in his name at Clancy's Bar."

"Well, I guess his boys will be looking after that for you. Clancy will give him a good send-off. Do you know his boys?"

"No. Gino wouldn't talk business to me. I wasn't even invited to his wedding." Jackie couldn't keep the hurt out of her voice. "Told me I was better off if Paula didn't know me."

"He was right about it. She would have kept hitting you up for money. She tried once with me but never tried again. I wouldn't let her past my front door."

"Will you call me when you know anything... about whatever they have for him?"

"Sure, but I won't be attending. I'm not about to offer my condolences to the person who killed him. I won't be a hypocrite. I can't tolerate even looking at Paula. You should stay away from her too. Gino gave you good advice. Follow it. He would be disappointed if you didn't."

"How can I stay away from my dad's funeral?"

"It won't be a funeral. It will be an excuse for Paula to get drunk and high. Do you want to be sitting beside the junkie who murdered your dad?"

"Will you call if you hear anything?"

"Of course, I will, honey. I know how much you loved him. And, Oh Lord, how much he bragged about you. He gave me your graduation picture. It's been on my dining room hutch all these years. You can't dust away memories. If you need my help, you just ask."

Jackie gave Henrietta her phone number before hanging up. Hearing her voice made Jackie homesick for old friends. Although she doubted if there were any left in the block who would remember her. Most people moved on; not Gino though. He was happy where he was.

Why hadn't Gino said Paula was moving out? If she was trying to get out before he came home, why shoot him? Just leave.

Jackie thought about her conversation with Henrietta and the words fire and brimstone repeated through her head. She didn't want that for Gino. He treated people better than most of them deserved. Her chin lifted upward and she spoke to the cottage cheese ceiling. "So, he better be up there with you God. Weed wasn't as bad as alcohol. Booze makes you mean, but weed makes you chillaxin." She used that logic a lot, whitewashing with justification, whenever neighbours painted Gino with off-coloured remarks. Her mother's eyes stared at her from the picture frame on top of the TV, reminding her, that lying to God is a sin. Jackie knew Gino sold heroin and cocaine too.

Picking up the frame, Jackie talked to the photograph. "I asked you to protect him."

Her mother looked at her with the stupid hat squashing down her hair. "Why didn't you keep him safe for me? It was the only time I asked you for anything. Why am I being punished again? Why can't I have a parent like everyone else? Gino treated people better than most of them deserved. So, he better be up there with you and God."

Jackie replaced the photo on top of the TV. The realization of feeling excited when she first read the newspaper headline brought a taste of bile. Shame and guilt made her stomach queasy. She didn't know it was Gino. But every article in their court case game over the years had been about someone's Gino.

Chapter 19

The interrogation at the police station was intense. Detective Anthony Murphy read off point after point from his notepad for the lawyer: Paula admitted firing the gun, Gino's blood was on her top, and her fingerprints on the gun.

The lawyer argued the gun was behind her back, the blood was on her back and not the front, no intent because Gino was the aggressor who yanked her hand behind her back which caused the gun to fire. The lawyer twisted each point to fit into the same conclusion. She was in fear for her life and couldn't have been the aggressor. The most damning evidence was the motive. She was moving out. She had no motive. But Gino did when he accused her of turning him into the cops. The lawyer hammered home this point, wanting to know which cop let it slip about her anonymous tip. He turned the tables on them: accused and demanded. Paula watched the one cop. He avoided eye contact. The lawyer hit a nerve.

Almost pissed my pants watching those shitheads sit there like a couple of dummies with nothing to say. Got them by the short and curlies. If their boss finds out, he'll carve them a new one. Cops—idiots! Least the lawyer was worth the money. Almost lost it when he'd chirped, "Who screams to attract attention before killing someone?"

Self-preservation. She knew it, lived it. They'd want to cover up their lack of professionalism. Assuming a struggle took place, would give them an easy out for self-defence. According to the lawyer, the coroner backed the theory.

Who said all she could do was waitressing? She outsmarted them all, especially Gino. She wasn't about to spend the rest of her life waiting on people and getting shit on for a lousy fifty-cent tip. The cheap bastards could complain to someone else about the service because she wouldn't take orders and clean up after people anymore. She put up with Gino's crap for two years and now he was gone, she wasn't taking it from anyone else.

***

It had been one day since the authorities officially ruled Gino's death a case of self-defence. Paula, the supposed grieving widow, walked away from any charges and straight into the insurance company to claim the payout but discovered she wasn't the beneficiary.

"Fuck! Fuck! Fuck!!!" She yelled at the insurance officer before storming out. She returned the next day and screamed again, and the reality was still the same—she wasn't the beneficiary.

When screaming and threatening didn't work, she tried to bribe one of the file clerks. The lawyer was no better.

Goddamn fucking rules!

Paula was served with an eviction notice soon thereafter. No amount of arguing and threatening swayed the situation. Paula demanded to know who owned the house. But like the life insurance policy, she wasn't privy to such information. The deed had to be in Gino's safety deposit box. With all that happened, she'd forgotten about it. Not like her at all, but between the cops, the insurance company, and the lawyer, she'd been overwhelmed.

***

Paula was surprised to find the safety deposit box empty. He had been on to her! After the credit card company swooped in and seized their share, not much was left in Gino's bank account. She sold off what was left in his showroom, used Gino's truck, and transported what was left of her life to a shabby two-bedroom apartment in a seedier part of town. Paula checked back on the house to see what was happening and scanned real estate listings regularly. When Gino's home was advertised for sale, Paula tried to find out from the Real Estate Agent who owned the house but like everything else, it was confidential information.

Under an assumed name, Jackie hired a company to make sure any possessions left behind by Paula were disposed of and the company cleaned the house for the new owners. Jackie became anonymous giving Paula no opportunities to find out who she was.

Drugs were a luxury Paula couldn't afford. She was worse off now than before she met him. *The son-of-a-bitch knew what he was doing to me. Cutting me outa everything. Never thought he'd screw over Theresa though.*

Always looking for a new angle, Paula asked the lawyer's secretary if she could collect UI sick benefits because her nerves were frayed and her hands shook so badly, that she couldn't carry dishes. Withdrawal was bad this time. She didn't have to fake the shakes.

The secretary looked at her hands. "I have a friend who works at the UI office. I could call and ask her."

After relaying the information, to show her gratitude, Paula took the secretary out for lunch. In no time, the two became friends, and the secretary arranged for her friend at the UI office and Paula to meet. Like with Gino and others, Paula worked a con and got what she wanted. It was better than sick benefits. Her friend offered the unexpected door, Paula needed opened. The friend worked in administration and was able to get her an interview for a job as a file clerk. The dream of cash for life didn't die with Gino. It was getting closer.

Visiting the Unemployment Insurance office, Paula found out about what the office offered. Walking to a stand with pamphlets advertising their services, she gathered up each pamphlet, a UI application, and a social insurance number application. She learned about their benefits, rules, regulations, and procedures. Her knowledge was impressive when she was interviewed for the position of Clerical and Regulatory Clerk by the UI Chief of Administration and his two assistants.

Paula started a new profession and even had Gino to thank for it. When she discovered where the records of employment forms were stored in the government office she was assigned to, she realized the potential for this con.

***

Paula walked through the corridor created by the maze of baffle boards to the open space which housed five long rows of grey metal filing cabinets. She peered down aisle after aisle at the thick walls of files that held the adjudicated unemployment insurance claims and thought of the money those files represented—the pot at the end of the brightly colour-coded docket rainbow. There was probably more money generated here in this office than a bank of the same size and yet there was no vault door or armed guards. Nothing to safeguard all the money.

The Benefit Control Investigative Unit was on the third floor while the fourth floor housed the administration staff, stock room, and large lunchroom. The first floor was the high-traffic area used by members of the public looking for work, filing for UI benefits or Social Insurance Number cards, and making any inquiries. The Enquiry Unit was the first line of defence a claimant encountered in the quest for benefits, and it was also the next level of advancement Paula hoped to achieve through the UI competition system.

It was now four months since Paula began work at the UI office on Rebecca Street. The supervisor commended her on how fast she learned the system and how ambitious she was to advance. Paula spent every night of the last two weeks in her bedroom studying manuals on sick, maternity, retirement, and regular UI benefits. Any questions she needed scrutinizing about the Enquiry Clerk job she wrote down and took to work so she could get the correct answers. Twelve people applied for the Enquiry Clerk position, but only the top four would be selected. Paula's goal was to become an agent but to achieve this, she first must secure the Enquiry Clerk position. Theresa didn't understand.

***

Paula explained. "I'm not ignoring you. I'm studying so I can afford to give you the same things other kids have."

Instead of appreciation, Paula got the cold shoulder and the silent treatment.

"I won't be home after work." Paula watched Theresa butter her toast. The knife went still. Melted butter slid off the stainless steel onto the golden crusty bread.

Theresa offered no reaction.

"I'm having dinner with the girls and won't be back until late. I'm trying you on your own tonight with no babysitter." Paula folded the last bit of toast and peanut butter and wadded it into her mouth. In between chewing and smacking, she said, "There's a TV dinner in the freezer for you. Don't forget to turn the oven off and don't wait up for me."

Theresa put her dirty dishes in the sink, gathered homework, and dumped it in a school bag.

"Get a move on," Paula yelled, waiting at the front door.

Paula's interview for the Enquiry Clerk competition was that day. She wasn't worried about the hypothetical situation questions; she was good at bullshit. She was told the interviewers asked direct questions looking for precise answers.

Every day, Paula and Theresa left home together and caught their buses a block apart, but this morning Theresa walked ahead of Paula.

"Do you have your key?"

Theresa pulled the chain with the house key on it out from under her shirt and showed her mother.

"Good. Make sure you clean up after yourself and do your homework. I don't need your teachers giving me shit because it's not done. Don't forget to lock the door as soon as you get in. I want you in bed by 10:00 p.m."

When Theresa's school bus pulled up to the curb, Paula said, "Have a nice day."

Theresa climbed the bus steps without answering or looking back. Paula walked a block and boarded the Barton Street bus, looking for an empty seat. The faces were becoming familiar. Most working people kept to a timed routine. Taking a seat, she opened her notebook and reviewed the list of frequently asked questions. As the bus got closer to downtown, the seats filled. People clutched the overhead bars. Feet positioned, listening to the grinding rhythm, they swayed, following the driver's lead like seasoned dancers—a shuffle of bodies.

It was two blocks through the gut of the city to the UI office, past storefronts, and bars, cheap ones with watered-down booze and expensive ones with hard liquor. But on Monday morning, the splatter of puke on the sidewalk looked the same. A trail of garbage and cigarette butts left by Saturday night revelers led Paula to the UI office.

Entering the building, she squeezed into an elevator stuffed with employees who arrived around the same time. She sat at her desk unable to concentrate on work, shuffled papers, and watched the clock. At 10:40 a.m. she stepped into the elevator and pushed the button for the fourth floor. There was no one in the waiting area when she got off the elevator. Paula took a seat next to the chrome ashtray stand, annoyed she'd left her cigarettes on her desk.

The door of the interview room opened, and a sombre-faced competitor walked out, puffing her lips up with an exhausted breath before heading to the elevator. A few minutes later, the door opened, and Paula was greeted by a supervisor who escorted her into the room and to a chair at a long conference table. It was a grey room lacking a personal touch. Plastic palm trees filled two corners and a photograph of the Queen hung lopsided to face the big round chrome clock on the opposite wall. This room didn't belong to a specific person or group, therefore no one took responsibility for its furnishing. Paula settled in the chair and noticed a pitcher of water with two empty glasses in front of the interviewers. Her throat was dry and there was no glass in front of her.

"Good morning," the unit supervisor said. "We will alternate asking you questions and will be taking your answers down in long hand. The interview is expected to last an hour and a half. For obvious reasons, we ask you not to discuss the questions covered in this interview when you leave this room. If you're ready, we'll get started."

The interview process was meant to intimidate, to see how she reacted under pressure.

"Name the types of benefits," the unit supervisor asked. Paula barely got the last word out when the other supervisor questioned, "What are the qualifying conditions for each?"

Paula's head turned back and forth as she answered rapid-fire questions from one supervisor and then the other, while her robotic responses matched the interviewers' speed of delivery.

"Translate this sentence," the older supervisor said. "The I.O. imposed a D6 for three weeks from the B.P.C."

"The Insurance Officer imposed a disqualification for quitting without just cause for three weeks from the Benefit Period Commencement."

Using rows of acronyms on micro-fiche tape readings, she interpreted the status of claims to their apparent satisfaction because they smiled and said, "We appreciate you trying out for this position. The list of qualified applicants will be posted in a week in the lunchroom."

Paula stood, remembering the conversation she had with Bill, one of the Enquiry Clerks. He told her, "It's not just about getting the right answers; it's about your demeanour too." At the time, Paula laughed, saying she could be de meanest. Bill didn't think it was funny. He said she had to have balls for this job. Ironic considering, he was the token male in a cackle of female Enquiry Clerks.

Paula walked toward the Queen's photograph and out the door to meet the next competitor's frightened stare.

"It was a breeze," Paula said, hoping to unhinge her competitor when she faced the unexpected intensity in the room.

Not being able to talk about this competition with co-workers was difficult. The interviews wouldn't be over for another two days. She was glad she organized a girls' night out with friends who knew nothing about the UIC because she would be able to talk about it with them.

Paula left the office at 4:30 p.m. and walked three blocks to the Running Pump Hotel on the main drag. Shoved between two buildings, it was nicknamed the Running Dump by the business core people. Cracked and chipped red brick was painted grey, and the lettered sign above the door hung faded and worn. Paula could go there without seeing anyone from work. Opening the heavy door, she watched the sliver of sunlight vanish, smothered by thick cigarette smoke, and then heard the door groan, to once again hermetically seal its patrons into the dank atmosphere of an old cellar swabbed by cobwebs collecting specimens of mold and mildew. The place was crawling with vermin of every type from two to sixteen-legged which made it the preferable watering hole for an unsavory downtown crowd.

Paula waved to her friend, Darlene, who was sitting at a table for four in the center of the room.

"What's with the getup?" Darlene said when Paula pulled out a chair. "I almost didn't recognize you."

"This is how they expect you to dress in an office."

"You look like a tight ass."

Paula undid three buttons on the white blouse, fanned the lapels out, stood, and rolled up the knee-length, charcoal grey skirt thigh-high. This new office wardrobe stood out in the closet amongst the hot pink, neon green, and orange miniskirts snuggling beside low-cut tops splashed with polka dots or slashed with geometric lines. Large, hooped earrings and bleached blond hair were the only remnants of her true personality.

"You got blue eye shadow?" Paula waited for Darlene to pick the lint off the plastic case she dug out from the bottom of her purse.

"Thanks." Paula looked into the round compact mirror and painted baby blue from eyelid to brow.

Both women laughed when their girlfriend Cathy came in flouncing her flesh. Most of the men stopped their conversation and watched her entrance. Cathy's cow tits hung low in a hot pink halter top and slapped her belly when she walked in a slow-motion rumba, which gyrated her thunder thighs. Cellulite oozed from holes and runs in her black fishnet stockings.

Paula leaned over and whispered into Darlene's ear, "Hard to believe men pay for that. She must do amazing tricks." They laughed at the pun.

"Maybe she stands on her head and spits quarters," Darlene said.

"She's too cheap to give change." Paula waved Cathy over.

Chapter 20

Habits were hard to break. Jackie opened the newspaper and turned to the court section. Their game was part of her life. She couldn't make a huge part of her life disappear overnight or within a week or a month or maybe even ever.

When she closed the paper, it felt like she'd closed a coffin lid. But there was no coffin, nothing that made Gino's death real, no one to mourn with, remember with. She didn't know why she bought the newspaper and tortured herself. She couldn't go to the movies because he should have been there with her. No more looking forward to the third Friday of each month and listening for his plodding feet on the stairs, picking the movie out before Gino arrived, and the feeling of satisfaction that she'd selected the movie he wanted to see. But it was more than the newspaper, and more than the table that reminded her of Gino.

Everything she did or felt was attached to a memory of him. Time was not the saviour, only the tormentor. Time provided more minutes, hours, and days to re-live the shock each time she opened a newspaper. Time provided more "what if" scenarios, creating a happy ending that was lost forever. No one would always be there for her anymore. Even husbands didn't mean forever. There was no one for her to call family. Gino was a whole family: father, mother, and brother.

She couldn't concentrate at work; her production rate went down. Since Gino's death, other than for work, Jackie left the apartment only when David complained and coaxed. She knew he was aware something had happened, but after five months he stopped trying to find out what was wrong. She knew she wasn't being fair to him or her friends she'd stopped seeing. The hollowness within her turned to not caring. When David presented her with a list of the two hundred and thirty-four guests he was inviting to the wedding, she didn't have the energy to argue. He claimed he couldn't leave his parent's best friends and business associates out. His mother and he made most of the decisions and arrangements, she was simply agreeing with them.

After a dinner date with David on Saturday night, they made love. Jackie left not wanting to stay the night to be dismissed on Sunday morning. At home the next day, still in her pajamas at 4 p.m., she curled up on the couch with her journal. Surrounded by an alone feeling, and disconnected from the world, their stories brought her comfort.

Afraid her childhood recollections of Gino would evaporate over time like the remembrances of her parents, Jackie had started a journal four months ago. Weeks were spent looking for the right book important enough to house her treasured memories. When she found a padded leather-bound book with the smell of steeped history, she knew it was perfect. She rubbed the leather cover. Would she ever be able to share this? Would anyone know who she really was? After pretending for so long that Gino didn't exist, having this journal cemented the history she hoped to share.

The pages looked dog-eared from the hundreds of times she had read them. She finished the last paragraph and closed the book with a sigh. Even those pages stopped offering solace when she considered the next entry she would write. Gino dead. She couldn't write the words to end his life. To end dreams. No longer tucked arm in arm walking down the aisle, not knowing his pride at holding his first grandchild, not seeing them play catch, fish, or boat. Everything was taken away.

Gino was all about blame, pointing the finger, with the accused punished. They argued too many times over his eye-for-an-eye mentality. She'd lectured him to bide his time and let consequences take their course because what goes around comes around. Assured him, whoever did whatever, would get theirs in the end. But now was the test. Did she believe it? Could she rely on fate? To just sit back and wait. And do nothing! Gino maintained nothing got solved when people sat back waiting for fate to come around.

"You grab the bull by the horns and make it come around," he asserted. She knew what he would have wanted. Retribution.

God damn fucking cops. Why couldn't they do their job and arrest Paula? Why couldn't they see she murdered Gino?

The need to release pent-up physical aggression was overwhelming. And there they were. The Correlle dinnerware. Bought just for this purpose. She told herself she'd never do it. Was too practical to let loose with emotions. But she had bought them just in case.

One by one, each piece of the four place settings was snatched from its neatly stacked pile and viciously slammed against the walls, bounced off the table, or crashed onto the floor.

Jackie panted, extended her arm as far over her head as possible for the strongest force, threw the cup like a hard ball, and then snatched the next piece before the first had time to hit anything. With loud banging, clanging, and rattling, her body released anger. She reached into the bare cupboard and looked down on the floor at the scattered plates and overturned cups, at the broken pieces.

She let out a deep, sad disappointed sigh. More dents and scratches than shattered pieces, which lived up to the manufacturer's claims. Even in rage, she'd gypped Gino. Pretending to break things. Wouldn't throw the good stuff. Like Gino wasn't worth the good stuff. She wanted to stretch out her arm and send *everything* smashing to the floor: the good china and crystal glasses—to show him, he was worth everything. But she couldn't do it; had worked too hard to get it. She got a broom and dustpan and swept up the broken dishes.

She was to blame. It was all her fault! It was her ROE scheme. It caused Gino's death. Paula found out about it. She gave Paula a reason to kill Gino. Even Henrietta knew Gino was dead because of Paula's greed.

Jackie had kept in touch with Henrietta and learned that Paula was now working for the UIC office on Rebecca Street in Hamilton. As soon as she heard the news, she knew for sure Paula murdered

Gino and was trying to work the con herself. After so many years of being a waitress, why would she switch occupations? And how she managed to get the position baffled Jackie.

For the last six months, Jackie expected the police to walk into the St. Catharines UI office and arrest her. Henrietta had told her, the word on the street, was the police picked Gino up at the docks with the stolen ROEs. But there was never any mention of it in the newspaper. She'd been smart enough to wear thin plastic gloves when filling out the forms. If the police found them, they would think the ROEs came from a Hamilton office. But with Gino dead, the police wouldn't have any leads.

Today was the third Friday of the month and marked the six-month anniversary of the last time Gino and Jackie were together at the movies. Jackie looked at the large poster of "Dirty Harry" which hung on the wall above the kitchen table. She paid the movie usher twenty bucks for the poster. It was her paper headstone in memory of Gino. Every morning, she ate her toast and peanut butter while Clint Eastwood's squinty-eyed accusatory glare demanded Gino's death be avenged.

Somehow, she must make Paula pay. Gino deserved justice. This anniversary was the breaking point. High noon. She looked over at the poster. Like Gino, Dirty Harry believed in an eye for an eye.

***

Jackie put in a transfer request from the St. Catharines UIC office to the Hamilton one Paula was working at. The transfer wouldn't take long, because the rate of unemployment in the Hamilton area was high which meant the office would need more agents to clear a backlog situation.

***

Jackie waited at David's apartment door for him to unlock the chain. She twisted and turned her engagement ring on her finger. She was supposed to spend the rest of her life with him. But this had nothing to do with David. Her feelings for him were the same. How could she make him understand? She couldn't stay and marry him until she put Gino's death to rest. She couldn't go through the motions of her life with this torn-apart feeling consuming her.

Her stomach flip-flopped when he opened the door. "I need to talk with you," Jackie said.

"Come in."

She sat on his sofa and stared at a stiff family portrait hung over his console, hi-fi stereo. His mother's smile was more like a nervous twitch and his father, sullen-faced but comfortable in his dark suit, looked annoyed he had to be dragged out of work to have his picture taken. David and his sister Catherine looked similarly put out. Not a picture Jackie would have enlarged and displayed. She thought it should have been captioned, "Smiling pretty, with frowning discontent."

"You know I've been upset for the last six months."

David moved closer so their thighs touched, and he held her hand.

"When I was orphaned, I was looked after by a man named Gino. He was a wonderful man. He just didn't treat me like his daughter; I became his daughter, and he was my dad." Jackie shook when she said the words. To voice Gino's existence to David made her feel light-headed. The closet door flung open, and the skeletons danced out, setting her free.

"He was killed six months ago." Jackie's body vibrated and David wrapped his arm around her back, caressing her shoulder. "His wife Paula murdered him, but claimed it was self-defence. But I know Gino, and he would never have hurt her. I didn't tell you about Gino because he didn't want my friends to know he was a drug dealer."

Jackie felt David's arm stiffen across her back, no warmth hugged or stroked her.

"Gino was the one who wanted me to leave Hamilton and get a fresh start where no one would know about him. I'm sorry I deceived you. I don't know if you'll ever be able to forgive me." She twisted and turned her engagement ring around her finger. "But I need you to know—I do love you very much."

Jackie looked at his family portrait and imagined their stern faces reacting to her revelations. David's arm dropped, and he shifted, their knees no longer touching. Jackie waited for him to say something, but he remained taciturn. She held her hand against her mouth and exhaled, breath heating her palm. Squeezing cheeks between thumb and fingertips the words slid through, "I'm sorry. I've just decided what I have to do."

"What is there to do? It's been six months already. Time enough for grieving."

David's callousness took her by surprise.

"So, if he hadn't died were you ever going to tell me? How do you think it would look at my firm if they found out my father-in-law was a drug dealer? Do you think I'd ever make partner then? You'd risk my vocation like this?"

"I'm sorry, I should have told you. I didn't mean to jeopardize your career. I am sorry for not telling you the truth from the beginning."

When Jackie reached for his hand, David crossed his arms. She felt the ache of his distrust.

"I was afraid to tell anyone about Dad in case someone turned him into the cops. I couldn't trust anyone with his secret. When we first met, I didn't know you, so I told you the same lie I'd been telling everyone for years."

"And after two years, I still didn't rate any higher than everyone else you'd been lying to? Two years. You had two years to tell me the truth!"

"After I got to know you, I knew you'd have a problem accepting him. And I couldn't kick my dad out of my life. He was everything to me."

"So, what was I? Where did it leave me? Was I only the schmuck you kept lying to?"

"I was afraid to tell you. Afraid we wouldn't be able to get past this."

She could tell by his disdain that the rest of her life was dying, disappearing like Gino. Avenging Gino's death was all she had left.

"I'm putting a transfer request into the Hamilton UIC office on Rebecca Street. I need to go back home and settle Gino's affairs. This is something I can't explain, but it's important. I have to do it."

"You can't explain a lot. I don't even know who you are anymore."

"I didn't either until now. I was living a lie and it was killing me. Gino was my dad and I loved him. And now he's dead. I can't pretend he didn't exist. I need to remember him." Jackie stood up. "He was who he was, and I am who I am." *I'm Popeye the sailor man, toot toot. A cartoon song playing in my head when I'm losing everything. Am I crazy?*

"So now you're leaving and I don't even get a say in it. You can't tell me why. And I'm supposed to wait when you don't even know how long you'll be gone. Or if you're coming back!"

Jackie couldn't say anything. There was no way to defend her decision. And she wasn't even sure what she was going to do when she got there. All she knew was that she needed revenge.

"What about all our plans? The wedding? The guests?"

"The invitations haven't been sent out yet. If you can't get the full deposit back from the venue, I'll cover the expense. I can't go through with the wedding. Not until I put things to rest with Gino."

"He's dead and already at rest. There's nothing to deal with! If you leave, don't bother coming back. I don't want you in my life."

Jackie twisted her engagement ring off her finger and placed it on the black smoked glass coffee table. Her reflection was pained truth, the smoke and mirrors exposed. "But I need you to believe I still really and truly do love you. I'm sorry, so sorry but I have to go."

The pain of leaving him tore her apart but she couldn't continue living with this depression. Taking action was the only way to escape it.

Chapter 21

Results from the competition were posted in the lunchroom a week after the last interview was held, and Paula placed second. She was to report Monday morning to the supervisor of the in-person Enquiry Unit.

It was odd when she walked by the closing elevator doors and saw familiar faces with whom she rode the elevator each morning. This time she did not step in. Out of one rut and into another, she continued to the back corner, where the supervisor's office looked out over the Enquiry Section. Paula was introduced to peers by the supervisor and then shown to her cubicle.

Baffle boards on both sides of the desks gave the claimants privacy. From her chair, Paula could confer with co-workers on either side if she had problems. She liked the reassurance help was close by, but not the trapped feeling of having her back against the wall.

"We work off the buddy system here," the supervisor said. "For the first week, Krista," she nodded to the girl whose desk was beside Paula's, "will sit in with you, and show you the ropes."

Paula's stretched lips turned into a fake smile. Even though she was probably fifteen years her senior, everything about Krista screamed old, plain, and boring, from the orthopedic shoes to the no make-up, and straight brown cropped hair.

Before turning on her heels, the supervisor said, "If you want to speak with me for any reason, my door's always open."

Krista waited until the supervisor was out of sight before saying, "The door is open, but she's never there, especially when you need help with an irate claimant. Good luck finding her then."

Krista pulled her chair next to Paula's. "This job comes down to one question: where's my money? If you can't answer it, then you fill out this form." Krista pulled the duplicate yellow and pink paper out of the desk drawer. "Then, you send the claimant upstairs to see an agent. You're in cubicle four. Ready?"

Paula nodded.

"Press the button on the corner of your desk." Krista shifted in her seat.

Paula heard the buzzer go off and their receptionist called, Mr. Sokoloski, number four, please. Listening to the complaint, Paula deciphered the codes on the micro-fiche tape and completed the appropriate form. "Take this to the receptionist on the second floor and an agent will talk to you."

A steady stream of claimants generated a flood of paperwork that made the day go by fast. Yelling erupted from Bill's cubicle on the other side of Paula's desk. It became louder. Bill leaped out of the chair and avoided the overturned desk as it crashed to the floor. The chair, with casters spinning, smashed into the wall. Broken plastic micro-fiche tapes, monitor pieces and paperwork scattered the area.

"You're getting faster." Krista picked up a stapler from the floor. "He went that way." She pointed toward the main doors.

Paula stood, got a better look at the mess, and snickered at Bill. "If you need balls to do this job, you might want to wear a cup."

"Ha ha." Bill looked annoyed. "Give me a hand with the desk, will you?"

Paula smiled. "Is that part of my job description?"

"It is when you sit next to Bill." Krista laughed.

Bill picked up the remaining pieces. "He was some pissed. As soon as I saw him grip the edge of my desk, I knew it was coming."

Krista seized the corner and leg of the credenza. "They should bolt your desk to the floor."

Paula took hold of the other corner. "How often does this happen?"

"One, two, three," Bill said, as they all hefted the desk upright.

Krista placed the stapler on the desk. "Often enough. But not to us. It seems to be something a guy does to another guy. But you never know. I've seen a guy hit one of our girls. You learn to keep your head up."

Over the next few months, Paula got to know her co-workers and became familiar with forms, rules, regulations, and office procedures. The days became routine. She scooted back to her desk when she heard their receptionist call, Mr. Ashton, number four, please. When the claimant walked into her cubicle, Paula saw sweat beaded on his forehead before it trickled down. From the look on his face, he was agitated. Mr. Ashton sat down and slapped the letter of disentitlement on the desk. "You cut me off. I'm a member of the labourers' union."

Paula greeted him with a stern look. "What local?"

"One Zero Two."

Paula reached for her list of union locals who were exempt from looking for work. His local wasn't on it. She could hear yelling somewhere down the row of cubicles. Then a claimant in Krista's cubicle raised his voice, threatening, and pounded the desk. Paula glanced toward Krista when she heard casters roll on the terrazzo floor. Krista pushed her chair a foot away from the desk. Out of reach, Paula assumed. She had been around long enough to observe how one incident sparked the next. One irate claimant can goad another into yelling, which provokes the next disgruntled claimant into action, resulting in a chain reaction that can only be explained by a full moon.

"One Zero Two is not exempt. It means you look for work like everyone else. You must have told our insurance agent you weren't looking for work, so you got cut off. It's the way it's supposed to work. You want the money; you look for a job."

"I'm on a waiting list with my union local. They call me when they got a job for me."

"So, great for you, but it's not a local we recognize. So, if you want benefits, you have to be looking for another job while you're waiting to get called back by your local."

Paula watched as his jaw clenched, his face turned red, and anger built. She was disinterested in him and his situation. She liked the feeling of power over him.

"This is fucking bullshit. I'm a union man! Call my local and they'll tell you I'm on the list."

"It doesn't matter to me what list you're on, you have to look for work if you want the money."

"If I don't get the money, I lose my house. I'm out on the street. What do I do then?"

Paula smiled. "Well then sir, you put in a change of address."

His face was going purple. If he came at her, she would make sure he got the worst of it. His eyes narrowed, pinching a thick furrow of skin above his nose. Paula's smile broadened. They both knew his attempt at intimidation wasn't working.

"What if I look for a job?"

"Then you have to appeal the decision."

"Appeal this, bitch."

He stood up, unzipped his pants, pulled out his penis, and let it rest on the desk.

Paula reached for the stapler. The only thing with weight to it.

She chortled, genuinely amused. She looked down at the wrinkled flesh. "You have to wield a bigger stick than that to scare me off."

She picked up the stapler and cocked it back so it would lay flat on the desk. "Unless you want it permanently stapled to my desk, I suggest you remove it."

In one swift movement, she slammed the stapler down an inch from his penis shooting a staple into the oak veneer. Mr. Ashton jumped back with a screech, stuffed the loose floppy stub back into his pants, and walked out. Paula laughed hard and long, while tears rolled down her cheeks.

After Krista finished with her claimant she said, "What was all that about?" When Paula related the story, Krista said, "I can't believe you did it. I would have been freaked out."

When Bill heard the story, he laughed and said, "Give me an overturned desk anytime." The story flew down the line of clerks, interrupted by sporadic laughter with each re-telling.

Being the last person to go for lunch, Paula hadn't realized co-workers primed the rumour mill pump with her antics. She was reading a posting on the wall for an Agent 1 competition displayed in the lunchroom when two employees came up to her wanting to hear the story. It surprised her. She'd never been popular before.

Paula wanted to apply for the Agent 1 competition but needed an agent who would help her study for it. *Maybe being popular now could work in my favour.*

Then she remembered the day she got pissed off at the agents and gave them shit. She watched how they skimmed through files and put the more time-consuming, complicated ones back in the "to-do" rack for someone else to do. Those files would appear on printouts as outstanding decisions she was responsible for clearing. She'd put the files on the agent's desks and find them again in the to-do rack. It made her look like she wasn't doing her job. With an armload of files ready to unload, and in a voice grounding out enunciated syllables, Paula announced, "Even though the more complicated claims lower your productivity rate, they still have to be done. You're getting paid to make decisions, so stop throwing files back in the rack."

Ever since then, the agents became standoffish with her so she wasn't sure if she would be able to get anyone to help her. Coming back to the old stomping ground on the second floor was uncomfortable for Paula. She didn't like to ask when it was easier to take. And she was aware she'd stomped on a few too many toes.

Paula stood in front of the agents' and addressed them since she had no one particular friend. "Well, have you missed me?"

The agents looked down at their desks, shuffled papers, opened files, and tapped pens.

"I'm looking for someone to help me study for the Agent 1 competition. Any takers?"

Paula was aware her arms dangled by her sides. She didn't eat humble pie delicately and wouldn't apologize for it. No one looked at her. It was like she wasn't there. The complete silence left Paula off balance, perched on her platform shoes. "No volunteers?" Still not a head was raised. "I don't need your help anyway."

When she turned to leave, Paula noticed a girl sitting at her old desk. Loud enough for everyone to hear, Paula said, "You can't get the files cleared, because the agents screen for the difficult ones and put them back in the rack. And they think the clerks are stupid enough not to notice."

Paula walked away. She would have to rely on the manuals now.

The next day, Paula was called into her supervisor's office and told that certain agents took offense to her inquiries. The supervisor produced an agent's duplicate copy. On the form, Paula had written simply, "Has claim been established? If not, why not?"

"The agents feel you are insinuating they're not doing their jobs when you question why a claim hasn't been established," the supervisor said.

"Aren't claims supposed to be established within six weeks?"

"Well, yes, but there are nicer ways to ask."

"I write it so agents can reply if there's a backlog. I figure if the supervisor monitoring the inquiries sees how much of a backlog there is, maybe they'll get more agents. Besides, this is the easiest way to write it. With the lineups we have, why waste a lot of time and ink stroking egos? I thought it was more efficient to cut to the chase."

The supervisor's face flushed pink. "It's a matter of office etiquette. I'm sure you don't want to ruffle any feathers."

Paula smiled at the supervisor. *What's to ruffle, when I already plucked the bird clean?* "As long as you're fine with my production rate tanking, I don't have a problem with flowering up my inquiries."

"I appreciate it," the supervisor said and escorted her out of the office.

***

Trying to make sense of the government jargon in the manuals over the last two weeks had been grueling. Just when she was ready to give up on the notion of becoming an agent, Paula learned a new agent was transferring in from the St. Catharines office on Monday. Paula knew she had to get to Jackie first before agents bad-mouthed her and spoiled their intended friendship. After all, she was her last hope.

Chapter 22

Jackie spent two weekends with a real estate agent in Hamilton looking for a place to live. Henrietta offered a place to stay while she looked. It was comforting to be back in the old stomping ground under Henrietta's roof. She was thinner than Jackie remembered, frailer, but her voice and attitude were still strong.

Henrietta picked up a crystal bowl from the doily on the end table and offered Jackie a hard candy. The candies were coated in dust and looked to be glued together.

"No thanks," Jackie said.

"What's the matter? Lost your sweet tooth? There was a time when I couldn't keep the bowl full when you were around."

"I'm trying to watch my weight."

Henrietta put the bowl back on the end table. "If you want, I'll introduce you to the people who bought your house. They seem like a nice couple."

"I can't go into my house again. It would be too hard—knowing Gino died there."

"I understand." Henrietta patted her hand. "When I look at your house, it breaks me apart too. I miss him. He stopped by at least once a week to see if I needed anything and to make sure I was alright. He was a good man. Shovelled my drive in the winter. Helped whenever I needed it."

Jackie wrapped her arms around the old lady and felt bones.

"You've got to train your mind to think of something else when you see your house. It's what I do. I like to remember the day Paula found out Gino left her nothing. She came stomping toward my house, nostrils flaring, ready for a fight. I got the poker." She pointed to the heavy rod leaning against the brick fireplace. "You should have seen her face. It was redder than the candy. She demanded to know who the beneficiary was on Gino's life insurance and who owned the house."

"I was worried she'd find out and come after me."

"Your secret was safe. No one's running roughshod over me."

"It's good to know some things never change."

"She still doesn't know anything about you. Gino made sure of it. Besides, I'm the only one left here who remembers you. They've all moved on or died."

With those words, Jackie felt empty, like her childhood had been erased.

"Paula was mad as a hatter, and it only got worse after the eviction notice. Sometimes when I think I hear the confounded noise from Gino's Pontiac, instead of missing him, I think of that day. Thankful Gino protected you from her. She would have stolen what was yours."

Henrietta hugged her and it ended with a squeeze. "Gino's up there watching over you."

"I hope so. I still can't believe Paula got away with it."

"She'll get what she deserves. Mark my words. What goes around, comes around."

***

With the money from the sale of her parent's house, Jackie bought a two-bedroom townhouse, on Paula's bus route. Hamilton felt at home. It gave her a comforting feeling she couldn't get in St. Catharines. It was where she wanted to be.

By the end of the weekend, the real estate deal closed and gave Jackie possession of the townhouse in a month. Time disappeared while she finalized the UIC transfer, arranged for the movers, and packed.

Before she departed, Jackie left a message on David's answering machine with her new address and moving date. David hadn't called. She took the Clint Eastwood poster off the wall, rolled it up, and wondered if she was making a mistake. She'd always believed fate handled all wrongs. And Henrietta reinforced her belief. This new life offered no direction except an uncertain end. She filled the last box when the movers arrived.

Saturday traffic would be heavy, and she dreaded the drive into Hamilton. With both parents killed in a car accident, she was afraid of driving and didn't get her licence until she was twenty. If it wasn't for Gino's nagging, she never would have taken her driver's test.

Highway driving was the worst. She followed the moving van. The mover drove 65 miles per hour, and passed cars freely, which forced Jackie to keep pace in her little red Horizon. It was the second of November, windy and bitter cold. Suffocated by the smell of rotten eggs, she choked and rolled down the window. Fingers stiffened around the steering wheel, as she passed yet another vehicle. A puff of black smoke puked out from under the dashboard, drifted upward, and put her head in a cloud. The radio cut out, lights dimmed, the horn faded to an insignificant moan, and smoke hissed through vents. Jackie swatted into the thick black smog and hoped she was still in her lane. The speedometer needle flopped down limp, and she was afraid the car would come to a rolling stop in the middle of the QEW before she got over to the side of the road. She put the blinker on and made a lane change but never heard the clicking sound. She guessed the brake lights didn't work either, and the mirrors were swallowed by the dark denseness. Smoke burned her eyes and made them tear. Hoping for the best, Jackie moved blindly into the next lane, and then onto the shoulder of the road. Smoke poured out the windows.

Jackie jumped out of the car as the moving van backed up on the shoulder of the road ahead of her. When the mover lifted the hood of her car, Jackie stood back as battery acid sizzled and spat in every direction.

"I was afraid I'd hit someone, or they'd hit me. My brake lights and blinker wouldn't work."

"Lady, with all the smoke gushing out the windows, if they needed a brake light or blinker to tell them to stay clear of you, they shouldn't be driving."

The driver radioed a tow truck and rescued Jackie from further driving. Taking an off-ramp into Hamilton, they crossed the swaying Burlington Skyway Bridge. Jackie covered her nose and mouth blocking out the stench as she looked out over Burlington Bay to the tall, black smokestacks. Bright orange flames, with the intensity of welding torches, shot skyward and pierced the permanent grey sky made by labourers who worked three rotating shifts to ensure the fires in the steel mills never went out.

The driver navigated through streets and arrived at the lawyer's office. Entering the lawyer's reception area, she was escorted into the office.

"You wouldn't believe my day," he said.

"Try me," Jackie said with a grin threatening permanent stretch marks.

"This house was never issued an occupancy slip, even though the previous owners lived in it for seven years; and the property taxes were paid under the wrong property. Please take a seat."

He pulled a stack of papers from the corner of his desk. "Everything is all sorted out now. We just need to review the papers; get your signature and you can be on your way."

Jackie gave the movers directions to the house. The movers were almost finished unloading the van while a plumber was in the kitchen hooking up the new dishwasher. She loved it when a plan came together.

The sound of loud, heavy breathing jolted Jackie's head out of the box she was unpacking. Sweat dripped from the plumber's forehead. His clothes were soaked.

Oh my God, is he having a heart attack?

Somewhere in the background, water gushed. *A waterfall in my house!*

"Do you have the number for PUC?" His panicked words gasped.

Running to the kitchen, Jackie saw water burst from the pipe underneath the sink. The wall phone was blocked by five large moving boxes. She jumped onto the countertop, ran to where the phone was perched, and dialed information, which connected her to the Public Utilities Commission.

"We need buckets and towels," the plumber said, as the movers came in to say they were finished and handed Jackie an invoice for payment.

She jumped down from the counter to find the box labeled "pots and pans." Water soaked the bottom of it.

"Here." She motioned to the plumber.

The movers smirked and shook their heads in disbelief, as the plumber rummaged through the box with his head swallowed up by the cardboard flaps, while Jackie wrote out a cheque and signed the invoice.

"Laundry tub," Jackie shrieked. "Bathroom."

When the plumber shuffled out of the kitchen into the hall, Jackie bumped past him, and into the bathroom. She snatched the metal tub and dumped the neatly wrapped bathroom essentials onto the floor. The plumber blocked the door frame.

"Look out." Running to the kitchen, Jackie placed the wash basin under the leak.

The plumber drilled through to the main water pipe, and there was no shutoff valve in the house. So, water flowed as they alternated emptying the tub and pots until PUC, with lights flashing, came to their aid. The workers found the shutoff valve in the driveway, partially paved over, so they turned the water off at a fire hydrant. Jackie met Colleen, her neighbour, when she came over to find out why she had no water to boil the potatoes she peeled for supper.

The plumber left and Jackie finished mopping up the last of the water when Colleen showed up with a bottle of wine, a burger, and fries. After the chaos of the move, Jackie wanted to be by herself without having to entertain someone surrounded by a mess, and it seemed Colleen understood because she said she had to get back to her girls. With all the commotion, Jackie forgot about missing lunch and was too busy cleaning to think about supper. She sat at the table, uncorked the wine bottle, tapped the corkscrew Colleen provided against the bottle, and toasted, "To a possible friend."

Chapter 23

Monday morning, Jackie woke before the alarm went off. Riding the bus to work made her feel like she was seeing flash cards of old, familiar buildings and haunts. The downtown had changed the most and maybe the least. The bones of the buildings were the same sturdy, aging structures, but much of the signage and businesses were different. Diamond Jim's, with all its flashing lights and glitter, was a new face on a tired, old building. Many storefronts exhibited fresh, stone-blasted facelifts or coats of paint. The walk to work wasn't enough time to satisfy her memories.

When Jackie tugged open the Unemployment Insurance office door, she was hit by the stench of beggary. Different city, same place. The homeless men arrived first. They wanted a few hours of work, enough to get them a bottle or two and some food. The anteroom was sunny and bright, but the atmosphere was shadowed by a dank depression which made Jackie eager to get into the main building. A large clock above the main reception desk read 8:10 a.m. A woman who stood beside the desk reached for two cups of coffee and headed toward her.

"I wasn't sure how you take it, so I got regular," the woman handed her a cup.

"You must have me mixed up with someone else. I don't know anyone here."

"You're the new agent, aren't you?"

Jackie grinned. "I almost forgot how good the rumour mill is. This is so sweet of you. Thanks."

Jackie raised her cup in a toast. She followed the woman's lead, moved over to the side, and cleared the way for other employees who came through.

"First days are always the worst. If you'd like, I'll meet you for lunch and give you the lay of the land. Which restaurants can get you fed and out the door on time. Where the best food is for the price. And where to find what kind of food. You're not a brown bagger, are you?"

"No."

"I have a 12:30 p.m. lunch, so meet me here at the front door. Oh, I'm Paula Amodeo by the way. I'm an Enquiry Clerk and work on this floor. The agents are on the second floor. Don't forget, twelve-thirty. See you then."

To stop the cup from shaking, Jackie wrapped both hands around it. Aware of the bustling crowd guiding her numb body, Jackie allowed herself to be led to the elevator. Paula's face loomed from the suffocating crowd of strangers who waited for the next elevator.

Jackie's anxiety built with the elevator's rising pressure.

Did Paula know who she was? What could Gino have seen in her?

Her look screamed used and abused. Head framed by bleached blonde hair, Paula's heavy makeup accentuated deep acne scars. Gino was a sucker for a sad story and Paula looked like she'd accumulated many of them. Jackie remembered the day in the park with the knife. He would have wanted to help and protect another unfortunate.

Jackie forced a "say cheese" smile without hearing much of what the new supervisor said, as she was led to a desk and introduced to peers. Without baffle board walls separating the agents' desks, Jackie felt like she was on display. Conscious of the stack of files on the corner of her desk dwindling too slowly, she opened another file.

Four floors of people and she meets Paula within seconds of arriving. It would have taken a day to find Paula, then a few more to get close to her. This unexpected role reversal from the pursuer to the pursued made her suspicious. Jackie's head throbbed as she flipped through the pages in the file before her. She closed her eyes against the pain before resuming work. Qualifying conditions and calculations interchanged with motives and intentions. Paula must know about their con. Henrietta must be wrong. Paula knew who she was! Was this a blackmail lunch?

A dusty plastic palm tree separated her desk from another woman's desk. The woman's thumb flicked the filter of a cigarette, missing the ashtray, and scattered fizzled sparkler bits of ash amongst the files. The smell of smoke was heavy.

Jackie looked up at the ceiling for a sprinkler system, then down at the woman. "Have you worked here long?"

The woman turned around. The cigarette lolled from her lips bobbing the words, "Too long."

She looked at the stack of files still on the corner of Jackie's desk to be done and then at her watch, cutting off any further conversation.

By 12:30 p.m. Jackie had completed the files and cleared them from the corner of the desk. At this rate, she should meet her quota for the day. She walked down the stairs to the first floor. When she skirted people waiting for the elevator, she saw Paula at the front door.

"I thought we'd go to the sandwich bar in Jackson Square," Paula said.

Although the little restaurant was crowded, Paula bullied her way to the counter, put in an order, and pulled Jackie beside her.

Paula handed the cashier twenty dollars. "I'll get this; you can buy the next time."

With a cup, saucer, and sandwich plate stacked waitress-style into Paula's one hand, Jackie followed, feeling inept as she juggled a purse and dishes while Paula cleared the way with her free hand. Glad to get to the table and set her rattling teacup down, Jackie pulled out a chair. *Maybe this wasn't a one-time blackmail lunch.*

Jackie ate her sandwich slowly to let Paula do the talking.

"So how long have you worked for the UI?" Paula asked.

"Three and a half years."

"How long you been an agent?"

Jackie bit into a pickle. "A little over two."

"Do you like it?"

"It's a job."

"A job I'd like to have. I'm studying right now for an Agent 1 competition. It's coming up soon. The money's great, a lot better than an Enquiry Clerk. The backlog is bad here. Transferring in is probably easy. I figure they still need about three or four more agents just to stay on top of the claim load. Nice money, especially with all the overtime agents have been getting lately."

Jackie kept eating. The conversation didn't seem like a shakedown.

"Who do you sit beside?" Paula asked.

"I was introduced to the agents all at once, but I think her name is Betty."

"Older, kind of grizzly, with brown hair, glasses, skinny, and a chain smoker?"

"Yeah."

"It's Betty. Get in good with her, because she monitors the claims. Not to say you make mistakes. But it never hurts to have a friend in your corner who can overlook a few uncrossed Ts, if you know what I mean."

"Thanks for the advice." Jackie's smile stretched uncomfortably over her teeth.

When they returned to the office, Paula said, "Want to do this again tomorrow?"

"Sounds good to me."

For the remainder of the day, Jackie stayed at her desk, missed a break, and reached the expected number of assessed claims. Filing out of the unit, she side-stepped the crowd in front of the elevator and took the stairs to the first floor. Snow crunched underfoot outside. Jackie was almost at the Barton Street bus stop when Paula ran up behind her, and then rooted inside a purse for change.

"So, how was your day?" Paula asked.

"Okay."

Even though things were working out the way Jackie hoped, she couldn't help feeling it was all too easy. Her plan was falling into place, but it was Paula who was orchestrating it.

Jackie had bought the townhouse mainly because of the location. She knew Paula took the Barton Street bus to and from work. It seemed plausible for a friendship to develop through routine. The bus door swished open. Paula boarded first, claimed the bench seat behind the driver, and motioned for Jackie.

"Are you married?" Paula asked.

Jackie tucked in her feet as other riders jostled for position. "No."

"Seeing anyone?"

"No. I just got over a bad break-up. I came here because I wanted a fresh start."

"I am a widow. I was married for two years. We were still in our honeymoon phase. Then he got sick. A true-life tragic love story."

Jackie settled her purse between them. "How did he die?"

"Cancer. He suffered in the end, so his death was a relief for both of us."

Jackie shuddered. *He suffered.* She felt her chin quiver and dimple like a golf ball. She squeezed her cheeks and puckered her lips. It never occurred to her, that Paula would make Gino suffer. Taking a few deep breaths, Jackie kept the hurt and hatred out of her voice.

"I imagine it's hard to watch your husband die."

No emotion flickered across Paula's face. She simply shrugged. "You learn to be strong. The medical expenses bankrupted us. He died penniless. The bank foreclosed on the house, so I was left with nothing."

Yeah right. "I'm so sorry you went through it. It must have been difficult losing someone you loved."

"Seems like I can't catch a break. And now with me back on my own again... well things just aren't easy. It's hard being a single mom on a clerk's salary. Theresa, she's my daughter, wants everything her friends have. But she forgets they got two parents pulling down a wage. With Gino gone, I have to do it all myself."

The bus jerked into motion again. Jackie clutched her purse before it slid onto the floor. She forced herself to relax her facial muscles and let the tightened hard lines of hatred soften.

"With an agent salary, I won't have to worry about the bills anymore. But I've tried studying from the manuals. It's impossible. I might as well stop dreaming now. Without help, there's no way I can figure out all the bullshit rules in those manuals. An Einstein, I'm not. We're just going to have to keep counting our pennies on my salary. But it's hard to tell a twelve-year-old kid 'no' all the time just because we don't have money. She talks about what friends have. I wish I could give her that stuff too. Sometimes, I feel like a failure as a mom."

Jackie's stop was coming up soon. She didn't want to be too eager. She waited until the bus was a block away from the stop before she said, "I guess I could help you study."

Chapter 24

After a week of riding the bus and being together most days, Jackie became exasperated with the submissive role Paula's friendship demanded. In their seats on the bus, Jackie and Paula kept their faces close. They shared an earplug each to Paula's transistor radio with the cord stretched between them as they mouthed lyrics from the latest countdown hits on CHML Radio. Like the glittery winter snow that concealed potholes and cracks in the deteriorated pavement, candy-coated conversations concealed Jackie's pretend friendship with Paula.

Getting off the bus together, they walked down the garbage-littered street. The plan was for Jackie to stay overnight, so they had more time to prepare Paula for the Agent 1 competition.

The house was small, old, and in need of repair. The front steps blanketed by snow, looked more like a ramp, except where boots had long ago blazed a trail. Jackie followed Paula's lead. So the snow wouldn't get into their boots, they stepped into the frozen boot molds to go up the stairs and onto the porch.

"Come on." Paula waved her in.

Jackie liked seeing the squalor Paula lived in. She deserved it. But then, she thought of her daughter.

She recognized Gino's brown leather recliner. It was more worn than what she remembered, but it had been years since she'd last seen it.

"I just love these old recliners." Jackie made a beeline for it.

Paula put the transistor radio on the coffee table. "It's filthy and stinks. Have a seat on the couch."

Theresa came in from the kitchen with a bowl of Froot Loops. "Mom hates it when anyone sits there."

Jackie tucked her face against the faded leather and thought of Gino's rough and warm touch: headlocks with playful noogies, her feet on top of his when they danced around the kitchen, being turned upside down, big bear hugs with lip-trilling wet raspberry kisses. Happy memories were soured like the chair.

Theresa ran into her bedroom, came back out, and cradled a photograph. "It's my favourite picture."

She held up a snapshot of her and Gino on the dock of a cottage.

"Oh, let me see," Jackie said.

Gino wore his fishing boots and plaid shirt. He held a full stringer and his grin said he knew where the best fishing holes were, but he wasn't telling. Jackie stared at the photo and memorized his face; those laugh lines, the crinkles around his eyes—his expression.

"It's Gino and me," Theresa said. "He was my best friend. Gino used to let me drive the boat. He taught me how to swim and we used to go canoeing too."

Jackie felt tears well up, but she wanted to hear more, because she remembered the same things, and coveted similar pictures. Theresa's serious, sad face mirrored her own. Jackie cherished all the pictures of her and Gino. Many of them were on display in the townhouse along with her parent's photographs.

"It's enough; don't bore us with any more of your shit. Go turn the TV on," Paula said.

"Are you sure you don't want to sit on the couch? The chair is disgusting and stinks. I can't believe you like it. I can't wait to get rid of it. It would have been gone already except Theresa made such a fuss about bringing it with us on moving day, I gave in. But it's time for the dumpster."

"No. Please Mom." Theresa popped up from the floor. "Please don't take Gino's chair away. I'll do the dishes every day and make my bed. You won't even have to tell me."

Paula picked up the photograph. "Is this where this thing belongs? Put it back where you got it. I don't need to be picking up after you all day."

Jackie watched silent tears streak down Theresa's cheek to the *meep meep* of the roadrunner. She hadn't considered Theresa in her plan. An innocent who loved Gino. And Gino had loved her.

Perched on top of the TV, a lava light cast a green glow onto Theresa's sandy-blonde hair. The green blob moved up and down mimicking the feeling in Jackie's stomach. To lose both parents was hard on a kid, especially at her age. Her plan would cost Theresa another parent when Paula was sent to prison.

"Don't throw away the chair. These things are expensive. The mechanics of it work well. It just needs to be recovered. If you don't want it, I'll take it off your hands. And Theresa can come visit me anytime and cuddle in the chair," Jackie said.

"Do you mean it?" Theresa wiped her runny nose.

"There's only one condition. Maybe two. You bring more cottage photos with you and stay overnight."

"Let's get started on this agent shit," Paula said.

Jackie got out of the chair and followed Paula to the kitchen table.

They spread out the paperwork. "Agents question claimants on why they quit or were fired from their jobs, then phone the employer to get their side of the story. Then this fact-finding information goes to a second agent to decide if a disqualification should be imposed."

"I know all this shit. I need you to show me how to calculate a claim."

They spent most of Saturday studying the calculation for regular and sick benefits. While Paula worked on the computation exercises, Jackie and Theresa squeezed into the recliner with the cottage photo album open on their laps. Theresa shared a story to go with each picture and Jackie couldn't get enough of them.

Paula came into the living room. "What are the two of you doing?"

"I'm showing Jackie the pictures of us at the cottage," Theresa said.

Paula looked at the album. "Remember this?" She laughed and pointed to the photo of Gino lying on the ground under a hammock. "By the time I found the camera, I missed the best part. Gino was in the hammock with a B.B. gun trying to blast the squirrels out of the tree. Shit was flying everywhere. The squirrels were running from one branch to another, pelting him with acorns and leaves. I thought he was going to hang himself the way he was jerking and twisting tangled in the hammock ropes, screaming and swearing at the squirrels, and flinging acorns back at them."

She laughed. "He used to tick me off sleeping in the hammock all day while I did the work, so I fixed him. When he was out fishing, I fed the squirrels on the hammock so when he tried to sleep on it, they would drive him crazy running up and down the tree, expecting to get fed." Paula's body shook with laughter. "They chewed the mesh pretty good, so I knew it was going to happen." Her words were sputtered between breathless giggles. "I was just glad I was there to see it. Funniest thing I ever saw. And I set him up."

Jackie and Theresa frowned at Paula who was bent over with laughter.

"His ass fell through the mesh buckling him like a folding chair. I laughed so hard, I thought I would piss my pants. Never thought I'd see his toes touch his head." Tears streamed down her cheeks.

Jackie's fists clenched the album while Theresa snuggled closer to her. Neither of them laughed or smiled. Jackie squeezed her cheeks into her molars and stopped the teeth-grinding motion.

"Enough with the pictures." Paula snatched the album and closed it. "You got to stop boring Jackie with them, and stop crawling all over her."

"She's not bothering me. I enjoy it."

"Well, it's her bedtime anyway. Theresa, you're bunking with me, so Jackie can have your bedroom. Get moving."

After Theresa left, Jackie looked for an excuse to retire early and picked up her overnight bag. The next morning, Jackie awoke disoriented and recalled other Sunday mornings when she wasn't in her bed. Except this time, she wasn't in David's bed either.

"I'll be down in a minute," Jackie answered Theresa when she hollered, breakfast was ready.

Jackie wanted to stay in bed and dream about David. She missed his soapy, fresh scent splashed with Pierre Cardin cologne, missed surprise outings on a boat or an overnight stay in wine country. She missed his take-charge attitude even though at times he could be too controlling. She missed the future she longed for. The life she wanted.

"I'm coming."

Breakfast was Cornflakes, Shredded Wheat or toast, and jam with peanut butter. Jackie found it hard following the conversation with Paula when all she could think about was whether David missed her too. Did he still love her? If he could forget about her so easily, was it love? Maybe he was dating again. She looked at her finger where the ring should have been. Maybe she should call him like a friend who wanted to catch up. But how could she chit-chat? What could she say? Wasn't it lucky they'd been able to get the deposit back from the venue? Was he able to cancel all the arrangements he'd made over the last six months? She thought of her beautiful wedding gown hanging in the closet. Because of the alterations, the bridal shop wouldn't take it back.

Jackie wasn't aware she'd eaten until she looked at the empty plate.

Paula cleared off the table and made room for the paperwork. "I said, we better get started if we don't want to be at this all day."

Jackie went through the calculations of regular and sick benefits step by step. When Paula mastered those, she moved on to maternity benefits. Calculations were plotted on graph paper. Anytime Jackie pointed out an error in Paula's work, she became defensive. When Jackie explained how the system worked, Paula countered with her version of how it should be. Because Paula found difficulty with calculating maternity benefit claims, she needed to prove the system was flawed and not her lack of ability.

After a grueling four hours, Jackie suggested they meet next weekend to go over everything again.

Jackie looked forward to getting back to the townhouse, and real life. A false friendship with Paula drained her. And getting attached to Theresa made the charade worse. Theresa was a sweet kid.

She was grateful for Colleen's friendship where she could be herself and still have a life without deception. No guilt. Just an honest friendship to look forward to.

This was the first opportunity to invite Colleen and her daughters over for dinner. She made the girls' favourite food, hotdogs, and macaroni and cheese. It was the perfect no fuss, first dinner party in the new home. Jackie loved belonging to a community again.

When she opened her front door, the girls pushed in together, each trying to be the first to enter.

"One at a time please," Colleen said, which made them fall in line. "Sorry, they're excited, especially since you cooked their favs."

"I got grumblies in my stomach," Barb licked her lips. "Mmmm, can't wait."

Jackie looked from one to the other of the identical twins. "So, who's the oldest."

"Mom says I must have pushed Michelle out of the way to get born first. It's why I'm so bossy," Barb said.

While the girls played in the living room, Colleen helped Jackie in the kitchen.

The table was set and condiments lined up when the guests took their seats at the dinner table. Jackie put a plate of hotdogs on the table next to the casserole with a big spoon in it. Colleen looked at the poster of Clint Eastwood while she poured milk for the girls.

"Dirty Harry? I feel like he's sitting at the table, ticked off because he didn't get a hotdog."

Jackie smiled, "He does have attitude."

"I love him too," Colleen said.

"You love him?" Barb asked.

"Well, not really. I don't know him."

"Then how can you love him? Daddy says you don't know what love is."

"Your hotdog is getting cold," Colleen said.

"Daddy says you're going to be sorry for kicking him out."

Jackie looked over at Colleen who rolled her eyes and shook her head.

"Did I smell cookies when we came in?" Colleen asked Jackie.

"What kind?" Barb and Michelle asked in unison.

"Chocolate chip."

"Yay, my yummiest."

"It's mine too," Michelle stuck out her tongue.

After dinner, Colleen shooed the girls into the living room so they could set up their Barbie house, while she and Jackie cleaned the kitchen. Wiping the table off, Colleen looked at Clint again.

"Good movie."

"It was the last movie I saw with my dad before he died. He was a lot like a Clint Eastwood character. Bigger than life, and fair, but a tough guy who believed in justice even though he was on the wrong side of the law. He looked out for a lot of people, and was a good guy but a drug dealer too."

It seemed like the most natural thing in the world to admit.

Colleen looked back at the poster. "I learned a long time ago, it's not what you do, it's who you are. As long as he treated people right, it doesn't matter what he did for a living. I'd rather know a nice drug dealer than a child molesting banker."

She hinted at an eerie hidden truth. Jackie thought of Gino's words from long ago, "pretty ain't always good." But she didn't want to know anymore, not now. She didn't want to spoil a perfect night. It was comfortable and easy. She loved the sound of girly giggles. When Colleen and the girls left, Jackie got out her leather journal. She skipped a few pages and wrote about the first dinner party in the new home.

Chapter 25

Even though the bus was crowded on Monday morning, Jackie spotted Paula and the seat she saved for her with a purse. Having spent most of the weekend together, there was little for them to talk about.

Once off the bus, they followed the trail of garbage on the sidewalk to work. Paula held open the front door to the UI office for Jackie and followed her into the anteroom. Homeless men huddled into a mosaic of bodies until one man stepped out to create a missing piece in their puzzle of poverty. His body was fermented in the droppings of city life. His clothes mopped up the refuse collected in the cracks of the sidewalk. He smelled of dirt gone moldy, trapped in the creases of him for too long.

"Remember me." He stood in front of Paula and blocked her way into the office.

"Move," Paula said.

"Been doing a lot of moving for you," he said.

When Paula took a closer look at the sallow-skinned man, Jackie saw a startled recognition in her eyes. Jackie was shocked when Paula rummaged through her purse, unfolded her wallet, took out a twenty-dollar bill, handed it to him, and then walked away.

"Do you think it's a good idea to just give him money?" Jackie said. "Once you start more will have their hands out. You'll go broke."

"Charity can't always begin at home."

Jackie's jaw slackened. Was this the same woman who just last week complained about these lazy stinking good for nothing homeless men who hung around the anteroom all day? She said the office should stop coddling them, throw them out in the cold, and give them the incentive to work inside and keep warm. To go from this attitude to here's a twenty, stunk worse than the odour from these men.

"Charity is one thing. This was more like a mugging the way the guy blocked your path and was aggressive."

Jackie knew Paula wasn't easily intimidated, so her rollover reaction wasn't right. Normally, she would have cursed at him and pushed him out of the way. Because the homeless man didn't look at Jackie for a handout, Paula was the intended target. She paid him for something, Jackie was sure of it. Or maybe for nothing, just to keep his mouth shut. She remembered Henrietta told her Paula hired two movers who looked like bums. With the reference to moving, he could've been one of them. He must have something on Paula for her to hand out money without question.

After she walked up to the second floor, Jackie settled in at her desk. She picked up a file and thumbed through it while walking to the elevator. When she reached the first-floor anteroom, the homeless man was nowhere to be found. He must have been sent out on a job or left, satisfied with the money Paula gave him.

Every day for the rest of the week, Jackie snuck down to the anteroom of the building searching for him. Each day there were different men, all with the same desperate look. It was impossible to predict when she would next see him, since homeless men came when they were up to it, somewhere between numb and involuntary detox, when their money ran as dry as their throats. If they worked too many hours they wouldn't be around the next day. More money meant more booze or drugs, so the next day would be spent in an alleyway heaving up some diner's special of the day.

It wasn't until Friday morning when Jackie and Paula walked into the office together that they saw the homeless man. Paula ignored him and this time he stayed on his side of the room. After starting work, Jackie went downstairs to the anteroom. She smelled, then saw, the puddles of urinated Old Sailor that warmed and festered in the corner and simmered in the sun. It wasn't written down anywhere, not in any manual, but everyone knew these men weren't allowed inside the main building. It was an understood rule. Since they couldn't use the washrooms, they pissed in the anteroom.

Spotting the man who confronted Paula, Jackie walked up to where he stood with three others. They weren't speaking, so there was nothing to interrupt. Their stink wasn't as discernable as body odour, but rather a clotted stench of backed-up sewer muck.

"Can I talk to you outside?" Jackie said.

Without a word, the homeless man followed her out and around the back of the building.

"My friend Paula said she wouldn't pay you off anymore. I know you helped her move the day her husband was killed."

Jackie took two twenty dollar bills out of her pocket, showed them to him, and then stuffed them back into her pant pocket.

"The twenties are yours if you tell me what you know."

The man squinted, lifted his upper lip much like a horse would, and showed off thick, white-coated gums with rotted teeth.

"She's not giving you any more money, so you might as well tell me. Or did you have something to do with the murder?" Jackie said.

"Didn't know nothing about no husband. Didn't even see him. We was in the shed and I needed to take a piss, so I went back to the house. She comes running out the house all crazy wild. Told me, I couldn't go in the house. Told me, I could shit on the lawn, it wouldn't bother her, cause she weren't letting me in. Knew right then, she hid them whiskey bottles in the shed for us. To keep us outta the way. Saw the gun in her pocket too and she knows it."

"You saw a gun?" Jackie concealed her surprise.

"Yeah," he nodded.

"Did you tell the cops?"

"No. Not my business."

"Did this happen before or after the gunshot?"

"Before."

"Are you blackmailing her?"

"Never said nothing to her about no money. Never asked for it. Not my fault she's got a guilty conscience."

Jackie handed him the forty dollars. "We never talked, okay?"

The man's story made sense. Paula was the one who brandished the gun. Gino was unarmed. No doubt she was the aggressor and planned every detail. It was why Henrietta didn't see the movers because Paula left whiskey for them. Gino must have been devastated when Paula pulled the gun on him. Life was always about family for Gino. And now after meeting Theresa, Jackie knew why Gino stayed. He loved Theresa. He would never do anything to hurt her.

The day slipped by. Jackie met Paula at the main doors for another weekend round of studying at Paula's house.

Theresa greeted them at the house with a big smile and a warm hug for Jackie, but not one for Paula.

"Do you have homework?" Paula asked.

"Just a bit. But it's Friday."

"I got to do mine." Paula pointed at the work bag Jackie brought with her.

"But I have all weekend to do it."

"Don't talk back. Get at it now."

Jackie set her overnight bag on the floor and sighed.

After three frustrating hours at the kitchen table teaching, Jackie was ready to quit. "Remember the formula. Maternity benefits are different than regular benefits. The claimant needs at least twenty insured weeks in the last fifty-two weeks, but out of those twenty or more weeks, ten of them, they're called the magic ten, must fall between the thirtieth and fiftieth week before the date of confinement, which is the due date."

"Why would they make such an idiotic formula?" Paula pushed the papers to the center of the table. "This magic ten shit is fucking stupid. It doesn't make any fucking sense."

"We can't change the rules. The rules are the rules, we have to go by them."

"As long as she has twenty weeks who gives a shit where ten of them fall."

Jackie covered her face with both hands and took a deep exasperated breath. "I think it was to make sure the claimant was working at the time she conceived. They don't want to pay out if she only worked after she found out she was pregnant. They probably figured she'd bilked the system then."

"What difference does it make? The woman is still pregnant, worked, and then has to stay home and look after the kid."

"I don't make the rules; I just tell you what they are. And you can argue about them as much as you want, but it still won't change anything."

"You can tell a man came up with this shit," Paula said.

Jackie put a blank UI application in front of Paula. "Now let's see what you've learned. I want you to fill out the application as if you are applying for maternity benefits."

"Why should I go through all this shit?" Paula said.

"You need a completed application to reference your calculations, and since it's important to familiarize yourself with the process from start to finish, this is the best way to do it," Jackie said.

"I think it's a lot of work for nothing. You should be able to tell me what weeks a woman worked, and what her due date is so I can figure out if she qualifies. I shouldn't have to fill out this whole fucking application."

"Humour me. This is the way I learned."

"Maybe you got a shitty teacher."

Jackie wanted to throw something at her, the ingrate. She was spending all her time teaching Paula and getting nothing for it.

"Back to work." Jackie tapped the application.

Paula stared at the form, laughed, and filled in the name, Cathy Ermeta.

"What's so funny?" Jackie said.

"Cathy hates kids, swore she'd never have any. She's the perfect person to make pregnant."

"In the address block, put in P.O. Box 1256, Hamilton, Ontario for all of them. It will be quicker," Jackie said. "And for the employer, let's use Arpico Steel."

With Jackie's guidance, Paula completed the rest of the application, along with the corresponding medical form, to show proof of the expected date of confinement. Paula signed the medical form, Dr. I. U. Duover. "Get it? I.U.D."

"Yeah, real funny. Don't forget to date and sign the application, Cathy Ermeta," Jackie said.

"You know you're anal making me do all this crap for nothing."

"Maybe, but this is what you'll get in a competition. If you're not used to working from the application, you won't know where to find the info and will be fumbling around. This way, you know what you're looking for and where it is. Since we don't have an ROE, using the application is the point of reference and it takes the calculation from theory to the actual intended purpose."

Paula mapped out Cathy's insured weeks on graph paper and calculated entitlement. She determined Cathy had 24 insured weeks in the last 52 weeks. She needed 20 weeks, so Paula concluded Cathy qualified for maternity benefits. Jackie checked over the calculations and showed her the graph.

"She has twenty-four insured weeks, but doesn't have the magic ten," Jackie said. "Only eight weeks fall between the thirtieth and fiftieth weeks before the due date. So, she doesn't qualify," Jackie said.

Jackie took Cathy's papers and put them aside. "Try again."

Jackie handed Paula another application form.

"Your coffee cup has sat here empty for the last hour. Do you think you could move it so I have room for all this shitty paperwork?" Paula said.

Without a word, Jackie picked up the cup, turned around, and sat it on the counter behind them. Jackie was amused by Paula's anger and felt great about usurping control. She was tired of Paula's, "my way, or the highway" superiority. Tired of how Paula picked the places they ate at and put down any of her choices as no good. Forced her to share an earplug to make sure she didn't listen to a different radio station. Apparently, there was only one good station and it was the one Paula listened to. No one was allowed to have different tastes. If they did, they were idiots. Jackie didn't know how Gino put up with this woman's obsessive need to control everything. Anyone with different opinions or likes than her was tasteless or wrong and needed to be corrected.

When Paula got to the question of first and last day worked, Jackie told her the dates to write in along with the expected date of confinement (EDC). After she signed and dated the application and medical form, Paula laboured over the calculation and concluded there were 21 insured weeks, and 10 of them fell within the magic ten formula, so the claimant qualified.

"You're catching on," Jackie said.

"I changed my logic and followed their screwed-up stupidity."

"It's just a matter of practice."

Another application was dropped in front of Paula. By the time the weekend ended, Paula completed 15 applications, with medicals, and calculated the maternity claims on graph paper. All of which, Jackie tucked into the briefcase. She felt Gino was by her side, and smiled down on her grinning the way he did when he told her how much money he'd made from selling the R.O.Es.

Chapter 26

The next day at work, Jackie went to the stockroom on the fourth floor and got records of employment, which according to the requisition form she completed, were to be mailed out to a payroll clerk at Firedime Inc. There was no one around, so she helped herself. Jackie only needed 15, but she didn't want to take the same amount to match up with the fraudulent claims. She put 23 ROE into her new foolscap-sized purse, but she would destroy the eight extra. The cops might check out the logbook looking for 15 ROEs taken and cross-reference the 15 phony claims.

Back at her desk, Jackie watched across the room as a person with a stack of newly completed applications disappeared behind a wall of files into a secluded claims prep area. This was the starting point where the paper became a working file to be adjudicated by an agent. A file folder docket held the application, supporting documents, and all other data and decisions collected along the way for an active claim. To create pseudo files, Jackie would have to steal what she needed from this section.

She tried not to be obvious when she looked over at the claim prep area and waited for the file clerk to go on break. After the clerk left, Jackie walked to the bay of files separating the claims prep workstation from the rest of the unit. A stack of applications sat on the corner of the clerk's desk. On the desk behind, plain tan dockets awaited personalization in thick, permanent marker with a claimant's name and social insurance number. Then it would be decorated in colour-coded social insurance number (SIN) labels duplicating the SIN on the application.

She peeked through gaps in the wall of files and made sure no one was around. Jackie counted out 15 clean new dockets and the same number of initial data entry sheets and slipped them into an old, battered colour-coded docket she carried. Hearing voices, she opened the file and looked to be studying it when two women passed by. She felt sweat break out.

Growing up, Jackie knew pickpockets and wondered how they stayed calm. She was sure she looked guilty. She remembered being shown how to palm items from a shelf although she'd never stolen from the stores, like her friends. Gino lectured against it. He was determined, she would be better than him.

She learned deep pockets were a must for this kind of deception. Jackie looked around before she palmed handfuls of SIN labels and stuffed them into her pants pockets. With bright pink cheeks, she walked out from behind the bay of files with a lowered head.

She plunked down in her chair and set the file on the desk. With Betty at lunch, there was no one within proximity. Jackie opened the side desk drawer, shielding against people who came and went and slipped the plunder into a wide-mouthed purse, propped open, underneath the desk.

Instead of going out for lunch, they ate sandwiches at Jackie's desk while she taught Paula how claims were finalized.

"After you calculate a claim, you put in the codes here," Jackie pointed to the spaces on the initial data entry sheet, "then you stamp it." She handed Paula her pencil with a detachable, personalized agent stamp on the end of it.

"Where do I stamp it?"

Jackie tapped at the space. "Every stamp has a different number that's assigned to an agent. This way, every agent is accountable for their work. Claims are monitored regularly so if an agent made a lot of mistakes, they'd know who it is by the stamp number."

At the mention of monitoring, Betty looked over at the two of them.

Paula waved at her. "Jackie's helping me with the Agent 1 competition. I may be coming back."

"You have to win the competition first." The hostility in Betty's voice was apparent.

Paula threw the sandwich wrapper in the garbage. "You're right. I do. But I'm getting lots of instruction. Hopefully, I'll be good enough to pass even your inspection."

Betty opened a file and ignored her. Paula left.

Jackie dropped the agent stamp at the end of the pencil into the purse with the rest of the pilfered items.

After she finalized a claim, Jackie lifted papers and files on the desk and searched for something. Opening the desk drawer, the thin one in front of her stomach, she rummaged through pens, pencils, staples, and white-out. In frustration, she pulled the drawer out and dumped the contents onto the desk. Breathing great exasperated sighs, Jackie rifled through another drawer before slamming it shut and then opening the next. Down on her hands and knees, under the desk, Jackie moved the purse and garbage can and felt around the carpet. She stood up and plopped files on the floor clearing off the desk.

"What are you doing?" Betty asked.

"I can't find my agent stamp. It has to be here. I just had it a few minutes ago to show Paula where the stamp goes on the data entry sheet. It couldn't have disappeared."

Betty snapped her tongue behind her teeth. "Did you check your pockets?"

Jackie turned them inside out so Betty could see, then tucked them back in, pleased she'd taken the SIN labels out of the pockets.

"How about files? You know how pens can sometimes get stuck in a file," Betty said.

Jackie picked the files off the floor and held the binding of each one over the desk before she shook it. The search went on for half an hour until she gave up and reported it missing to her supervisor. Carol Baggott from Benefit Control was called in to question Jackie and made a report. The supervisor reprimanded the negligence and then issued her another stamp.

***

Paula placed second in the agent competition and secured the promotion. A lot changed during the three weeks of agent training, which included Paula's hair colour—now a vibrant red.

She equated the elevator ride to the second floor with climbing the proverbial ladder that would take her to the pot of gold and her new position amongst the other agents and Jackie. The supervisor escorted Paula into her office, unlocked a cabinet, and got an agent stamp. She wrote Paula's name in a ledger and beside it the number imprinted in the rubber stamp. It looked like one of those hollowed-out erasers attached to the end of a pencil.

"You're responsible for this stamp. Don't let anyone use it and keep it in a safe place."

The supervisor led Paula to a desk across the room from Jackie's. Paula adjusted the chair, tried it out, readjusted it, set up binders, and filled desk drawers with office supplies. While gathering up files, Paula proclaimed to the posting clerk she'd take any outstanding files that needed to be cleared because she knew the importance of timely decision-making. Having worked so hard and come so far from her waitress days, she felt like trumpets should have blared marking this new prestigious career.

Paula opened a file. She read the application. The claimant, Tim Bared, worked for Don's Trucking and quit. Using graph paper, Paula calculated the claim. Tim had 32 insured weeks in the last 52 weeks. More than enough to qualify, but he quit his job, so she called the employer and found out why he quit. Tim was a trucker. The employer, Don, told her, Tim quit because he heard he was getting fired. According to Don, Tim was lazy, never could get anywhere on time, wouldn't fill out his paperwork, and couldn't tie down a load properly no matter how many times he was shown. Tim was her next call.

"Why did you quit your job with Don's Trucking?" Paula asked.

"The guy was forcing me to run all the long hauls."

"Don says you were lazy," Paula said.

"The son of a bitch would have me running fifty hours straight if he had his way."

"Don said you couldn't get anywhere on time."

"It's because if I went over the goddamn speed limit his truck would shimmy and shake. He never put any decent money into it for repairs, only patch jobs. The guy should be reported to the safety board."

"Why didn't you get your paperwork done?"

"I told him if he wanted me to lie about the number of hours I drove straight, then he was going to have to do it himself. I'm not fudging the hours for him. If he didn't like it, too bad."

"Don told me no matter how many times you were shown how to tie down a load, you couldn't do it right."

"It's just plain bullshit. You should be investigating him on account of the way he runs his business."

Paula loved this "he said—she said" part of the job. It was a long way from taking restaurant orders and cleaning tables. She loved pitting one against the other, wielding power over decisions. She wrote both conversations and then put the file in the contentious rack for an Agent 2 to make the final ruling on whether Tim would be disqualified for quitting.

Surprised at the number of claims she completed before lunch, Paula felt she would meet her quota for the day.

***

The week before Jackie went to Paula's home to help her study for the Agent 1 competition, she'd rented PO Box 1256 in Paula's name at the post office.

With Paula in her new position, Jackie started to put her plan in motion. At home, for references, she listed the social insurance numbers on each of the dockets she would put together. Pasting colour-coded social insurance numbers onto the fifteen phony files, she wrote the names in black marker. Gathering up the documentation for each claim, she finalized the initial data entry sheets and stamped them with her supposedly lost agent stamp.

Over the next two weeks, she hid three files at a time into her over-sized purse and took them into the office. It was easy to slip them into the clutter of files on her desk, input the information into the computer, and file them into the bays with the other adjudicated claims. Everything was underway.

Four days after all fifteen phony maternity claims were slotted into the bays of files, Jackie scanned the microfiche tapes to see when the first report cards would be mailed out. Jackie would go to the PO Box, pick up the report cards, fill them out, and send them back. Then she must allow another four to ten working days for the cheques to be processed and a few more days to receive them in the mail.

It was all in the details, Gino liked to say. And she hoped she hadn't left anything out. It made sense to set up a con using phony maternity claims because the claimants would never be expected to report to the office and would never be set up on a job search or interviews. Therefore, the likelihood of being caught was slim, unless the perpetrator was an inexperienced agent who made wrong calculations on a claim.

Chapter 27

Jackie found herself telling Colleen about David, their engagement, and the split with him. The two women became like sisters, with Colleen sharing her separation, and then divorce from her alcoholic ex-husband. They were each other's support system.

Colleen worked from nine to five as a receptionist for an insurance company, then as a bartender, getting paid under the table. She took the bartending course, because the job paid more than a cocktail waitress, and she could go to work after tucking her kids in bed. On the nights when she bartended at Tommy's Tavern, her brother, Stephen, would babysit. It was a nice arrangement. Jackie offered to look after the girls if Stephen couldn't make it, but so far, her services hadn't been required.

Jackie admired Colleen—a single mom who worked hard and spent her free time with her kids. From the kitchen, Colleen and Jackie watched the twins play in the living room with their Barbie doll house.

Colleen reached for a handful of potato chips. "Even though we fought like cats and dogs growing up, Stephen and I were still close. If someone picked on me, Stephen was there to flatten them. He never liked my ex." Colleen looked up to make sure the girls couldn't overhear.

"I wondered what it would be like to have a sibling. Because my dad was only eighteen years older than me, he was kind of a dad and brother. And he was always protective."

"Stephen threatened my ex more than a few times, afraid he might hit me when he was drunk. But Joe was all mouth. He bragged a lot and liked to ridicule me. But I only took his insults for so long then hurled them back at him. I did the tit-for-tat thing for years thinking I was getting back at him."

Colleen's husband Joe could never compliment anyone, but always patted himself on the back. It took a long time before she figured he had an inferiority complex and needed to put her down to make himself look better. She didn't realize it changed who she was.

Colleen looked over at the girls. "Excuse me," she said to Jackie and turned towards the children. "Barb let Michelle's doll have a turn driving. The car is big enough for both Barbies."

Returning to Jackie, "I grew up in a family who believed that if you don't have anything nice to say then don't say anything at all. It's how I was. With every tat, I became more like him—negative and critical. One day, after our divorce, I said something to Barb, and she said I sounded just like daddy. And she was right. Even though he was out of my life, I let him be part of me. It was the worst thing she could have said to me. So, I made a list of the five things I hated about Joe and worked on getting rid of them in myself. After eleven years of marriage, you don't realize how much you become the other person. I adopted the—see how you like it—attitude dishing out what he gave me."

"Is it why you're not interested in dating?"

"Yeah. You know the song from South Pacific, 'I'm gonna wash that man right out of my hair?' Well, I think I'm up to rinse, then repeat. Until I'm back to who I was, I'm not ready to take on anyone else's bad traits."

"With all the pictures on your walls of Joe with the girls, I thought you might be hoping to get back together."

"Never. I left the pictures up so the girls wouldn't think I hated him."

"I don't think I could be as nice..." Jackie looked over to see if the girls were listening and mouthed the words, "to the SOB."

"Have you noticed how much the girls look like Joe?"

"Actually, I have."

"From the time they were born, everyone has told them how much they look like their father. Because the girls are like him, if I hate Joe, I'm afraid they'll think I hate them too."

The phone rang. Picking it up, Jackie was shocked to hear David's voice. She had hoped for so long he would call but gave up because she couldn't put herself through the gut-wrenching disappointment anymore. When he asked how she was doing, she wanted to break down and cry. She turned away from the concern in Colleen's eyes and hid her pout-a-puss face. She couldn't cover up the half cry of, "Good."

Both girls stopped playing with their Barbies and spun around. Jackie covered her face with her hand, unable to trust herself to speak without crying.

Colleen stood up and said to the girls, "Pick up your Barbies, we've got to go." She waved bye and closed the front door.

Jackie broke down and cried, "I've missed you so much."

"I just crossed the Burlington Skyway Bridge and I need directions. I'll be there soon," David said.

After she hung up the phone, Jackie went next door. She was practically gushing when she told Colleen the news. "And he'll be here soon." *Carried off into the sunset by my white knight. How hokey! Stupid, childish. But maybe....* "How do I look? Oh, my God, I have to get changed and put some make-up on."

"Relax, he's coming to you, remember?" Colleen said. "Don't be too quick to react. Take time to think about what you want."

On her way out the door, Jackie heard Colleen holler, "You have to leave room to negotiate."

Jackie finished applying mascara when the doorbell rang. Her smile spread as she invited David in. He presented her with a dozen long-stemmed red roses and a box of chocolates. While she put the flowers in a vase, he hesitated at the armchair and couch as if wondering where to sit. Jackie had never known him to act so uncertain before. He chose the armchair. Jackie sat across from him on the couch placing the presents on the coffee table between them.

He sat forward in the chair. "I've had time to think about the way things were left between us. I think it was the shock of you moving that made me react so badly. I understand now, people process grief differently. Some need more time. I expected you to get over it too soon. That was my fault."

Jackie waited for him to say something about how deceitful she had been in keeping Gino a secret. When he didn't broach the subject, she assumed, he had forgiven her. Overwhelmed by his understanding, Jackie couldn't say anything. She cried. He came over to the couch, sat down, and gathered her into his arms until she recovered.

"How is it coming with finalizing your dad's estate?"

"I sold the house, but I still have a lot of other things to do. It's a slow process."

"I know it's hard to do but this might help you to move on. Maybe this is what you need. Will you be moving back when things are completed?"

"I'm not sure."

"Do you think we could have a second chance? I'm sorry that I let my mother take over the wedding plans and shouldn't have. I should have gone along with you and settled for a small wedding instead of turning it into something you didn't want. I made mistakes that I regret."

Jackie didn't regret hiding Gino's existence from him or telling him about Gino after he died. She told him the truth when Gino couldn't be harmed by it, so there was no wrongdoing to confess. Nothing for her to say.

"It's not a far commute for me. Can we start over? Forget about the past. Chaulk it up to our first big fight and make-up?"

Jackie was stuck in a different lie now. She couldn't tell him how she was setting Paula up for fraud and that she was defrauding the government to do it. Could she handle the guilt of deceiving him again? How could she put him in that same predicament? She was torn and didn't know what to say. The uncomfortable silence made her fidget out of his embrace and sit up straight.

Like a fairy-tale romance, he came back for her. He did love her. Since moving to Hamilton, Jackie hoped for this day. She had stayed awake in bed at night and dreamt of this very moment. She wished so hard for it. She wanted her life back again with him.

David turned her chin so she was facing him. "You know we are perfect for each other. You are all I've thought about." He kissed her passionately. "I love you."

Swept up in his embrace, responding to his familiar touch, clothes scattered when she succumbed to his persuasion.

Lying in bed, she listened as David snored softly, and thought of Colleen's advice. Negotiate! She hadn't said anything—afraid to confess her plan. But what did this mean now? Should she tell him she suspected Paula had murdered Gino? But she had no proof. Should she tell him the real reason she came back? David was not a vengeful person. He wouldn't understand. He would never forgive willful deceit a second time. She let her emotions take over and was now perched in a precarious spot. Was the engagement back on? How stupid! Why hadn't she listened to Colleen? Why couldn't she trust him with the truth?

David rolled over and scooped her into his arms. Jackie snuggled closer. It felt so warm and right. Maybe nothing needed to be analyzed, but only enjoyed.

He whispered, "I love you. How about in the morning, I take you out for a big breakfast?"

Jackie thought about the morning after he proposed and how it was what she wanted to happen. Maybe this could be a new start, without all the ugliness that followed.

They went to the Holiday Inn for breakfast then back to her place. Parked at the front of the house, he leaned over and gave her a deep lingering kiss.

"Save it for when we get inside," Jackie said.

"It's Sunday—files are waiting. I'll see you next Saturday," he said.

Jackie opened the car door. *And don't let the door hit you on the way out.* The new start ended the same way. Would work always come before her? Or maybe Sunday was just a rut and routine that could be broken once they were married. He waved goodbye and she blew him a kiss.

After David's car pulled away and was no longer visible on the street, Colleen showed up at Jackie's door.

"Want to talk?" Colleen said.

Jackie nodded.

Colleen waved her hand away and said to the girls, "Stay out and play."

After the re-cap about David ended, Jackie announced, he was coming back next Saturday. By the look on Colleen's face, she knew something was wrong.

"Oh my God, I forgot we promised to take the girls to the zoo next Saturday," Jackie said. "Not a problem, I'll call him and tell him it's what I'm doing, and if he wants to join us, he can, if it's alright with you and the girls?"

"Of course, it is," Colleen said. "I'd love to meet him."

When Colleen told the twins, they jumped up and down and cheered. Barb was always louder and more exuberant than Michelle. This could be the fresh start Jackie needed, where what she wanted mattered. Where she just didn't go along with whatever David wanted.

For the last three months, whenever Colleen was off work on a Saturday or Sunday, they'd take the twins on outings. They visited the zoo, watched movies, bowled, and hiked in the woods. The outings reminded Jackie of the places Gino took her and their long walks into the bush around the cottages he rented.

***

The next Saturday, David was back as promised with stuffed animals for each of the girls, which won them over. It was a crisp, sunny day and the walk through the zoo was enjoyable for all. Afterward, Colleen invited them over for wine and hors d'oeuvres before the couple went out for dinner. Colleen's kitchen table was cluttered with her income tax return and a T-4 slip.

"Sorry, I'll get this out of your way. I hate doing this crap. Government red tape is the worst paperwork to get through."

David smiled. "This is ten minutes of work."

"For you maybe, but I can't decipher it," Colleen said.

"If you want, I can take this home, do it, and bring it back next weekend."

"Are you serious? I would love it. But I don't want to put you out."

"He wouldn't offer if he didn't want to do it." Jackie beamed.

"This is what I do. I'm an accountant," David said.

"Oh. I knew you worked at a business firm, but Jackie didn't tell me what you did. I'm sorry, but I can't pay you for this, so I'll have to muddle through it."

"There won't be a charge. Let's just say it's to show my appreciation for you sharing your day with me."

Colleen warmed up to David all day, but this unexpected generosity won her over.

Chapter 28

The office was backlogged, and it took longer before Jackie got all the report cards completed for the fraudulent maternity benefit claims and sent them back. The week dragged on. She couldn't wait to see David tomorrow. She envisioned the menu in her head and checked off the ingredients when a clerk handed her a file to do an in-person inquiry.

Jackie read the complaint. The claimant got cut off from receiving benefits for a failure to avail. She walked to the reception area into the tight maze of cubicles where the claimant was seated. She was glad the seat closest to the doorway was free. His broad leather-jacketed chest dominated the tiny space, while his arms spread out as he took over the desk and made her feel like an intruder in her turf. A long scar sliced through his Italian, olive-tan complexion.

Jackie opened the file. "I understand you want to know specifically why you were cut off."

She looked at the date of birth on the application. Even though he was a few years older than her, she imagined long hours of squinting into the sun on his motorcycle left those deep creases around his eyes and above his nose that belied his age.

"You came into our job bank area on March 7th and got a job referral for an interview at Allisiam Industries for a position as a forklift operator, then never showed up for the interview."

There was something familiar about this man. Jackie closed the docket to look at the name on the file. Emanuel Miceli, all grown up. Jackie traced barely visible scars in the palm of her hand from when Emmanuel tried to run her down with his bike when they were kids. She was aware that Gino wasn't around to protect her.

Jackie smiled at him. "As the letter said, you failed to make yourself available to a job opportunity you were qualified for in the area, so you got cut off."

"It's bullshit. You people set me up."

Jackie shifted in her seat and presented more of a profile. He was right. Anyone from the street could recognize this "gotcha" mentality. He would never have been cut off if he hadn't used the job bank in the first place. And he used it voluntarily. If he wasn't trying to find a job this never would have happened.

She argued the unfairness of this very situation with her supervisors claiming, you can't offer to hold a claimant's hand and then slit their wrist and still be seen as helpful.

Emanuel unzipped his leather jacket and exposed a tattooed snake wrapped around his neck.

"I was the one who picked the job off the board."

Jackie knew how tough Emanuel was; she didn't need the tattoo to remind her. She licked her lips.

"Then you should have gone for the interview." The words were quieter than she intended.

"I didn't know who the employer was until the counselor told me. The place is notorious for ripping people off. They hose you out of hours. Make you work overtime but don't pay the overtime rate. They think 'cause there's no union they can do what they want. If you people put the name and address of the employer on the job card, I wouldn't of picked it up. Then there'd be no harm, no foul and I'd still be getting my money." Emanuel lit a cigarette. "You look familiar. Do I know you?"

"I've never seen you before. I just transferred here from St. Catharines. Maybe you know me from there." Jackie angled her face more.

"Even though I don't like the employer, I didn't go to the interview because I had another one on the same day for better pay at the Esso gas station on Barton Street."

Jackie flipped through the pages in the file. There was no referral slip for Esso. *Back-peddling again.*

"And did the interview last all day? The referral we gave you stated only the day you were expected, not the time. You were given all day to get to Allisiam Industries."

"You people set me up. If I hadn't looked on your board, I wouldn't be cut off."

"Then appeal it," Jackie said. "If there's nothing else?"

"How do I appeal?"

"Read this." Jackie handed him an appeal pamphlet and then walked back into the unit.

Normally, she would have explained the whole appeal process, but she didn't want the agent's decision to be rescinded. Sometimes life worked out the way it should. And other times one must prod life in the direction one wants to go in.

Jackie sat down at a desk with a monitor and microfiche tapes lined up on the side and checked the fraudulent maternity claims to see if any cheques were mailed out. She looked around at the cleared-off desks, then at the clock, and was surprised it was 4:25 p.m.

Paula stood beside the desk. "Get a move on, we don't want to miss the bus."

Getting off the crowded bus away from Paula was always a relief. The three-block walk to the townhouse invigorated her. Jackie enjoyed the bit of exercise at the end of the day. It cleared her head, unwound the day's clutter, and made arriving home a fresh start. She smiled at the satisfaction she felt with Emanuel, the bully, getting what he deserved.

Walking past a black iron fence that surrounded church property, Jackie heard a familiar, yet somehow different sound behind her. She moved closer to the curb and expected the kid who used a stick or broken twig on the iron fence like a xylophone would run past. The rhythmic sound was the same, but instead of a hollow thud of wood on metal, the sound was a clang, like metal on metal.

Jackie turned when the sound was so close it played up her spine. A hunting knife glided over the steel rungs and sparked the blade in Emanuel's hand. When she saw the smile curl his lips, her numbed body froze. There was no one around. No one to help. Her legs softened like plastic melting. She had no voice to scream. For a fleeting moment, she considered climbing over the iron fence to get to the church. But there was no cross rung to climb, and the fence was too high to vault over the spear-like rods. She imagined herself impaled on those spears.

Emanuel's muscled girth bulged his black leather jacket and emphasized a weightlifter's physique. Jackie bolted pumping her arms to keep ahead of him. Her gasping breath fell in step with his pounding feet, and she heard the swish of leather before she felt a tug on the winter coat that held her in place. Icy blasts of cold air heaved from her lungs, stung her throat, and puffed out cloudy ragged breaths. A leather glove was wadded into her mouth and held in place by a scarf he wrapped and then tied around her face. Jackie tasted sweat and motorcycle grease, while her arms and legs flailed wildly, as she kicked, and clawed at him.

Making a tether, he twisted a handful of Jackie's long auburn hair around a hand. Emanuel forced her head back and laid a knife along her neck. Beads of perspiration, now frozen, dotted the stubble under his nose.

"Did you think I wouldn't remember Gino's pet? It didn't come to me right away where I knew you from until I saw Paula and thought of Gino. I asked Paula when she started working there. And the timeline didn't fit. Then it hit me. Gino must a got them record things from you. Heard how much he charged for them things and thought he was crazy. Till I heard people paid the price. He raked in the dough. So, I figure now I'm cut off pogey, this is a good business for me to get into. Or I can go to the cops and tell them it was you who supplied Gino. Your choice."

Flicking his wrist, Emanuel wound her hair tighter burning Jackie's scalp. The fetter of hair was the only thing keeping Jackie upright when he dragged her to the side of a house and hammered her back against the brick wall. Pinned down with his beefy arm across her chest, Emanuel tugged on her winter coat and pushed it aside. Jackie's tight-fisted punch hit his cold leather jacket without a reaction. She imagined Gino's voice teasing, *you hit like a girl.* Jackie brought her knee up as hard as she could and tried to nail him in the groin, but his leg blocked it. An arm pushed into her throat and forced shallow panting breaths.

"You think I've never done this before?" He ripped open her blouse, used the edge of the bra cup as a guide, and sliced into a breast. "Just a reminder."

When he removed his arm, Jackie's body slid down the brick wall and puddled into a heap. Blood splattered the grey slush.

Emanuel laughed. "You never were much of a fighter. It's only a flesh wound. Not deep. We couldn't have you going to the hospital to get stitches. It would attract attention. I'll give you till the second Wednesday to come up with those record things."

Jackie wrapped the wool coat around herself.

"More than enough time. I figure a hundred isn't too many to keep you out of the joint. If I take the scarf off, can I trust you not to scream? It's not like we won't be seeing each other again, especially if we become partners. And let's face it, the way you fight you wouldn't have a chance against them bitches in prison."

He smiled as though they were exchanging pleasantries. Jackie understood there was no point fighting him. Emanuel untied the scarf and jerked her head when he whipped it out from around her mouth.

He bent down and picked up the glove. "Maybe our next meeting can be a little more civilized. I'll be watching you. Remember, the second Wednesday from now, I'll expect them record things. I want the same deal you gave Gino."

He walked away. Jackie sat in the slush, pants soaked, and rolled onto shaking hands and knees and got herself up. She couldn't go to the cops. And he wouldn't go away. He would always need another hundred. Emanuel would never let it end.

Chapter 29

The key in Jackie's hand vibrated and scratched the lock numerous times before it was inserted. She sprinted toward the bathroom and yanked off her coat along the way. There wasn't a lot of blood. Most of it was absorbed into the bra's padding.

Emanuel is back in her life again. Why now? He would watch her. Find out about David and Colleen and the girls. She wouldn't let him touch them. But how could she stop him? The police weren't an option. Not while she orchestrated this scheme. Gino's friends would help her. But if Emanuel was connected, she couldn't put them at risk. Gino avoided the local mafia. Said he stayed small-time, and it kept the mafia from his door. He was a nobody, not worth their time.

Jackie took off the blouse and bra. Her hand trembled and her body stiffened against the pain when she followed the rounded contour of her breast and cleaned the two-inch slash with warm soapy water. It wasn't deep enough for stitches. Even though it was long, he was right, it didn't need stitches. The cut was precise. An expert butcher, Jackie imagined.

She settled back onto the couch with a large glass of red wine to calm her nerves and swabbed a melting trail of ice cubes over the cut to take the sting out. Wine soothed her mind until the phone rang. She jumped, afraid, and picked it up—frightened it would be Emanuel. Needing to show him, she wasn't the terrified little kid he remembered, she snarled, "What now?"

"Who pissed in your Corn Flakes?" Paula asked.

The relief of hearing Paula's voice made Jackie laugh. "Sorry. I've just been getting crank calls."

"I feel like going out tonight, what about you?"

If she stayed home, she'd be worried about Emanuel and what he would do. And she didn't want to be alone. "Sounds good."

"I'll meet you at The Jockey Club around eight."

Jackie took a taxi. Paula was seated at a table for four near the band. Jackie spotted an empty table near the door. If they sat there, she would be able to see everyone who came in. Emanuel couldn't sneak in without her noticing.

"We're too close to the band." Jackie pointed to the table near the door. "Let's move over there."

"I didn't come here to be shoved in a corner. This is the best seat in the house. Sit down."

Jackie pulled a chair out. "Are you expecting someone else?"

"Here's hoping." Paula raised a beer glass in a toast. "Because so far, this has been my lucky day."

Jackie ordered a beer. Paula's large, hooped earrings now made sense paired with a too-tight, mini-skirt and tighter lemon-lime neon halter top that plopped her breasts onto a shelf-like protruding belly.

Paula picked up her glass and surveyed the room. "I'm ready for a little action tonight. I feel lucky. What do you think about the guy over there? Little black tie and polyester pants. I'll give him my come-hither look. Men can't resist it. And I'm wearing my, come fuck me boots. Take a look at him. What do you think?"

Jackie turned and looked at him. Behind her back, Paula waved him over and pointed at Jackie making out she was the one interested in him.

"I saw that," Jackie said when the guy stood up and looked at them.

"I just need to get him to the table. With your good looks, you're the perfect bait. There isn't a man in the bar who won't come after you if you give them a nod."

Jackie's pursed lips gave Paula a disgusted look.

"Once the guy is at the table and realizes, you don't want anything to do with him, then I'll have a turn at him. It's the old bait and switch."

"Yeah, I get it."

"You might be book smart, but you don't know people."

"He's coming over." Jackie crossed arms over chest.

"Natch. Didn't I tell you they can't resist my come-hither look?"

When the guy sat at their table, Paula cozied the chair up to him. He was the perfect guy. Not good-looking enough to be choosey. And the kind who gets overlooked. So, he'd feel flattered sitting between two women.

"Loosen up." Paula undid the guy's tie and stuffed it into his pocket. "It could be your lucky night." She scraped her teeth over her bottom lip and revealed bright pink lipstick stuck to her front tooth.

Jackie excused herself and went to the washroom, while Paula's fingers ran down the guy's thigh. "Play your cards right and you could have both of us tonight. My friend is into threesomes. She likes you. She told me so. You won't get any better than her. Some body eh? Pretty great. When are you ever going to get something like her?"

Paula was easily spotted on the dance floor. The gyrating halter top glowed under a rotating glitter ball casting a sickening yellow-green blush onto the guy. Jackie couldn't imagine Gino dancing with Paula. She was wild, uninhibited, and all over the poor guy. She was sure Paula was on something. Even under heavy baby blue eyeshadow and clumpy black mascara, you couldn't miss the dilated pupils. And she talked non-stop all night. It was jibber jabber, not a conversation.

When Paula went to the washroom, the guy came back to the table and sat beside Jackie. His shirt was stained with darkened loops of perspiration under the arms, and he smelled of sweat. He leaned in too close. Crooked yellow teeth parted passing the stench of skunky beer and pickled eggs. He touched her bare arm with his sweaty hand. "Do you want to dance?"

Jackie covered her nose and mouth with her hand. "No thanks."

People packed the tables and spilled out into the aisles. A twenty-something girl ground out a beat on the way to the dance floor and bumped Jackie's elbow. She turned; the bandage tugged on her skin. Her fingers rubbed the sore spot above the bra as she scanned the bar for Emanuel.

"I could get it for you." The guy leered at Jackie's breast.

Hand by her side, she glared at him.

He winked. "I've been told I have magic fingers."

"That you better keep to yourself unless you want to be all thumbs."

He laughed as if she wasn't serious. "Paula tells me you're looking to hook up."

"With you? Not on your life."

"Well, you don't think I'm hanging around here for her, do you? I can do a whole lot better than her."

"Then do yourself a favour and go trolling somewhere else."

After he left, it was a while before Paula came back to the table.

"Where did the guy go?"

"Dance floor. What took you so long?" Jackie asked.

"Nosebleed." Paula held a tissue to her nose. When the waiter came around for last call, and the lights came on, Paula had no takers. "I know a place that's open after hours. I need to get laid. I was hoping to pull an all-nighter."

"What about Theresa?"

"She's fine."

Jackie worried about Theresa being alone overnight. She slipped bills from her wallet into her purse and then opened the wallet and showed Paula. "I'm all tapped out."

"Well, I still want to party."

Jackie was nervous about leaving alone and wanted Paula home for Theresa. "How about we go back to your place? We can party there."

"Okay, I got a bottle at home. You can spend the night?"

"Sounds good."

When they walked up the front steps of the house, the living room light went off. Paula put her key in the door. "I don't know how many times I told that goddamn kid to be in bed before I got home."

"Maybe she got scared. It's hard being alone. Sometimes I turn the TV on for the company."

When Paula flicked the kitchen light, they heard Theresa's footsteps scurry down the hallway to the bedroom.

"I don't give a shit. If she can't do what I say, then she can get out. See how she likes it then. Maybe it's what it'll take for her to listen to me."

"She's only twelve."

"I was thirteen when I ran away."

"Why?"

"My mother's boyfriend raped me. Wouldn't leave me alone. My mother wouldn't help. She was jealous he wanted me instead of her."

"Do you still see your family?"

"Nah. My dad was a boozer. Liked to beat my mom when he got drunk." Paula unscrewed the cap to the Canadian Club bottle and poured them each a shot. "He left when I was nine. Coke or ginger?"

"Coke."

"Do you know where they are?"

"No. I didn't keep track of them. I ran into my dad about eight years ago. I almost didn't recognize him. He looked like a skeleton with the shakes. Wasn't so big and threatening then. I could've easily beat the shit out of him, but he wasn't worth the trouble. I'd be surprised if he's still alive."

"What about your mother?"

"She didn't look out for me so why should I bother with her."

"Do you have any brothers or sisters?"

"An older brother. He left as soon as he could. He never tried to protect us. Me, I fought back. Before Dad got home, I always made sure I found a weapon close by. I'd seen what he'd done to my mother, and I wasn't about to turn into her. Theresa doesn't know how lucky she's got it. I never beat that kid. Never even a spanking. I was too afraid if I started spanking her it would turn into a beating, so I never did."

"Where's Theresa's father?" Jackie took a long pull on her drink.

"The bum left us when Theresa was three. Never said a word, just didn't come home one night. Gino might have been a controlling SOB but at least he was a great father."

Jackie poured another shot for herself.

"I used to razz Gino about being a short shit. It was great fun," Paula said.

Jackie topped the rye with coke.

This could be the start of another one of her rambling rants. She must have been snorting something in the washroom because she seemed more wired than before. The nosebleed was a giveaway. Jackie knew how sensitive Gino was about his height and felt bad Paula would use it against him. She felt bad, she'd done the same thing.

Back when she was a kid, Gino used to keep a pack of cigarettes rolled into the sleeve of his T-shirt. In the fifth grade. after school, Gino caught her smoking behind the bushes along a path the school kids used as a shortcut to the corner store. Gino said it would stunt her growth. And she, being a smart ass, mouthed back, "I guess you'd know about it."

She tucked her chin against her collarbone squinted her eyes closed and waited for the hit. When it didn't come, she opened her eyes and saw Gino's boots, then the denim material bunched at his ankles where the pant legs were turned up a couple of times. She looked at him. He ran his fingers through his slick-backed hair, wiped the grease on his pant leg, and laughed before walking away.

Jackie finished the drink, chewed on the ice cubes in the bottom of the glass, and waited until Paula's babbling ended.

Setting the glass on the table, Jackie said, "I think I'll turn in now if you don't mind."

The next morning, Jackie experienced a dull headache, and she wasn't sure if it was from the booze or the restless night thinking about what would happen to Theresa if Paula went to jail.

Paula took the bacon out of the fridge and handed it to Theresa. "Because you disobeyed me last night and stayed up until I got home, you can make breakfast for us. We'll have BLT's."

Paula hovered over Theresa telling her when to turn the bacon, and how to cut the tomato. It was either too thick, or the bacon was too crisp; the lettuce needed to be dried off better because she didn't want soggy toast. There was too much butter, and not enough mayonnaise. The whole instruction made Jackie's head hurt even more.

"No mayo for me," Jackie said.

"You can't have a BLT without mayo. Try it. Just a little on hers," Paula said.

Theresa looked over at Jackie, not sure what to do. Jackie could see the relief on her face when she nodded her consent.

"Now, isn't it better with mayo on it?" Paula said.

"No. I don't like mayo."

"You don't know what's good. Your taste is in your ass."

Theresa brought the orange juice and milk to the table. When Theresa reached for the juice, Paula said, "Milk is better for you. Leave the juice."

Jackie poured a glass of milk for Paula and handed it to her.

"I don't want milk," Paula said. "I want orange juice."

"Drink the milk, you just said it's better for you."

Jackie imitated Paula, and gave a back-at-you attitude, hoping she would see how unreasonably controlling she was. Then she thought of Colleen's story about tit for tat and turning into her ex-husband. When Jackie saw the look on Theresa's face, she regretted the tactic since it made her like Paula.

"The kid needs milk just because kids do, but us, we got a choice. Juice is better with a BLT. But what did I tell you, your taste is in your ass?" Paula's tongue flicked the roof of her mouth and made a disapproving clicking sound while she shook her head as if she'd made the point.

Theresa cleared the table and soaked the dishes in the sink. "When can I have a sleepover at your place? You didn't forget, did you?"

"No. I've got plans for today." Turning to Paula, "How about she comes over after lunch on Sunday?"

"Fine by me."

Theresa poured the grease from the bacon into an empty coffee can.

"We can spend the day together; you can sleep over and I'll take you to the bus stop for school Monday. How does it sound?"

"Great."

Jackie looked over at Paula who nodded her consent.

"It's a date then. I'll see you on Sunday. I have to get home, got lots to do." Jackie ruffled Theresa's hair on the way out.

Before Jackie got off the bus, she looked out the window to see if she could spot Emanuel.

Chapter 30

David arrived later in the day than expected with apologies, more flowers, and Colleen's income tax form completed.

"This is so sweet of you. I appreciate it. Colleen just can't afford to have it professionally done. You're a nice guy." Jackie kissed him.

She went to the kitchen and checked on the spareribs hoping they weren't dried out from being in the oven too long. The sweet tangy garlic vapour whooshed, steaming her cheeks when she lifted the lid off the roasting pan. Tilting the pan, she scooped the rich, dark, alcohol-laced sauce and drizzled it over the meat. Simmered in brown sugar, soya sauce, barbecue sauce, and vodka, the meat fell off the bone.

"It smells great, and I'm starved," David said.

The kitchen table's ink-smudged memories were disguised by a white linen tablecloth. Matching white napkins tucked into silver-plated ring holders sat on white dishes edged in silver. In the center of the table, a fluted silver-plated vase offered up a cluster of red roses entwined with white baby's breath.

"Would you open the wine?" Jackie asked.

While David uncorked the bottle and poured the wine, Jackie plated their food and set it on the table.

"Looks great." David ripped off a meaty bone from the rack.

She smiled and watched while he licked sauce from his fingers before he picked up another rib. A satisfied moan escaped his lips as he savoured the taste of butter-roasted potatoes. Engrossed in the meal, David's conversation was limited. Jackie poured more wine.

"It was incredible. I don't think I've ever eaten so much." David wiped his mouth and hands on the napkin. "Before it gets too late, do you want me to take Colleen's income tax forms over to her?"

"She's not there. She's working. I'll drop them off tomorrow."

"Isn't the insurance company closed by now?"

"It is, but she's working a second job."

"What's that?

"She's a bartender at Tommy's Tavern."

"Has she been there long?"

"Two years."

"But I didn't have a T-4 slip from there."

"It's because she works under the table."

"Why would you keep that from me?"

"It's working under the table. Everyone does it."

"It's fraud!"

"She's a single mom and doesn't get any support from her ex-husband. She needs the money."

"I have a 'Code of Conduct' to uphold through the Institute of Chartered Accountants."

The words and superiority of his tone shocked Jackie. "So, you say you knew nothing about this second job and was only provided a T-4 for her full-time job with the insurance company. What's the big deal?"

"I could be penalized—lose my job."

"It's not like it was billed through your company. No one will know."

"I swore an oath. That may not mean anything to you, but it does to me."

"No one but me knows, and I won't rat you out."

His eyes burned with anger, while clenched stomach muscles made his breathing heavy.

"If you feel so strongly about it, then we'll get a new income tax form and she can copy everything over from yours. She fills it out so it has nothing to do with you."

David's face flushed. "I'll know. She's defrauding the government."

Jackie thumped the glass on the table. "Are you going to report her?"

"I must, according to the Rules of Professional Conduct."

"You'd be taking food out of the kid's mouths? This isn't some textbook case. These are real people who you spent the day with."

"Why should you and I have to pay income tax when she doesn't?"

"Why should her ex-husband not have to pay anything for the kids? She didn't create them alone."

"Rules must be obeyed."

"And kids have to eat. If she has to work under the table, too bad."

"So, only certain," he extended the last word and emphasized it, "people should have to obey the law?"

"It's only working under the table. Please tell me you won't turn her in for this. I couldn't stand it if you did."

"We must be reasonable. After all, it's my reputation on the line. Our future. I have to think about what's best for us."

Jackie's hand knocked the wine glass.

Pompous self-centered asshole!

"Colleen will hate me."

"So, let her."

"Leave."

"I'm not the bad guy."

"Your position! Your job. Your company. This isn't getting billed to your firm. It has no impact on your company. Stop using it as an excuse. All you have to do is rip up the forms, turn a blind eye, and forget about it. I don't think that's asking a lot."

"You weren't the one who took the oath."

"How can you be so cold? How can you talk about being loyal to some oath? What about loyalty to me?"

His voice was cold. "You expect me to disregard the principles of my career, my life, for a person I don't even know or want to know?"

Her fist curled into a tight ball. Jackie wanted to punch him. He didn't want to know Colleen because she couldn't advance his career. Wasn't part of the "right people."

She pounded the table. "No. I expect you to do it for me."

David scowled. "This is the second time you've put my job in jeopardy without any consideration for all the years I have put in to achieve my goals."

"I thought you came back because you'd forgiven me for it."

"Drug dealers. Now fraud. And you expect me to condone this?"

David could take his highfaluting morals and stuff them up his upper-crust ass. She snatched the envelope with Colleen's income tax forms in it before the trail of red wine stained it.

"If you report Colleen, I'll have some of my daddy's friends pay you a visit and shoot his product into your veins." *Oh my God— shoot his product into your veins—who talks like that?* "Then I'll report you to your firm for using and suggest they give you a drug test. You can forget about becoming a partner there or anywhere else."

The threat surprised even Jackie.

Jackie gripped the tax form tighter and put it behind her back. "Get out now."

They scowled at each other before David turned, walked away, and slammed the door behind him. Jackie's body shook. She wasn't sure if it was from rage, disappointment, or loss. David didn't know her. Even believed she could follow through on the crazy threat. How did she come up with it? She laughed. The laughing turned to tears. Why was she crying? How could she be sad about losing him, when he offered no compassion for anyone except himself? Still, she cried even harder.

Colleen would feel bad if she broke up with David because of her. Maybe it was best not to tell her. But then how would she explain it? Another lie? The lies must stop. She was lucky she found out how unfeeling David was thanks to Colleen's income tax forms. Why couldn't she see this side of him before?

But conflicts with friends never came up before, because he never got to know her friends. They went to his functions with his friends. Jackie was relieved he'd asked no questions about her life. She failed to comprehend how every topic of conversation centered on him; his likes and his needs. He never asked about the books she read, her friends, work, growing up, or anything. It was easy to keep secrets because he wasn't interested enough to know her. She'd been happy to find the perfect guy Gino described, so she overlooked a lot. Gino wanted her to find someone who was the opposite of him.

Chapter 31

An hour after David stormed out of the house, Jackie was settled enough to take the income tax form over to Colleen. She heard music playing before reaching Colleen's front door. When Stephen opened the door, she looked past him to the twins dancing in the living room.

"Sorry, I thought Colleen would be home. I just came by to drop off her income tax forms and to invite the girls over tomorrow."

"Come in. You must be Jackie. Do you want a beer?"

"Actually, I could use one right now, thanks."

"I thought you were on a date tonight?"

Jackie was cognizant of her face giving her thoughts away.

Stephen blushed. "I'm not a Peeping Tom."

"How did you know about my date?"

"You know Colleen." He walked to the kitchen, got the beer, and shouted back, "She lets things slip every once in a while. She's just happy for you." Stephen set the beer on the coffee table in front of her. "She likes your guy."

"Well, she shouldn't. I just broke up with him."

He lost his smile and looked uncomfortable. "Oh, I'm sorry."

Although he was younger and bigger-boned than Colleen, it was easy to tell they were brother and sister. They looked alike but his soft features didn't distract from his manliness. Nothing could do that. Not with the triangle-shaped torso filling out the t-shirt.

Stephen guzzled the beer. "Did this just happen?"

"As it turned out, this form," she waved the income tax papers, "probably saved me from making a big mistake."

After relating the argument to him, Jackie said, "I'm sorry for dumping all this on you, but I just needed to vent. It's the only way I can get the anger out."

"The guy's lucky he's gone because if he were still here, I'd punch his lights out. What a jerk."

Jackie wasn't prepared for this reaction. But she should have known better. Colleen said Stephen protected her. When Jackie told him about her threat, he said, "Who talks like that?"

"Exactly."

"And he fell for it?"

"He almost ran out my front door." They both laughed.

When the music stopped, Barb put another album on the record player. "Come dance with us," she coaxed.

Stephen looked at Jackie. "Maybe later."

"I really should be going." Jackie gulped down the last of the beer. "Could you ask Colleen to give me a call when she gets home? I'm having a sleepover tomorrow for a twelve-year-old and figured it would be nice if we could get the girls together."

"Sorry, she can't. She's coming to my place with the girls for dinner. I'd cancel, but I've invited a friend of mine over too."

"Are you setting Colleen up on a date?"

"I'm just having a friend over while she and the girls are there."

"Does she know?"

"No."

"It's a date, isn't it?"

His scrunched face answered.

"I won't tell her anything," Jackie said.

"Okay, yeah, it's a date. But if she knew it, she wouldn't come."

"When she gets there, she'll be some pissed off at you."

"Not when she meets this guy. He's perfect for her. And it's about time she got back to a social life. Do you think she'll be mad?"

"Oh yeah. But I think it's what she needs too."

"I've got an idea. Why don't you all come to my place? This way the girls have someone to play with."

Jackie turned around when the twins squealed and cheered their approval.

"What's her name?" Barb asked.

"Theresa."

"What school does she go to? What grade is she in?"

"Central Elementary, Grade Six." Jackie turned back to Stephen. "You're just looking for backup."

"Damn right. Have you seen her when she's mad? At least with you there, she won't be tempted to leave when she finds out she's been set up."

"Need help with the menu?"

"No. It's burgers and dogs on the barbecue. But tell you what. I'm no good at dessert. How about you bring dessert?"

"Sounds good."

"Great. It's settled then. I'll tell Colleen."

***

"They're here." The girls chimed in unison.

Locking the front door, Colleen looked over her shoulder at the girls running and dive-bombing into the car. Barb, the first one in was sprawled across the bench seat when Michelle plopped onto her stomach.

"Get off," Barb screamed and pushed Michelle to the floor.

Theresa stood, hand on the open car door, and waited for them to sort it out when Colleen arrived.

"Barb sit up, and Michelle get off the floor so Theresa can get in."

"It was nice of Stephen to invite us," Jackie said, as they drove through Stephen's well-established tree-lined street.

"He's such a nice guy. It's hard to believe he's still single," Colleen said.

"So, why is that?"

"He was in a long-term relationship, but she cheated on him. It's been a year, but he hasn't shown any interest in dating. But it works for me because he's always available to babysit."

When Colleen pulled into the driveway in front of Stephen's single detached home the back doors flew open, and the kids jumped out on the run.

"They're excited." Colleen reached for the pan of brownies. "I'll get this."

With purse slung over a shoulder, Jackie picked up the dish of apple crisp. Before closing the door, she backed up while talking. She was as excited as the girls. She couldn't wait to see Stephen's guy and Colleen's reaction to the setup. Stephen was fun and easygoing, so she assumed his friend would be the same. Taking a step back, Jackie's heel slipped off the edge of the pavement. Her body teetered on the cusp before she pitched backward, purse hitting her face while she and the apple crisp landed in the ditch.

"Where did you go?" Colleen asked.

When Jackie realized nothing was broken or injured, she started laughing.

Colleen walked around the back of the car and looked into the ditch. "What the hell are you doing down there?"

The apple crisp was upside down on the front of her coat. She knew what would happen as soon as she picked the pan up.

"Oh my God, what a mess." Colleen climbed into the ditch and gave her a hand up.

Jackie held the dessert to her coat. "Maybe if I lean over just right, I can still salvage it." She bent over and it miraculously fell back into the pan.

The kids let out the dog on their way into the house. The dog ran up, paws on Jackie's shoulders, and lapped up the dessert from her coat. She laughed when he licked splattered bits on her face. Jackie grappled with the dog as he tried to get his nose into the pan. Stephen arrived, pulled the dog off, and took the pan from Jackie.

"It's okay." Jackie laughed. "Let him go. It's too late now, and he's cleaning my coat."

Stephen laughed. By the time things calmed down and Jackie was cleaned up, any awkwardness at meeting Brian, Stephen's "friend," was nonexistent for Colleen. Jackie could tell Colleen was attracted to him by the way she flirted with him. He was much more attractive than her ex-husband Joe who had a bulbous drinker nose. Brian drew people in with those big blue eyes that showed he was interested in what anyone said to him. It was wonderful to know you were heard and what you said mattered. He brought out the best in Colleen.

After dinner, Stephen got a fire started in the living room fireplace and then called for Jackie to join him in the kitchen.

"How do you think it's going?" he asked.

"I think Colleen likes him. He seems like a really nice guy."

Stephen touched Jackie and pointed to Colleen and Brian laughing in the dining room.

"I got it. You did well." Jackie replied, smiling.

The laughter continued.

Stephen took a can of apple pie filling out of the cupboard along with six slices of bread.

He handed her a knife. "Butter these for me, will you?"

"What's all this for?"

"My version of apple pie. It's a replacement for your apple crisp."

He went to the fireplace and got an apparatus leaning against the brick. "This is a pie iron." He opened the double-sided small square box attached to long blackened rods with wooden handles and put a slice of bread in the hollow. He then scooped pie filling onto the bread.

"Do you have some flour, brown sugar, cinnamon and butter?" Jackie mixed them and globed spoons full on the apples.

When he topped it with another slice of bread and closed the irons, Jackie could see the edges of the bread crimped and held the pie-filling sandwich in place.

"Guests first," Stephen said and handed the pie iron to Theresa. When Barb groaned, Stephen added, "Everyone gets a turn."

Theresa stuck the iron in the fire, while Jackie joined the other couple at the dining room table. Colleen dealt out cards for Euchre while Stephen brought the beer. Across the room, Jackie heard Theresa say, "It's like being at a cottage."

Jackie listened to the instructions Theresa gave the girls to an old campfire song she recognized from her summers spent at camp. She had taught it to Gino and made him sing it when they traveled to a cottage. But he was bad at rhymes.

Brian picked up the King and said, "Hearts are trump," then discarded.

Theresa flipped over the pie iron and sang the song. "My gal's a corker, she's a New Yorker, I buy her everything to keep her in style," Then Theresa pointed to Barb who was supposed to make up a rhyme. It was the first time Barb was stumped for words.

Jackie chimed in from across the room. "She's got a long, long nose, just like a rubber hose." And together Theresa and Jackie chorused, "Oh boy that's where my money goes."

Both sides of the room erupted with laughter. The warm sweet smell of cinnamon and caramel apple filled the rooms and nestled the group in familiarity.

When the song was repeated, this time Barb piped up with, "She's got a big round ear, just like a big fat rear."

Jackie wiped a tear. Gino had left part of himself behind in Theresa. Stephen gave her a strangely knowing smile. Like he knew this was the best night in a long time.

Chapter 32

As soon as the new microfiche tapes were delivered Friday morning, Jackie scanned through them. With the whir of the tapes spinning on the reel, her stomach felt queasy as she searched for the phony maternity claims. Ever since the sleepover with Theresa, Jackie was having second thoughts about the con. But she wouldn't betray Gino. An eye for an eye was what he expected. And what he deserved.

Scenes flashed, blurred like the spinning numbers, as she re-lived the fight with David, while thoughts of Emanuel lurked and threatened. She wondered what he would do if she stalled him. An eye twitched. She covered it, gave it a rest, and hoped it would settle down. So far, out of the 15 fraudulent claims, 13 cheques were processed and mailed out to P.O. Box 1256.

The exhilaration of the plan coming together was overshadowed by her fear of being discovered. If the plan didn't work, she could be the one sent to prison. It was a plan that seemed good when first baited. But what if the cops were too lazy to investigate and were content to conclude Jackie's stamp had approved all the claims? After all, it would be the easiest and fastest way to close the case.

She kept the plan in motion. All the cheques should be in the P.O. Box by Wednesday next week. Wednesday, the day Emanuel expected the ROEs and applications. Everything happening on the same day! Jackie felt a meltdown coming on and it wasn't even time for the first break of the day. Her eye twitched, like she was in distress, winking out SOS signals. She kept her head down.

When Paula was in the washroom, Jackie dropped a file beside Paula's desk. Paperwork spilled and scattered underneath it. Jackie's tongue snapped, expressing loud annoyance as she bent under the desk and picked them up. Opportunity created, she taped the supposedly lost agent stamp to the bottom of Paula's desk.

Jackie walked over to the wall of adjudicated claims, pulled out the Cathy Ermeta file, and walked back to her desk. She opened the claim, checked the calculation, and made sure it was one of the practice maternity files Paula had created with errors. When Betty went on break, Jackie slipped the file into the to-do pile on her desk. Now the con was ready.

Paula came up behind Jackie, making her jump. "Watch my back."

Using the large plastic palm leaves as camouflage, Paula leaned over Betty's desk.

"What are you doing?" Jackie pulled Paula away from the files, untucking the blouse from her skirt.

Paula slapped Jackie's hand away. "Look what you did."

Jackie's eye twitched. If Paula found the Ermeta file, she would know something was wrong. Her heart jack-hammered with a dizzy effect.

Paula stuffed the blouse back into the skirt. "Betty picked up the files I worked on. I want to see if she's monitored them."

"Get out of here. She's coming!" Jackie's frightened words made Paula jerk her hand away from the desk. She brushed against the palm tree while pivoting toward Jackie's desk in a rush. But it took Paula only a moment to realize Jackie's false alarm.

"What's with you? Calm down." Paula said.

"This isn't a good idea." Jackie felt the warm stickiness under her armpits spread. "You don't want to get into trouble in your probationary period."

"Well, I..."

"Do you want to be written up—demoted? It's too much of a risk. You'll know soon enough if you screwed up."

"Okay, already. Stop your nagging. Where do you want to go for lunch?"

The adrenaline rush left Jackie drained. "How about the salad bar?"

"I feel like pigging out."

"Sandwich store?" Jackie felt the heat leave her face.

"Eaton's cafeteria is so much better."

"I just started a diet."

Paula nodded her head in Betty's direction and alerted Jackie. Betty was returning this time.

"See you at lunch," Paula said and headed back to her desk.

Jackie opened a file and forced herself to concentrate. She jotted down numbered codes onto a data entry sheet. If Betty noticed the shift of files at the corner of the desk, she didn't let on. Jackie wasn't sure how many files were on top of the Ermeta one or when Betty would get to it.

After lunch, Eaton's cafeteria lasagna and garlic bread became a bloated, gassy lump of heartburn. Jackie tried to make out the colour-coding on the dockets to see if she could pick out the Ermeta file, but the plastic palm tree blocked her view. Betty spent a lot of time on one file, flipped pages back and forth, and made Jackie wonder whether this file was *the one*. When Betty picked up the phone, she was sure. For the most part, phone calls weren't required for monitoring claims.

Betty would be upset if an agent allowed a maternity claim without the magic ten.

Jackie stared down at the open file and strained to hear the conversation, when Betty's raspy smoker's voice blurted out, "What!"

Her voice got louder with excitement. "Are you sure? There's no mistake? No one by the name of Cathy Ermeta ever worked for you? Maybe she just got married and she's still under a maiden name?"

Like a musical conductor who struck a baton with an anxious rat-a-tat-tat, Betty's pen, although muffled by the pages in the file, riveted Jackie's attention.

"Let me speak to the payroll clerk who completed this ROE. The name is Fin Hartley."

"Are you saying you have no payroll clerk by this name?" Betty's words resounded into a crescendo of disbelief. "I need to speak with your supervisor. The signature on the ROE is Fin. That's right F I N, Fin."

The conversation repeated.

Jackie smiled.

Betty's tapping intensified. Jackie hoped there wouldn't be an employee with this unique name who would end up being investigated by the cops. She didn't want to get anyone else involved nor have the cops sidetracked.

Betty hung up the phone, picked up the file, went into the supervisor's office, and shut the door. No one else in the unit seemed aware of anything out of the ordinary until three men from Benefit Control showed up at the supervisor's door. One knock and the door opened. The door remained closed for the rest of the day. It was a small office for five people.

Chapter 33

On Monday morning, Betty was nowhere in sight and the desk was in the same state of disarray as when she left it on Friday. The supervisor's door was shut. This would be a distracting day for Jackie, so while things were quiet, she worked hard and got as many claims finalized as possible. An hour later, the supervisor emerged from the office and carried printout sheets which she gave to a file clerk. The clerk referenced the printouts, pulled armloads of adjudicated claims from the file bays, and delivered them to the supervisor. When the file clerk came out of the office, Jackie followed her into the washroom.

"You looked busy," Jackie said to the clerk.

"Yeah, as if I don't have enough work, they dump more on me."

"What are you doing?"

"Pulling files from a printout."

"What for?"

"Who knows? They're just maternity claims."

People trooped in and out of the supervisor's office with files for the rest of the day.

"Break time." Paula knocked on Jackie's desk.

As they walked, the supervisor's door opened, and a couple of men strolled out. Paula pinched Jackie by the arm and stopped her. "See those two guys," she nodded in their direction. "They're cops. This place has been crawling with people. I bet it's another bomb threat."

"Maybe. But how do you know they're cops?"

"I saw them at the police station when the cops investigated my husband's death. I hate it when they won't evacuate us."

"I wouldn't worry about it," Jackie said.

"Do you want to get blown up while they decide if it's legit or not?"

After returning from break, people spilled out from the supervisor's office into the unit. Jackie willed herself to concentrate on work. They could be coming for her. She was glad she wore a blazer so they wouldn't see her sweat. Gino always said she had no poker face.

Damn you, Clint Eastwood!

From Paula's assumption of a bomb threat, Jackie learned innocent people made wrong conjectures leading to inaccurate conclusions. Like the natural confusion, she felt when she read about Gino's death in the newspaper and thought he was protecting Paula. Confusion was ignorance interpreted as innocence.

Jackie didn't hear the police officer who walked up behind her. She caught the end of his sentence. "Sorry, what did you say?"

"We need a word with you."

"Sure." Jackie felt an imaginary fist punch, as she forced herself to stand up straight. He took her into the supervisor's office and sat her on a chair in front of the desk.

"I'm Detective Anthony Murphy and this is my partner, Detective Gretzinger." Murphy sat.

"Do you remember working on this?" Murphy handed her a file across the desk.

The name, Cathy Ermeta, stood out in black magic marker. Jackie opened the file and flipped through the pages. "No."

"Take your time. Study it."

After a couple of minutes, Jackie said, "The claimant doesn't have the magic ten, but this claim was allowed."

"You don't notice anything else?" Murphy asked.

"No."

Murphy scratched his head. "Recognize the number twelve stamped in red?"

"Yeah."

"It's the stamp you were assigned."

Jackie turned at Gretzinger's comment. "I wouldn't have allowed this claim."

Gretzinger pulled his chair too close to Jackie's. His breath stunk of garlic, and it wasn't even time for lunch. "How does your stamp get on this file?"

"You'll have to ask the supervisor."

"We did, and now we're asking you." Gretzinger's voice sounded impatient.

"How should I know?" Her confusion imitated someone with no idea of what they wanted from her. Innocent until proven guilty.

"It was your stamp, right?" Murphy's voice was more congenial.

"Yeah. But it went missing. And if it was found and re-issued to someone else, I don't know who she issued it to."

Murphy undid the button on his jacket and leaned over the desk. "You were the only one with access to it."

"I told you already, I don't know who the supervisor issued it to, ask her. She keeps a log of all numbered stamps issued to agents."

"We know. We've seen it," Murphy said.

"Then why are you asking me?"

Gretzinger pounded the desktop. "Because it was your stamp."

Jackie quelled hyperactive jitters and tempered her words so she wouldn't be seen as a bad actress in a B movie over-selling.

"Well, it wasn't me. The date on the claim is *after* I reported it missing."

"Oh, so now it's a setup?" Gretzinger brought his hand from his lap, rested it on the arm of the chair, and leaned toward Jackie. "So, you're being framed?" He leered.

Murphy turned the file in her direction. "Are you saying there was someone after," he read the date the file was adjudicated on, "the twenty-fourth of February who was given this stamp?"

Shocked Jackie blurted, "Well, then who's using the stamp?"

Murphy flopped back into the chair. "It's what we're trying to find out."

"My stamp is on my desk. I was assigned number four. It's all I know. I lost the number twelve stamp and reported it to the supervisor the way I was supposed to."

Gretzinger shook his head. "That's convenient. Do you mind if we search your desk?"

"Go ahead."

When the detectives left, Jackie felt she could breathe again. She hoped Betty remembered Paula was at her desk before she lost the stamp. She wondered what co-workers would think about her desk being ransacked and blocked out the thought. Fear spiralled through her. Despite setting this up, she wasn't prepared for the gut-twisting nausea.

The detectives came back into the room. "Do you mind if we search your home?" Murphy said.

"No."

Jackie expected it. Everything she used to put the files together was disposed of a while ago. Gino's number one rule: get rid of the evidence.

"We'll need the key."

"Of course. It's in my purse. Am I supposed to go with you?"

"It's not necessary. You can go back to work."

Jackie's desk was scattered with files when she left, but now the contents of the drawer were dumped on top of them as well. She tucked her hands into her pants pockets and wiped the sweat from them before handing him the keys.

"We'll be in touch," he said.

At the next break, Paula made a beeline for Jackie's desk which was still in disarray. "What did they want?"

"I don't know. They just wanted to search my desk."

"Were they looking for a bomb?"

"They didn't say."

"Why wouldn't they just evacuate the building?"

***

By the end of the workday, the detectives hadn't returned, so Jackie assumed they were still at her home. She anticipated a barrage of questions and rehearsed her answers on the bus and while walking home. Embarrassed by the police car parked in front of her home, she was glad Colleen and the girls got home later.

Jackie noticed a huge difference when she opened the front door. Cushions were off the couch. Kitchen cupboards and drawers were open, contents were dumped onto the countertop. When she heard voices, she went upstairs to the bedroom. Clothes neatly folded in the dresser were now strewn in a heap on the bed. Her underwear drawer was open; granny panties were exposed, pawed, and tangled with her bikini briefs. They had touched her most intimate things and violated her privacy. *Did they find my vibrator?* Jackie felt heat on her cheeks. She was unable to meet Gretzinger's gaze when he said, "We're just about finished."

A night table was turned on its side. Murphy pulled more boxes down from the top shelf in the closet—their lids scattered everywhere.

Jackie folded clothes on the bed and rearranged them in the dresser. Within ten minutes the opening and shutting of doors stopped, and the search ended.

"We'll be in touch." Murphy handed back the keys.

Before leaving home, Jackie looked around and made sure there were no police cars in sight. She drove to Papa's, a nearby pizza place because there was a secluded pay phone booth in the back. Although the cops didn't say anything about the P.O. Box number, she assumed they would be staking it out. She dialed Paula's number and hoped Theresa wouldn't answer.

"Evening Mrs. I'm calling from the post office, if you wouldn't be minding, could I speak to a Giovanni Amodeo?" Jackie said to Paula, disguising her voice in the best Scottish accent she could muster.

"He's dead."

"Oh dearie, 'tis so sorry I am for your loss. A nod's as guid as a wink tae a blind horse."

"What?" Paula let her irritation show in her tone.

"Lost me head. Wouldn't be expecting you to know. You people would be saying, that explains it, why his P.O. Box is full to overflowing."

"So, why are you calling?"

"We can nae put one more letter in there. Tis not good for us. It must be cleared out. And who would you be?"

"Paula Amodeo, his widow."

"I'd be needing to speak to the executor of the estate then."

"It's me."

"We worry since there seems to be some cheques."

The pregnant pause, signaling greed working its magic. "But I don't have a key for the box. It's been a while since his ...his death. I can't even remember the box number anymore," Paula said.

Jackie put her hand over the mouthpiece of the phone when a loud couple strolled by.

"I must be confirming Giovanni's personal information with ye first." Jackie made Paula answer a series of questions.

"Gino's been dead for a while. Would the cheques be stale dated?" Worry registered in Paula's voice.

"There'd be nae telling dearie."

"If I had the key there'd be no problem. Right?"

"Aye, there'd be no problem then."

"I could just go there and pick up the mail."

"Aye. But you dinnae have the key."

Jackie smiled at the desperation in Paula's voice.

"As his wife, and executrix I'm responsible for the box, right?"

"Aye."

"If Gino called and said he misplaced the key, would you give him another one?"

"Aye, we would."

"So, I'm telling you, I misplaced the key. So, you should send me another one."

"I suppose... I could be having the mailman drop the key in your mailbox."

"That would work perfectly."

"But I dinnae say for sure," Jackie stammered.

"Thank you so much. You've solved everything."

"Ah, well ...I dinnae..."

"Please, you have to help me."

Jackie sighed into the phone.

"Please," Paula begged.

"Aye. I'll give it to the mailman in an envelope. What's your home address?"

"Oh, wait. What was the box number again?"

"Would ye be having a pen? It would be box twelve-fifty-six. One, two, five, six."

"Thank you. I appreciate it," Paula said.

"'Tis best sometimes to rule with the heart. Good day to ye."

Jackie replaced the phone.

Chapter 34

Jackie took the later bus the next morning. When she entered their workplace, Paula raced to meet her.

"You're late! The cops are looking for you. When you didn't show up, they questioned all of us. I told them you normally take the bus with me, but you weren't on it this morning."

Earlier in the morning, Jackie had waited outside Paula's house for them to leave. When they were no longer in sight, Jackie dropped the envelope with the P.O. Box key to number 1256 into the mailbox.

"I took a sleeping pill last night and slept right through the alarm. Being late for work is not a crime."

"It isn't." Detective Murphy blocked the entranceway. "Don't bother taking your coat off. We're taking a trip down to the station."

Jackie had never ridden in the back of a police car before. It's all part of the plan, she told herself. They must get her before they get Paula.

The police station was dingy and hummed with fluorescent lights. Murphy escorted her passed a miserable older cop at the front desk, and down a narrow hallway into a small room. Detective Gretzinger was seated at a table with a stack of UI files in front of him. Murphy sat her down in a wooden chair. He settled into another across the table.

"When did you lose your agent stamp?"

Jackie avoided looking at the files in the middle of the table. "A while ago. I told you already. It'll be in the supervisor's logbook. She'll have the date. Oh, and Carol from Benefit Control wrote up a report. The date will be on it too."

"How did you lose it?"

"One minute it was there, the next it disappeared. I turned my desk upside down looking for it. Betty probably remembers. She helped me. Well, not physically help me. She gave me some ideas on where to look. She thought maybe it got stuck in a file. But I shook out all the files and nothing fell out."

Gretzinger closed the file he'd been reading, stared at Jackie, and smiled. He rose and left the room.

"What were you doing just before you noticed the stamp missing?" Murphy said.

"Nothing. Just adjudicating claims."

Detective Murphy stood, stretched, and walked behind her. "What did you do with the twenty-three ROEs you took from the stock room on February 19th?"

He must have seen the requisition form. Jackie sat stiffly in the chair with her head bent and brushed hair off her face. "I would have mailed them out to the employer who requested them. It will be on the requisition form. Check there."

Murphy leaned down, his head almost resting on her shoulder. "We have. And we spoke to the payroll clerk."

Jackie bristled when she felt his warm breath on her ear. She tugged the hair from behind her ear and let it drape like a curtain between them. Grey paint-peeled walls surrounding her gave the illusion she was already in prison.

She'd been right to pick a large company with many layoffs. If this part of her plan was proven right, then maybe the rest would too. Murphy straightened, walked around the table, and stood in front of her.

Jackie folded her arms on the tabletop and rested her head on them. The porous wooden table felt oily, and Jackie knew it wasn't from furniture polish. With no windows in the small room, body odour and sweat from guilty suspects permeated the furniture and seeped back into the room with the changing seasons and temperatures, aged like a good Limberger, and fouled the air. Repulsed by the stink, Jackie sat up straight again and dropped her hands in her lap.

Gretzinger walked back in and motioned for Murphy who joined him. In whispered tones, Gretzinger said, "Betty said Paula Amodeo was there when Jackie lost her stamp."

The detectives walked across the room and joined Jackie at the table.

"Was anyone with you when you lost your stamp?" Gretzinger asked.

Relief overwhelmed her, but she forced a deadpan look before she answered. "Paula Amodeo."

"What happened?" Gretzinger asked.

"I remember now. It was lunchtime. I showed her how to complete a data entry sheet and where to place the stamp. I let her do a couple of entry sheets on her own. She used the stamp! Are you saying Paula stole it? Why would she, when she'd be getting one of her own soon? Why take mine?"

Murphy interjected, "Did Paula say or do anything odd?"

"No."

"Did she ask any questions?"

"I don't remember. We talked about where to go for lunch."

"Did she seem nervous or off?" Murphy questioned.

"No. She was bossy as always. I wanted to go to the salad bar because I just started a diet, but she didn't want to go there. We always have to go where she wants. I can never..."

Gretzinger's shoulders slumped. "We don't need to hear all this crap."

"You're free to go, but don't say anything to Paula," Murphy said.

Gretzinger stood, grabbed Jackie by the elbow, and faced her. "If you do, it would be construed as interfering with an investigation, punishable by jail time."

Murphy escorted Jackie to the door and opened it for her.

With only an hour left of the workday, Jackie didn't return to the office. The day was hectic enough and she didn't want to be grilled by Paula.

Tension and fear left Jackie with stiff, sore muscles, and a persistent headache that twitched her eye. When she headed home on the bus, she went over and over the interrogation questions and convinced herself, she had given appropriate answers.

Opening the front door, she sighed when the "It's great to be home" feeling came over her. She hung up her winter coat, kicked off her boots, and went to the fridge for a beer. The thought of soaking in a hot bubble bath made things better. Going into the bedroom, she smelled cigarette smoke before Emanuel stepped out from behind the door. Her knees went weak. This was Wednesday!

"How did you get in?" Jackie took a step back.

Emanuel flipped the toothpick on its end inside his mouth. "Are you shitting me? I supplied Gino with his stolen crap. B & E is my thing. Why did the cops bring you in?" The toothpick lay flat in the corner of his mouth.

"How did you know?"

"Knew something was fucked up when you weren't on the bus this morning."

"You've been following me?"

"Have to keep an eye on my meal ticket."

Jackie looked around the room for anything she could use as a weapon.

Emanuel swaggered toward her. He grabbed the beer from her hand, stretched an arm over her shoulder, and slammed the bedroom door closed. Yanking buttons off her blouse, he pushed the material back to expose skin. "Hmmm. No wire."

Jackie jerked away and turned toward the door just as Emanuel's hand slammed against it.

"Have a seat." Emanuel nodded toward the bed. "When I saw the cops bring you out, I figured you got nabbed."

When she didn't move, he pushed her onto the bed.

"This has nothing to do with us. The police are investigating a maternity fraud case."

"What did you tell the cops?" Emanuel asked.

"They wanted to know about my agent stamp that went missing."

"Did you give them my name?"

"No. Why would I? This has nothing to do with you."

"You think I'm fucking stupid? Like the cops just show up on the day you got to get me them forms. I know you got nabbed."

"No, it's not what happened. The cops were there, so I couldn't get them. It was about fraudulent maternity claims. I told them what I knew, and they released me."

"Yeah, I bet you did."

His punch knocked the wind out of her, and she doubled over.

"Told them what you knew. Like about me?"

"No." Jackie sputtered and gasped. "It wasn't about you."

He slapped her hard across the face and knocked her to the floor. "Think you're ratting me out?"

He jerked her up by the arm and flung her back onto the bed. Jackie waited until Emanuel lowered himself on her with legs straddled, and then she seized the beer bottle on the night table and shattered it on his head. She scrambled off the bed, as he rolled over and held the side of his face while blood oozed between fingers from the jagged cuts. Jackie dashed out the bedroom door, and down the stairs.

She heard snorted breath and heels thumping as he gained speed behind her. Afraid of being tackled if she slowed down, she didn't pause for boots or a coat. When her hand reached the front doorknob, his large hand clamped over hers like a vice and pried her fingers from the knob. He hurled her into the living room. Her back hit a magazine rack and knocked it over. It framed her in a bright collage of cover photos. Emanuel stood over her. Blood trickled along his laugh line and pooled into the corner of his mouth. Leaning on the magazine rack, she got herself up, and half staggered toward the kitchen.

Emanuel gave one powerful yank on the phone cord and pulled it from the wall. She was an arm's length from the knife drawer when Emanuel grabbed her. A hand clamped around the back of her skull. She couldn't move her head even when she saw the tight fist coming at her. Her face exploded in pain. Jackie screamed once before the second blow hit. Propelled into the air, she slammed against the stove. Crimson spurted from her nose and mouth and splattered the white enamel appliance.

Splayed across the cooktop, Jackie jerked her hand off the burner afraid he would turn it on. She peered at the kitchen cabinets. Her vision was like a camera lens creating diamond-shaped sparkles and shutter-speed blurs. She groped for the brassy knob on the knife drawer and felt for the thickest-handled blade hoping it was the butcher knife. She turned at his laughter.

Emanuel bent from the waist, lifted a pant leg, and unsheathed a long slender hunting knife strapped around an ankle. Jackie's hand barely came out of the drawer in time to fend off the first upward thrust. Vibrations from the force shook her hand and the sharp clang of steel against steel rang in her ears when the blade sliced from elbow to wrist. She cried in pain. The butcher knife clanged against the stove before hitting the floor.

Cowering in front of him, Emanuel's arm flexed and then tensed. He prepared for the exertion needed for a downward thrust. Jackie stared at the knife poised over his shoulder. A blurred halo-like shadow crowned Emanuel's head. She heard the dull clunk the snow shovel made when it smashed his skull. His body folded to the floor and revealed Paula as she brandished the shovel. Gripping Jackie's arm over a shoulder, Paula wrapped the other arm around her back and propped her up. The two women walked to Colleen's house while the shovel dragged behind them.

***

Jackie focused on the wavy, white popcorn ceiling, but her head throbbed. Pain stabbed her eye and made her dizzy. She heard Barb ask, "Why is her blouse ripped? Will she be alright?"

Someone pulled her blouse together and draped a blanket over her. She was relieved when she heard Stephen answer, that she would be fine, and not to worry. She trusted Stephen. Even though Michelle, in the background, cried she was going to die. Vaguely aware of her arm being wrapped, she sensed something tight above her elbow, like when she gave blood, and they knotted a rubber band around the arm.

Drifting in and out of consciousness, she awoke each time startled when she perceived the wadded-up towel in her mouth and the pain in her face and eyes. Michelle pleaded, "Don't go, don't leave us." Stephen commanded her to lock the door behind him. Paula soothed their fear. The next time she woke, the towel was being removed from her mouth, and she heard Paula say, "She'll need a few stitches. Her teeth went through her cheek."

Uniformed men leaned over Jackie, and discussed a prognosis before they lifted her onto a stretcher and took her out the front door.

Spindly dark tree branches stretched out and scratched at a thick grey pasty sky above. Before Jackie closed her watery eyes against the stinging wind, she heard Paula's insistent voice. "She needs me to ride to the hospital. I'm her best friend."

She wished it was Colleen saying those words, but she knew Colleen was at work.

Tucked tightly into a sheet, Jackie struggled and freed her good arm as she blocked out a glare. Blinded—metal flashed. The stickiness of blood dripped down her arm. A luminary steel blade stretched out, got closer, and sliced again when the shaft was blocked by a broad-shouldered silhouette who whispered in her ear. Was Emanuel being sarcastic when he said, she would be alright? Did he mean this time, but he wouldn't miss the next? Her thrashing body was restrained by a blue arm. Wide black straps tightened across her chest and hips when the thrusting steel blade diffused overhead and splintered into silver glitter revealing shiny rays from the streetlight's beam when she was lifted into the ambulance.

Chapter 35

Distracted by whining sirens when the two ambulances drove away, Paula didn't notice the detectives until they flashed their badges, stuffed her into the back of an unmarked car, and took her to the station.

It had been a while since Paula had been hauled into a cop shop, but the anxiety always elicited her mouthy side. She sat at the table in the interrogation room, and smiled at the detectives before asking, "Is this going to take long?"

Murphy smiled back. He picked up a pencil and tapped the eraser on the table. His smile broadened while he waited for hers to disappear. He didn't seem to like her smug attitude, especially since her rap sheet was long.

"What happened?" Murphy said.

"I stopped by Jackie's place after work."

"Is this something you would normally do?" Murphy asked.

"No."

"So why did you go there?" Gretzinger asked.

"She's my friend. I wanted to find out why you guys picked her up."

Gretzinger stretched an arm out on the table in front of her and closed the gap between them. "Is it any of your business?"

"No. But the rumour mill in the office was working overtime. I wanted to get the scoop. Squash the gossip and set people straight. Protect my friend."

"Tell me what you saw," Murphy said.

"From the porch, I heard a scuffle. It was not a yelling fight, more physical. Then I heard Jackie scream."

It was as though Paula was a teenager again when she heard the banging, crashing, and screaming. She expected to go in and see her dad beating her mother. And her mother doing nothing to defend herself, only cowering in a corner, waiting for the next blow. Paula would never let him hit her like that. She never went into the house without a weapon. She even kept a hammer stashed under the bed.

"Right next to the door was a shovel. I don't know what kind of shit was going down, so I figured I better take the shovel to protect myself. I went to the kitchen and saw this Neanderthal slicing Jackie up. He'd got the knife raised, going in for the kill when I slammed him with the shovel. He's a big guy, so I come down with everything I got. I know I got to take him down the first time because if he had a chance, he'd kill me too. As soon as he went down, I grabbed Jackie and headed for the neighbours. It's all I know. Don't know what it's about and it's not my business."

Gretzinger sat up straight in the chair and crossed his arms over his chest. "You come to her house to find out why we bring her in for questioning, but a guy tries to kill her and you're not curious?"

Paula rolled her eyes. "Does a bear shit in the woods? Yeah." The long drawled-out syllables emphasized the point. "Of course, I am. But I'm going to find out from her, not you."

"Something to hide?" Gretzinger asked.

"Nah. It just doesn't add up. A beating like this is personal. Why didn't she tell me about the guy? I'm her best friend."

"We're waiting to hear how he is. Lucky for you, he's still alive," Murphy said.

"Lucky for him it wasn't a pickaxe near the door."

"We could charge you with aggravated assault," Murphy said.

"Damn right, I was aggravated. Look at the size of the motherfucker. And all I got is a shovel to his knife. You should be thanking me for doing your job."

Murphy's eyes met Gretzinger's scowl as he opened the door for Paula. "I'm sure you know the drill. Don't leave town in case we have to interview you again."

***

Painkillers made Jackie drowsy, and every time she woke, Murphy was by her bedside. She remembered him asking questions, but she was certain she never answered him, just moaned, held her head, and went out again or pretended to until she could think of the right answers.

"Water," Jackie said.

Murphy cranked her bed, poured a glass of water, and handed it to her.

"I want to hear your version of what happened," he said.

Jackie finished the water and handed it back for more. Murphy put the glass on the nightstand out of reach.

"How do you know this guy?"

Jackie licked dry lips and picked at a sliver of crusted blood in the corner a nurse missed in clean up.

"He's a claimant. It was an inquiry. He wanted to know why he was cut off."

She spoke slowly, and deliberately and got the well-practiced words out. Long hours in bed with only thoughts provided feasible answers.

"We referred him to a job through our job bank and he didn't show up for the interview, so he got cut off. He figured we set him up and got pissed off at me."

"When was this?" Murphy said.

Jackie licked her lips. "I don't know. A while ago."

Murphy refilled the cup. "A month ago?"

"No, maybe a couple of weeks."

"You ever see him before?"

"No."

"He didn't hang around the office?" He handed her the cup.

"I don't know."

"Why did you let him in?"

"He was in my bedroom when I got home."

"How did he know where you lived?"

A drop of blood turned the water pink. "I don't know."

Murphy took the cup and handed her Kleenex. "Sure, you didn't know him before?"

She dabbed her swollen lip and looked at the red on the tissue. "I've never seen him before."

Murphy went to the bathroom, wet a washcloth, and handed it to her. "Put some pressure on it. What did he say?"

"He slammed the bedroom door and told me to sit on the bed. He was on top of me going to rape me." The cloth muffled some of the words. "I fought him off and got downstairs but couldn't get out the door."

He took the cloth she offered and handed her a fresh cup of water.

Jackie gulped the water. "I ran to the kitchen to get a knife. We fought. He tried to kill me."

"Why would he kill you, if he wanted to rape you?"

"How should I know? He held the knife over me and was coming down with it when Paula hit him with the shovel. She saved my life."

"Were you expecting Paula?"

"No."

Jackie couldn't keep her eyes open. She was thirsty, but the glass was empty. She thought she said the word water, but she didn't hear it. Her eyes rolled back.

This time when she woke up, Murphy handed her water without having to ask for it. The bed was propped up.

"What time is it?" Jackie asked.

Murphy checked his watch. "Nine-thirty."

Jackie looked out the window. It was daytime. "It's Thursday, right?"

Murphy nodded, yes. "Does the name Emanuel Miceli mean anything to you?"

"No."

"It should, you answered a complaint he made. He's our guy."

"I do lots of inquiries. Who remembers names?"

"Well, you even noted in your reply he was extremely irate."

"Most claimants are when they get to me. How is he?"

She was almost afraid to ask. He wouldn't go down alone. He would tell the cops about her ROE con with Gino.

"He has a bad concussion. Can't even count to ten. The doctor says he'll recover, but he's not sure how long it will take before the memory comes back. Are you ready to press charges?"

"I just want this all to end. If I press charges how much time will he get?"

"It's hard to say. There were signs of forced entry. So, we have him on break-and-enter and attempted murder. His lawyer might plead the charges down to assault with a deadly weapon."

"And what will happen when he gets out? He did this because he got cut off his unemployment. Imagine what he'll do if I send him away for years. Anyway, I won't find out, because I'm not filing charges."

Murphy's radio crackled when a voice at the other end alerted him to something specified by a number code.

"Roger," he said. "I'll give you some time to reconsider. If you don't lay charges, he could come back and finish the job. No need to decide yet. I have to go. We'll talk later." Murphy left the room.

Chapter 36

When Paula got home and checked her mailbox, she was surprised to find an envelope with the key to Gino's mailbox. All night, she tossed and turned in bed, and went over all the payouts she collected from Gino's estate, and nothing was outstanding, except for his life insurance policy. She never found out who the beneficiary was, only that she wasn't. She wondered how much money there could be. Enough mail to fill the box. Maybe a bunch of cheques. So, why wasn't she contacted sooner? She figured he must have been running some other scam she'd known nothing about.

People are fucking gullible. Or, maybe, I'm just that good!
She kissed the key.
Should I go to work or call in sick?
Paula looked like it was a rough night. She watched every illuminated hour on the wind-up alarm clock, so when she called in sick there was no need to fake grogginess. Finally, at 8 a.m., she crawled out of bed.

***

From the entrance to the post office, Paula headed towards the three metal walls at the back of the building. She scanned the metal boxes, followed the numbers, and ended her search at the center wall, third row from the bottom, sixth in from the left. Paula bent down and slid the key into P.O. Box 1256 and looked into the cubby hole, surprised at the dozen similar grey-brown envelopes inside.

She took a handful out and stared at the name Cathy Ermeta through a window envelope. Hair at the nape of her neck bristled. An achy hollowness permeated her stomach and raised goosebumps. Hard-soled shoes struck the tile, as men rushed toward her. Paula looked over at the other person at the mailboxes who stopped and looked back at them too.

"I didn't do it," Paula barked just before she was thumped against the metal wall.

Murphy frisked Paula for the key. He snatched the envelopes out of her hand and cuffed her. She heard him blurb her rights before walking her outside into an unmarked car—one she had passed on her way into the post office.

Sitting in the same chair, in the same interrogation room as yesterday, Paula felt as though she never left the police station and wished she hadn't.

"I'm telling you I didn't do it," Paula said, for the tenth time. "I know how it looks, but I was set up."

"Yeah, well it's the usual story, except we caught you red-handed with the cheques, so there's no point denying it," Gretzinger said.

"I'm telling you I didn't do it."

"We'll have handwriting experts who will verify you filled in the applications and forms."

"I did. I wrote them out, but they were for practice."

"So, your defence is, I needed to practice cheating the system. The cheques just happened to come." Gretzinger laughed. "Well, you didn't practice enough, because you screwed up on the math. Practice didn't make perfect."

"Those were practice samples for an Agent 1 competition."

"Come on. It's your PO Box number on the cheques and applications."

"No. It was Gino's PO Box number, not mine. I don't have one."

"According to the Post Office, this box was issued to you."

"They're wrong. It wasn't."

When Murphy came into the room, he slapped down an agent stamp on the desk. "Guess where we found this?"

Paula and Gretzinger both looked at him.

"Taped underneath your desk at work."

"I didn't put anything there. My stamp is on my desk."

"Yeah, that one was there too," Murphy said.

"What are you talking about?" Paula screamed.

Murphy tossed the stamp onto the table. "It's the stamp you used to approve all those maternity claims."

"What's the number on it?" Paula asked.

Gretzinger stamped it on a piece of paper.

"That's not my stamp."

"We know it isn't. It's the stamp you stole from Jackie. We have a witness who can corroborate you were the last person at Jackie's desk when the stamp went missing."

Paula's head was too heavy. Everything blurred. There was no way to explain it. No way to prove innocence.

"I didn't do this. Jackie set me up. I don't know why. She told me the P.O. Box number to put on the applications. I never did anything to her. I only met her a few months ago when she transferred to our office."

"She set you up! Why?" Gretzinger scratched his head.

"How should I know? This wasn't my plan."

"She's got no motive. You were the one with motive, opportunity and most importantly, the one caught red-handed with the cheques."

"I was called by the post office and told to come in and pick up cheques from Gino's box. I didn't even know Gino had a box or the number for it. She arranged for the mailman to leave the key in my mailbox while I was at work. Go ask her. She'll tell you she called me to pick up the cheques."

"Who was the woman you talked to?"

"I don't know. She didn't tell me her name, but she has a thick Scottish accent."

Detective Murphy left the room to check out the story and then returned twenty minutes later.

"There's no employee with a heavy accent either Scottish or Irish. They said, it's office etiquette for anyone calling to identify themselves. They also said it would not be proper procedure for any employee to drop a key off for you that belongs to someone else's P.O. Box. In the case of a deceased customer, certain protocols must be followed. A death certificate is required, and all the paperwork has to be completed by the executor of the estate. It's a big rigmarole and takes time. So, nothing you've told us is true."

"I'm telling you a woman called me from the post office. Or at least she said she worked for the post office. Can't you see I've been set up?"

Hours later the interrogation was getting nowhere. Not any closer to a confession, Gretzinger found himself starting to believe her story. He left Murphy to continue the interrogation while he stepped out of the room to do a background check on Jackie.

Gretzinger came back into the interrogation room and confronted Paula. "Funny you don't know who your stepdaughter is."

"What are you talking about? I have no stepdaughter. Gino was never married."

"Gino was given custody of Jackie by St. Michael's orphanage when she was eleven."

Paula took a sharp breath and choked on a build-up of saliva going down the wrong pipe. Through sputtered breaths, she gasped, "What?"

"Government records show for years Gino got a baby bonus cheque for Jackie."

"He never said anything to me. How could he not tell me? We were married for two years. He never said a word about having a kid. Why didn't she ever visit or call? He didn't even have a picture of her."

The startled look on her face made Gretzinger lean back in his chair.

"Fucking life insurance! That's who got it and the house too. Gino got a life insurance policy, but I wasn't the beneficiary. The insurance company wouldn't tell me who was. It must have been Jackie. The bitch set me up."

"Why?" Murphy asked.

Paula's face turned paper towel white, and her breathing was heavier. *Jackie must know I killed Gino.*

"How should I know? I didn't even know who she was. Arrest her. Make her talk."

"All the evidence points to you," Murphy said.

"You have to do something. I'm innocent. She framed me."

"You're the prime suspect here," Gretzinger reminded her.

"Yup, the sure bet," Murphy chimed in.

The look in Paula's pleading eyes caused both men to look at each other.

Chapter 37

Jackie woke to the clatter of breakfast trays being delivered to rooms. She looked into a mirror. Her face pulsed imitating throbbing constant pain that made it seem as though she winked. She dreaded washing her face and brushing her teeth. It would be painful.

Splashing water on her face, she swished mouthwash, until her gums stung from the open wounds, then spat it out. She applied red lipstick on the lopsided fat lip. It made her look like a crazed villain; she thought of Batman's Joker as an eye twitched back at her. A cut with two black crusty stitches stuck out from a lumpy, swollen bruise covering most of the left side of her face. Poufy, long clown-like hair accented the sinister look. She wiped the lipstick off.

A long line of stitches flashed in the mirror when Jackie brushed her matted bed-head. Lucky for her, Emanuel's knife was razor-sharp and had sliced cleanly down the arm. If it weren't for Paula... She never even thanked her. Paula asked to ride along in the ambulance, but Jackie didn't remember her being there and couldn't recall any later visits. The brush caught in frizzy tangles when someone knocked on the door.

"Come in."

Stephen pulled a chair to the end of the bed and handed her a book. "How are you feeling?"

"Better than I look. Harold Robbins! How did you know I like him?"

"Colleen told me you had a couple of his books."

"Thanks." She set the book on the table. "Colleen and the girls were here after you left."

"I know. We couldn't convince Michelle you were alright. She needed to come and see for herself. She's been upset by this. We all have. If only I hadn't let the girls turn their music up so loud, then I would have heard the attack."

"You don't know that. There might've been nothing to hear. I don't even know if I screamed. Can't remember. Isn't that weird? It happened so fast. I just wanted to get away."

"I should have been there to protect you."

"You were."

When Paula dragged her into Colleen's house that night, she remembered Stephen scooping her into his arms and carrying her to the couch. She remembered the anguish in his voice when he asked who did this. Then the twins cried and begged him not to go, but he left anyway.

"If you weren't there, he might have come after us."

He picked up the book from the corner of the table and pretended to read the back-jacket cover. "I couldn't let him get away before the cops got there."

Jackie sipped water through a straw. "I remember when I was on the stretcher outside, Emanuel whispered in my ear, I was alright for now. Meaning, he was going to get me."

"It was me. I told you, you were alright, but there was no other meaning to it. I wanted you to know you were safe. He couldn't hurt you anymore. Emanuel was out cold on the floor when I left him. They carried him out of your house on a stretcher."

Stephen turned when the door opened, and the nurse came in. "Time to take your vitals," she said and rolled the pole, with the blood pressure cuff attached, toward her.

He took the cue and left.

***

After dinner, a nurse came and took Jackie for a stroll down the corridors as she dragged the IV pole beside her.

Jackie trudged up and down halls in every direction. "No one made me do this before."

"We like to make sure your legs are strong enough before sending you home."

"Does that mean I'll be going home soon?"

"You have to ask the doctor."

Jackie's breath was heavy. She noticed the nurse checked her watch regularly. "So how long have we walked for?"

"Twenty minutes. Time to head back."

By the time the nurse helped her into bed, Jackie was exhausted and slept soundly through the night.

***

The next morning, the heavy door creaked open, but Jackie snuggled on her side tucked into the covers.

Where was the good girl, Gino said I was? I've transformed into someone else. Is Paula's penance paid?

"I came to break you out," Paula said.

Jackie turned and sat up.

"When I called to find out what room you were in, they told me your doctor signed your release papers, so you'll be free to go soon."

A tiny sob caught in Jackie's throat when relief escaped. "Where have you been?"

"Got you a coffee." Paula set it on the bedside table. "The cops hauled me in for questioning over fraudulent maternity claims. They just turned me loose this morning."

"What did you tell them?"

"What could I tell them? It has nothing to do with me. But they gave me the line about not leaving town like they were expecting me to flee. So, I'm probably the number one suspect."

"Did they have any evidence?"

"Nothing they told me about."

Paula moved out of the way when a woman came into the room and deposited a breakfast tray on the bedside table.

Jackie felt a lone tear puddle in a deep crease under her eye. *Paula saved me. I can't repay her by sending her to prison. It's my turn to save her.*

"Can you imagine if they put me away? Poor Theresa would be stuck in some orphanage. It would've killed Gino to see it. She wouldn't have anyone."

Paula lifted the chrome dome breakfast lid, "No bacon and eggs. Lousy cereal is all you get?"

"It's what I ordered."

Paula picked up the hospital coffee cup. "Dishwater crap," and replaced it with the Tim Horton's coffee cup.

Jackie's stomach felt like a hollow pit. Had she condemned Theresa to the life she should have lived? There was no satisfaction in what she did. Only guilt and regret. She remembered the frightening feeling of being alone at the orphanage. Jackie's lips flatlined, void of emotion and she looked at her lap.

"Drink your coffee." Paula handed it to her. "Don't let it get cold."

Jackie's nose crinkled. "It's a little bitter."

Paula plucked the packet of sugar from the tray and poured it into the coffee. "Sorry, they must have forgotten the sugar."

Paula waited for Jackie to drink. "Is it better?"

"Yeah."

If Jackie didn't confess and Paula was convicted, even after being released from prison, she would never be able to work for the government again. Did she also sentence her to life as a waitress? Jackie couldn't tell Theresa her mom killed Gino. Theresa didn't deserve to be devastated by that reality. What had she done? She was no better than Paula.

"When did they bring you in?" Jackie brought herself to ask.

"Who?"

"The cops."

"Oh, Thursday."

So, the cops detained her before she got a chance to go to the mailbox and get the checks? It wasn't too late to stop this whole thing!

"Even though those phony claims have nothing to do with me, the cops are trying to pin it on me. And imagine poor Theresa. Alone. To have the only person you love in the world taken away from you."

Jackie didn't have to imagine. She knew how it felt.

Paula removed a newspaper from the end of the bed and sat down. "Do you know how long I'd be gone from Theresa's life? How long she'd be alone?"

Jackie looked at the morning edition of the newspaper Paula held and thought of their game, name the crime and Gino could tell you the time you'd do.

Maybe seven years. Federal crimes carried longer sentences. Time to confess. Set things right and do my time.

"I'd bet you'd get seven years. Not long enough, my father Gino would have said, if he were still alive."

Paula smiled when Jackie set her empty Tim Horton's cup on the table. Jackie expected Paula would have been shocked. But instead, her lips stretched into a perma press smile.

Paula set the paper aside and shook her head from side to side. "Gino's daughter. You're as stupid as he was."

Jackie stared in disbelief and wondered when she found out. The whole situation drained her, as she fell back onto the pillow.

"He fucked me over, but I got him. Planned it out and waited for him. Even used his gun. He cried like a baby in the end. And the cops were so stupid, they thought it was self-defence."

Pressure from Paula's eyes and jawline compressed her nose and mouth and turned her face red. Jackie had never witnessed rage like this before.

"You screwed me out of his life insurance. It was my money. I was entitled to it not you. And to the house."

"It's my house." Jackie's words slurred from exhaustion.

Paula picked up the Tim Horton cup and put it in a plastic bag, into her purse. "And now, I got you too."

Jackie's eye sockets felt like they were on fire, pinpricks seared her skin, but she felt chilled at the same time. Pain throbbed and shot to her temples. "I'm going to be ..." Jackie gagged from dry heaves, doubled over, and clutched her stomach.

Paula laughed. "Poison does that to you. So, who's the stupid one now?"

The door banged open. People spilled into the room shouting commands.

"Cuff her," Murphy said.

Paula jerked her hand away screaming, "Fuck, fuck, fuck."

A white-coated doctor ordered a nurse. "We need to stabilize her."

Murphy read Paula her rights before escorting her out.

Overhead lights blurred as Jackie's bed raced down hallways into another room. She faded in and out and heard disjointed words, ventilate, resuscitate between mechanical heartbeats and blips. Someone asked what her vital signs were before she went unconscious.

***

The next morning, Jackie was stabilized and back in her room. She felt a tap on her foot and opened her eyes.

Detective Gretzinger stood at the bottom of the bed. "How do you feel?"

"I've seen better days. I'd say I was lucky but have no idea what or why this happened. Do you mind explaining?"

"We arrested Paula when she picked up the fraudulent checks at the post office on Thursday. She said, you framed her. I believed her. She tried not to react when we told her you were Gino's daughter. But she couldn't hold back the rage. It showed on her face. We figured she'd be coming after you."

"So, you used me as bait?"

"No. We were here to protect you."

"But how did you know when to come in?"

"Wiretap on the bed."

Huh! The long walk with the nurse yesterday.

"So, you used Paula, to get to me, but got her instead."

And I was so close to confessing!

"We have enough evidence to charge Paula but wanted to see how this played out first. Good thing for you we did."

Gretzinger moved closer and confronted Jackie. "I still believe Paula. I think you set her up because she murdered Gino. I spoke to the DA about bringing you in on fraud charges. But there's a catch. They must prove you intended to deceive the UIC for personal gain. It's not possible to prove because the checks were addressed to Paula's PO Box. Which means you wouldn't financially gain. Paula would. And seeing how Paula was caught red-handed, the DA said that's the winnable case for a conviction. He's not interested in my theories when the evidence won't support them. My gut tells me, you're behind both ROE scams. Unfortunately, I can't prove either one. But we both know I'm right. For now, you're free to go. But I'll be watching you." Gretzinger left.

***

Jackie was released after three days in hospital. Stephen came and took her home. Children's Aid allowed Henrietta to look after Theresa until Jackie, her step-sister, recovered and took over.

When Theresa heard her mother was in jail, she was more than willing to be taken in by Jackie.

Unable to protect Theresa from sensationalized front-page headlines that told how Gino's death went from a case of self-defence to one of murder, Jackie offered to take Theresa to see her mother, but the girl wouldn't go—never wanted to see her mother again. Jackie felt guilty about getting Gino's life insurance money. Benefiting from his death was wrong. She used the money for Theresa and established an investment account payable for when she was twenty-four. She thought Gino would like that.

Theresa and Jackie snuggled together into Gino's recliner flipping through photo albums from his safety deposit box. Jackie reclaimed her life. She looked at a picture of Theresa with Gino, and said, "I can't believe he still wore the plaid shirt I gave him years ago for Christmas."

"He said it was his lucky shirt. Always brought home a stringer when he wore it. Mom tried to throw it out a couple of times."

An irregular but distinct knock on the front door made Theresa bolt from the chair. "They're here," she yelled. And tapped the same code back on the door before she opened it.

Jackie loved how Theresa passed on signals and secret sign language to the twins like Gino had done with both of them. Jackie went to the kitchen and got the picnic basket she packed for their hiking adventure with Colleen, the girls, Brian, and Stephen. On the wall above the table, Clint Eastwood gave her the Time for Vengeance look. Before picking up the basket, she took down the poster and threw it in the garbage. Maybe an eye for an eye wasn't about justice or vengeance, but more of a warning. With payback, you become the person you hate.

—End—

Author's Note

My story is fictional but based on two real ROE scams that happened when I worked for the Hamilton Ontario Unemployment Insurance Commission from 1973 to 1988. In real life, I was one of the file clerks who used a printout and pulled fraudulent maternity claims with PO Box numbers for my supervisor. It was an employee in our Hamilton office who caught the fraudulent maternity claim and investigated it. The employee who perpetrated the crime was from another UIC office.

I'd love to hear what you think of the story. Drop me a line, a word, or just a rating through a review on Goodreads or Amazon. Thanks.

If you want a sneak peek at my next work in progress, tentatively titled, *Is it Obesity or Cushing's?* Check my website under memoir to read sample chapters at www.janicebarrett.ca

I left my husband, but he drove the getaway car.

Happy reading.

Acknowledgements

Thank you, to my publisher, Shane Joseph, for his insightful suggestions that greatly improved my book.

Thank you, international New York Times bestselling author Linwood Barclay for the wonderful blurb. I love your latest book, *I Will Ruin You*. Masterful!

Thank you, Maureen Jennings, author of *The Murdoch Mysteries,* for your encouragement.

Thank you, Barbara Baker, author of *Jillian of Banff XO,* for your keen editing eye and attention to detail.

Thank you, Brian Henry, of *The Quick Brown Fox*, for your critiques that improved my writing skills.

Thank you, to the members of The Canadian Authors Association, Niagara Branch. Special thanks to Sylvia Barnard, James Bryan Simpson, Tom Wood, Sharon Frayne, and Cynthia Colby for their brilliant critiques.

Author Bio

Janice Barrett is a proud mother of three. She is a novelist, journalist, playwright, and ghostwriter. Her debut novel ***Authorized Cruelty*** (Blue Denim Press) was published in 2023.

www.ingramcontent.com/pod-product-compliance
Lightning Source LLC
Chambersburg PA
CBHW070632170726
48291CB00003B/980